WINTER'S DEMON

ERIC R. ASHER

FOR JAMES,

LIVE. LOVE. DREAM.

www.daysgonebad.com

Produced by ReAnimus Press
www.ReAnimus.com

Edited by Laura Matheson
www.plainstext.com

Cover typography by Bookish Brunette Designs
brunettedesigns.wordpress.com/

Cover design © Phatpuppyart.com – Claudia McKinney

ISBN-13: 978-1500170936

First print edition:June, 2014

10 9 8 7 6 5 4 3 2 1

For the love of all things Worrible.

Acknowledgements

The past two years have been an amazing journey, and I can't wait to see what the next two bring. It wouldn't have been possible without the incredible support from the community, and all the readers who charged headlong into battle—and chimichangas—alongside Damian.
Thank you.

An enthusiastic thank you goes to my beta readers: Amy Cameron, Jason Cameron, Angela Shafer, Vicki Rose Stewart, and Ron Asher.

Thanks to the Critters.org workshop and their superb critiques.

Thank you to The Patrons of Death's Door.

Thank you to my editor, Laura Matheson, who kindly reminded me characters ought not teleport around battlefields, unless of course, they're actually teleporting.

CHAPTER ONE

There are days so great, you wish them to never end,
There are days gone so bad, you wish them never to
have been,
And there are days when hell kicks in your front door.

"Damian!" Sam's voice screeched over the phone. Adrenaline wracked my body. "They're at our house, Mom and Dad's, get here as—" Fear bled through my sister's words before they were cut off by a scream and the roar of gunfire. The line went dead.

I didn't think as I hurtled out the door and down the stairs. I strapped on my gun holster and the black body armor Hugh had given me, tossed my staff into the car, and tore out of the apartment complex, with little recollection of what I'd done to get there. It didn't matter. Mom and Dad mattered. Sam mattered. I pushed the accelerator to the floor and my supercharged '32 Ford Vicky screamed the rage and panic I felt.

I knew it should take almost thirty minutes to get to the house, but there was no way in hell it was taking that long. The highways and signals vanished in a blur of color and horns. Tires screeched as I slid around one car and slammed the accelerator to the floor. Nothing was going to keep me from my family. I should've been stopped by the cops. I wouldn't have stopped for anything.

My heart plummeted as I bounced into the driveway of my parents' old brick two-story home. Sam and I grew up there. Safe, cozy, it had been a calm haven in a crazy world. One of the Pit's black SUVs was upside down on the lawn, trailing black smoke. I was sure it was Sam's, but a glance told me she wasn't in it. I turned to the house. The front door was in splinters. I focused my Sight as I ran toward the gaping wound in my childhood home and saw nothing but a cacophony of broken ghosts, a rainbow of residual power, and dead auras rising and falling like smoke. I had little doubt there were necromancers nearby.

Inside was so much worse. I cursed and slipped on a smear of black-green zombie goo, barely catching myself with the staff in my left hand. The smell tickled my gag reflex. I started breathing through my mouth. I heard something scrape in another room and the pepperbox holstered at my waist almost sprang into my right hand. Body parts littered the foyer. The walls were covered in scratches and tiny holes. My brain registered what the holes meant a second later — shotgun.

"Dad!" I yelled as I moved through the house. Some part of my brain screamed to stay quiet and hunt the bastard that dared to do this. The other part just wanted to find my family. Remnants of a battle were strewn all around me. The dining room to my right was obliterated. Fallen zombies were sprawled throughout the hall, trailing toward the kitchen. Beyond that was the den. I could just make out the blood and gore sprayed across the short dividing wall. "Mom! Sam!" My voice was shrill and my heart hammered as I plowed through the corpses. I passed another corpse with every step. Some were long dead, others had probably enjoyed dinner not long before. Something clattered in the kitchen. I took two quick hops over the shotgunned detritus and leveled the pepperbox at the man at the table.

"Holy shit." My hand twitched before I lowered the barrel. I holstered my gun and leaned my staff against the wall. I flexed my fists to stop the shaking. "Dad."

He sat at the kitchen table with a glass of whiskey, a smoking shotgun, and a pile of ammunition. The room was choked with exploded zombies and one very, very dead necromancer. Dad stared at me over the rim of his glass, threw back the last of the whiskey, and slammed it against the table so hard the glass cracked.

"They took Andi."

"What? They took Mom? Who did?"

My dad shook his head and then closed his eyes. "I don't know."

"Philip did. It was Philip," a voice croaked from the far corner, close to the patio door.

Philip. One of the worst humans I'd ever had the pleasure of meeting. Zola swore he hadn't always been such a bastard, back when they'd been lovers during the Civil War, but everything I'd seen firsthand was a testament as to why dark necromancers deserved their reputation. He'd raised a demon, gotten Carter and Maggie killed, and forced me to unleash a forbidden soulart. I still felt stained by that act, and some part of me worried I'd follow his footsteps into madness.

"You okay?" Dad asked as he stood up, took a few shaky steps, and knelt down by the bloodied form. It took me a moment to realize he wasn't asking me. He'd wiped some of the gore away from her eyes and smoothed her hair back before I even realized it was my sister.

"Sam! Jesus, shit, Sam … what the hell happened?" I slid across the blood and gore that surrounded her, stopping to kneel across from my dad. Her black hair was thick with human and zombie gore. I couldn't tell whose blood was where and fresh panic clawed at my throat.

"Where's Foster?" she said, reaching for my hand. "It hurts." Her other hand tightened around her waist.

Wounded. "How bad?"

She grimaced.

I was on the phone before she could say anything more. I needed Foster, Cara, Aideen … anyone. No one picked up at my shop. Sam shifted her arm and I could see a ragged tear across her stomach. I ground my teeth and looked away. "Dammit." I dropped the phone into a pants pocket and took a deep breath. The wound might not be enough to kill her, but I couldn't be sure. It wasn't closing, and that was bad. Real bad.

I closed my eyes and pushed my aura out harder than I ever had before. The ghostly gray webwork of the city's ley lines shimmered into my mind as my aura ran across them, searching for the only creature I'd learned how to speak to without words. I found him, eventually, curled up by a red panda in the zoo, and I formed my thoughts into a summoning. It probably wouldn't have worked if the damn bear didn't like me, but as soon as I made contact, Happy's pale ghost was standing in my parents' kitchen. Dad didn't even jump. He may have blinked, but then he just shook his head and went back to the table.

"Sam's hurt, we need Foster or Cara or…"

The bear nodded once, made a chortling whine, and vanished before I even finished rambling.

"Been practicing," Sam said. She tried to smile but it fell off her face a moment later. I started rolling up my sleeve and she shook her head.

"Don't make me make you bite me. You bloody well know I'll do it." Sam had some resistance to my necromancy since she'd fed off me before, but if I was really determined, I could still get her to do things. I would imagine that's most siblings' worst nightmare. I stuck my wrist in her face.

A tiny smile cracked the dried blood on her lips before she bit down.

I winced, but that was all. I looked up at Dad. He didn't grimace, didn't flinch. For all the times he'd complained about Sam's "condition" and how there had to be a cure, he didn't make a single comment. I nodded once and he returned it.

"Did they say anything?" I asked.

"Only that they wanted a blessing," he said, "whatever the hell that means."

"A blessing?"

Dad inclined his head as he pulled a clean glass from the cabinet and filled it with water.

"What are you wearing?" he asked.

"This?" I said as I pointed to my chest with my free arm.

He nodded.

"Body armor."

"Why does it say 'Cub'?"

Sam snorted and I yelped as she jerked her fangs to the side. "Sorry," she mumbled into my arm, and went back to feeding.

I smiled at Sam and blew out a breath. "Hugh's sense of humor."

His right eyebrow cocked in question for a moment before laughter rumbled out of his gut. "The werewolves, ah, that's good. Your mother likes Hugh. Seems like a good man." His smile faded as he mentioned Mom.

"We'll get her back," I said. Sam's grip on my arm tightened as I spoke. My mind trailed back to what Philip had done to Zola when he'd taken her last year. My teeth ground together. There was no sense in talking about that now.

I felt a surge in the ley lines before Cara stepped through a black whorl. It snapped out of existence as soon as Aideen followed behind her.

"Philip is after the nail," Cara said as she flashed into her full size in a burst of fairy dust. Gray and white wings brushed the ceiling as she knelt beside Sam. "The Blessing of the Seelie Court."

I closed my eyes and took a deep breath. "Shit."

"You're not sneezing," Aideen said with a small frown.

"Allergy medicine," I said.

"What about allergy medicine?" Dad asked, unable to see or hear the fairies.

Sam let go of my arm. "Hi, Mom," she said. Her voice wasn't much above a whisper.

"Christ, is she losing her mind?" Dad asked.

"No, she's just—" I started.

"I am not waiting for you to explain everything that happens here," Cara said. "Aideen."

"I hope your father is ready for our help," Aideen said as she placed a tiny o-shaped stone in her hand. She whispered an incantation and the stone filled her palm with a thick, syrupy liquid. She slid the stone into a pouch on her belt and stepped toward my dad. She blew across the liquid in her hand, sending small bubbles floating into my dad's eyes, granting him the Sight, showing him the Fae.

His eyes widened as he saw Aideen and Cara for the first time. Golden armor and fine white linens hung around them, framed by their gray and white Atlas moth wings. His hand scrambled for the edge of the table and he sat himself down on the chair with a thump. Sure, he'd met werewolves and vampires, but seeing a seven-foot fairy materialize with brilliant armor and enormous wings can be a bit jarring.

"It is a pleasure to meet you properly, Dimitry." Cara said.

"Christ, you're big." His eyes trailed from the wingtips at the ceiling down to the armored boots on their feet.

"Sometimes we are, sometimes we are not," Aideen said. "Regardless, we must heal your daughter."

"Yes, enough talk. Stand aside, Damian," Cara said.

I nodded and Sam released my arm. Cara leaned in and pulled Sam's shirt up, exposing the gash beneath. It was smaller, but not by much. Cara let the blood-soaked fabric fall back onto the wound, and placed one hand on Sam's shoulder and the other over her heart. *"Socius Sanation."* The incantation was only a whisper, but the explosion of white light was a sun that burned away every shadow in the room.

When I could see again, Sam was standing. Cara had Sam's shirt pulled up enough to reveal my sister's flat, muscled stomach, free of wounds and blemished only by unwashed blood.

Aideen swabbed away as much of the blood as she could with a white kitchen towel and nodded to Cara before dropping the bloody cloth into the sink.

"My god," Dad said as he stood and stepped toward Sam. "It's really true."

He didn't even seem to notice as Aideen and Cara flashed into their smaller forms, only a few inches tall, in a burst of white that emitted no luminescence. His hand brushed the scraps of Sam's shirt to the side. Her black eyes glanced to me and I shrugged. Who knows what runs through someone's mind after surviving a supernatural hailstorm like that? Dad's mind was an open book as he reached out and crushed Sam in a bear hug. Tremors shook his body and I didn't need to see his face to know he was crying. Sam looked shell-shocked for a moment before tears started down her own cheeks.

We stayed still for a while, destruction and death all around us in our childhood home. Cara and Aideen perched on the owl-shaped salt and pepper shakers at the edge of the table and Sam whispered into Dad's ear.

"We'll get her back."

CHAPTER TWO

Dad stood abruptly and the whiskey glass shattered when it fell from his hand as he reached for his shotgun.

"Don't shoot him!" I said.

"What the hell?!" he shouted when Foster materialized in the living room, roaring a battle cry from Happy's back, sword drawn and rage twisting his face.

Sam rewarded the fairy with a snort from the couch. "They're all dead. Calm down."

Foster blinked, looked around the room, and then sheathed his sword with a sigh. His wings drooped a little as he slid backwards off the panda. Happy trundled over to Dad and nosed him in the face. Sam laughed as Dad jerked back.

"He's not exactly a ghost," I said. "You can pet him."

The expression on Dad's face—one raised eyebrow and an uncertain smile—raised a small chuckle from the group. He reached out and scratched Happy behind the ears.

"You may go, Guardian. Find Cassie," Cara said. "Tell her danger is coming."

Happy backed up a few steps and bumped me with his hip. He chortled before vanishing with a quiet, hissing pop.

"What the hell?" Dad said again. He was much more reserved about it this time as he lowered himself back into his chair.

"Cassie has the Blessing again?" I asked. "Is it at the History Museum?"

"Of course not," Cara said. "Don't be daft."

Sam smiled and then bit her lip. I'm sure she was keeping her sibling-insulting impulses in check.

I rubbed my face. "Where do we find her?"

"We don't know," Aideen said. "Zola had an idea for hiding the Blessing, but she only told Cassie. Cassie is hiding it somewhere even Zola won't know about."

"Damn that woman likes her secrets," I muttered.

"And only Zola knows where Cassie is," Cara said. "Cassie is more friend to your master than she ever was to us." She paused and looked at her hand as it curled into a fist.

Something in Cara's voice struck me as odd. She sounded disappointed, or regretful. I suspected there was a history there I didn't know.

Foster shrank and glided over to sit below Aideen. He fluffed his wings and scratched his head. "That's great. Philip doesn't know who has it. He won't think Cassie has the Blessing again. He'll come after all of us, pick us off until he finds out who really has it."

"That's why he took Mom," Sam said. "Isn't it?"

"What?" Foster said. "He was here? He took Andi?"

"It wasn't Philip," Sam said. "It was three necromancers. Two of them I'd never seen before, but the other was a leftover from Stones River, Volund."

"Where's Zola?" Cara asked.

"At the cabin," I said. "I'll call her."

I flipped out my cell and called my master. She picked up in one ring, but was silent. In the background, I could hear the low, gravelly growl of rocks speaking.

"Dark times, Adannaya. They drew on much power in the city today."

"Hey, Aeros!" I shouted into the phone.

"Dammit, boy. Ah'm hard enough of hearing," Zola said with a snap in her old world New Orleans accent.

I could hear Aeros's rumbling laughter in the background.

"We have problems," I said with all humor gone from my voice. "They took my mom. They're after the Blessing."

The string of curses that erupted from the phone would have sent a demon running for a bomb shelter. "I'm coming."

The phone went dead.

***

I heard the rumble of Zola's car two hours later while it was still half a block away. I was standing in the dim night when the motion-activated floodlight over my parents' garage lit up her flashy, blue 1957 Chevy Bel Air. She steered past my car, into the driveway, and stepped out. Her gray cloak lifted briefly in a cold breeze and her gnarled hands contrasted sharply with the pale knobs on her old cane.

My eyes widened as Edgar Amon stepped out of the passenger side with a bowler tucked under his arm. He was dressed to the nines in a black three-piece suit.

"Oh, shit," Foster said. I looked toward his voice and saw him perched in one of the shattered windows.

Edgar glanced at the overturned SUV and rolled his eyes.

"Hey, Eddie!" I said cheerfully as I affixed the best fake grin on my face I could muster.

"You litter the streets with corpses, destroy a prized sculpture, burn an entire city to the ground, and let's not even start on Stones River."

I was fairly certain he wasn't talking about the mess we'd made during the battle at Stones River. I was pretty damn sure he was not-so-subtly referring to the soulart I'd destroyed Prosperine with.

Edgar looked up and met my eyes. His own were black pitch in his sandy face and close-cropped hair. "And now you drag this catastrophe into your parents' home."

My false grin faded into a snarl.

Zola put a hand on Edgar's shoulder. "Enough, Amon. That is enough. The Watchers can't win this battle without us, and we can't win without you. We are past this petty nonsense."

Edgar closed his eyes slowly and took a deep breath. "I forget myself. My apologies, Damian."

My jaw was still hanging loose as he walked by and followed Foster into the house, back to the relatively clear living room.

I grabbed Zola's arm and whispered into her ear. "What's he doing here?"

She glanced at my hand, plucked it off with the strength of a bodybuilder, and narrowed her eyes. "He's a friend of the best sort."

"What does that mean?"

"Once he was an enemy, many years ago."

I shook my head. "How long have you known him?"

"Long," she said as she stepped into the house and we picked our way into the kitchen through the carnage.

"My god," Edgar said. "They struck like this in daylight?"

"Sunset," Dad said as he held out his hand and shook Edgar's. "We were sitting down to a late dinner when these things came in."

Edgar leaned down and studied a few of the headless zombies. "You are a surgeon with a shotgun, Dimitry."

Dad's eyes narrowed. "How do you know my name?"

"I am a Watcher. It's my job to know things. Has Damian not spoken of us before?" Edgar flipped the bowler onto the glass stovetop with a flick of his wrist, not waiting for my dad to respond. He turned one of the kitchen chairs toward the living room. I was half irritated and half glad he didn't want to get into it with Dad.

I sat down next to Sam on the old, blue corduroy couch as she finished wiping most of the blood off her face. Some still trailed down her neck. I watched her for a moment as she brushed her hair back, revealing the darker patch of skin where a vampire named Dale had ripped out her throat. I'd turned him into confetti and used the leftovers to stitch Sam back together with a soulart.

I ran my hand over the tightly woven bumps of the fabric on the cushions. We used to sit on that couch as kids, back when Saturday mornings were still reserved for cartoons and Fruit Loops.

I stared at the floor and muttered, "How the hell did we end up here?"

Sam smiled and squeezed my knee, as though she knew exactly what I meant.

Zola sat down on the dark leather recliner while Dad took up a post at the edge of the kitchen, within arm's reach of his shotgun, a fact I don't believe Edgar missed. The fairies formed a loose circle on the surprisingly intact glass coffee table.

"Where is Cassie?" Cara asked.

"She's with the Piasa Bird," Zola said.

Edgar rubbed his face and sighed. "Never boring around you people, is it?" Everyone ignored him but Zola. She shot him a smile.

"Just wait, Edgar. Just wait." Zola's quiet laugh was utterly unnerving.

"You mean the painting on the bluffs?" Sam asked. "Over in Alton?"

"Yes, that's where she is, but within the cliffs, in the lair of the bird."

"That thing is real?" I asked.

"It is one of the last of its kind," Edgar said. "There were many more, in darker times. A hybrid of Native American lore and twisted Fae magics."

"Hardly," Zola said. "You know what he is."

Edgar frowned and glanced at the fairies.

"Does Philip know about the Piasa Bird?" Foster asked.

Zola rubbed her chin on her shoulder. "He may."

"There are no Ways into that lair," Cara said.

"There is one," Aideen said.

Cara shook her head. "Anyone appearing in front of that creature would be devoured in an instant."

"So we get to travel by car?" I asked, unable to keep a little edge of glee out of my voice. "No nauseating ride through the Warded Ways?"

"What are we waiting for?" Foster asked.

"The hour is late," Edgar said. "It would be better to travel tomorrow morning, after some rest."

"Enough," Cara said. "It is already tomorrow and Andi is missing. Load up, we are leaving."

CHAPTER THREE

"Hugh?" I asked as soon as someone picked up the line.

"Damian, your call is welcome brother. What do you need?" Hugh—River Pack Alpha, and all around Native American werewolf badass—had inducted me into the pack in the summer, after our battle with Philip and Prosperine the Destroyer. Now he's my Alpha too, in a way, but I don't turn furry.

"I have some Indian questions for you."

"I don't know much about Indian questions," he said, with a particular emphasis on Indian.

"Ah, right. No disrespect intended," I said. "I have some questions about a Native American legend. Or possibly myth? Maybe creature? I'm not sure."

"That seems to be the usual reason for calling me. I begin to wonder if your sister was correct. Perhaps I should employ a secretary?"

Sam snickered from the driver's seat of my '32 Ford Victoria. It felt wrong to call my car Vicky anymore, now that the little ghost had taken the name. I studiously ignored Sam as we started across the bridge over the Mississippi River. Huge swaths of cabling draped across the center towers of the bridge and out to the edges on either side, creating skeletal sails against the cloudy blue sky.

"It's a quick question, I swear."

Hugh sighed. "Very well."

"What's the Piasa Bird?"

"A quick question? That is a very complex question. It has many meanings to many people."

"But what's the real bird?" I asked.

Hugh paused. "That is a dangerous question with a perilous answer my friend. Why do you need to know such things?"

"We're on our way to meet it." I heard a strangled cough from Hugh. "Cassie is staying with it and we have to find her."

"The fairy?"

"Yes," I said.

"That is good. You may avoid being eaten. It would be better if you did not venture out in situations such as this without the help of the pack." He sighed again, and I could practically see him rubbing his eyebrows. "Very well, the Piasa Bird may seem an enormous bird to your eyes, but it is not. It is balance, and a force against the underwater panthers of the Mississippi."

"The what?" Sam asked. I didn't think my phone was turned up all that loud, but Sam could hear Hugh well enough.

"The Mishupishu, underwater panthers," Hugh said again, with his voice raised a bit higher in volume.

"That's what I thought he said." Sam shook her head.

"The panthers are many, dragging hunters and animals alike to their doom. Without the Piasa Bird, humans would be cut down before they reached the river's edge. At first glance, you may see a bobcat, or a cougar, but focus on the panthers long enough and you will find horns, scales, and claws long enough to gut bison.

"The Piasa Bird eats underwater panthers. I do not know all the stories. Many are kept by the Society of Flame."

"Koda's group?" I asked.

"The same," Hugh said. "The Fae guard the Piasa Bird, but it is not theirs to control. Be wary my friend. You deal with powerful beings. I must greet the pack."

"Thanks, Hugh," I said as he clicked off the line.

"What's the Society of Flame?" Sam asked.

"Best I can tell, they're keepers of lore," I said. "I've spoken to a ghost of the society off and on since I was a teenager. His name's Koda, one of the elders Hugh knew. Koda told me about a time when necromancers were celebrated. 'Gifted with the ability to speak with ancestors,' he said. That's sure changed, hasn't it?" I couldn't keep the bitterness out of my voice.

Sam glanced at me from the corner of her eye. "There are a lot of idiots out there, Demon. I still think you're all right for a corpse-loving zombie groper."

"Look who's talking," I said as I gave her a small nod before turning my attention back to Hugh. "The Society of Flame was made up of commoners and Fae alike. I've run across mentions of them in some old books, but nothing recent. A few books even hinted the society knew more about the magics of our world than the Fae courts did."

"Seems unlikely," Sam said.

I shrugged.

The brake lights on Zola's car lit up as we took another exit and started through downtown Alton. It was homey, with much the same charm as Saint Charles, though there were many more modern buildings invading the old city. A farmer's market bustled on the street corner, white tents catching the sun in a brilliant contrast to the aged brick behind them.

"I want to stop there," Sam said.

"If we're still alive later, I'm game," I said.

"You think it's okay Dad's riding with them?"

I nodded. "He wanted to. Hell, he hasn't seen Zola in what, five years? Six? He sees us all the time."

"Not all the time," Sam said. I could hear the tinge of loss in her voice, some piece of her still struggling with her change. "And he lost Mom."

"For now," I said, watching Sam. She frowned slightly before all emotion left her face. I'd seen the look before. She was choking something back that she didn't want me to see.

The town vanished. A sheer, white rock bluff rose up on our right, speckled with green brush and crowned by trees and power lines. The Mississippi River hurried past on our left.

The bluff drew away from the road a short while later and Zola began to pull off. The rocks curled back around and started for the road again. A dry inlet, filled by an asphalt parking lot and a small tourist kiosk, greeted us as we parked. Gray landscaping stones lined the base of the bluff before a small patch of grass.

Above it all, on the rocky face of the bluff, the painting of the Piasa Bird loomed. It was not frightening, but when Sam turned the car off and my foot found the earth, power spiked around me. My Sight flashed up by instinct alone. The explosion of electric blue ley lines was almost blinding. The tangled lines of power lead to a massive cavern to the left of the painting. I let my Sight fade and stared at the cliff painting. I have no idea why they call it a bird. It looked more like a griffin, almost, but adorned with red wings and covered with golden scales. Red eyes bored into me, framed in a disturbingly human face, crowned with a deadly pair of horns. A tail crossed from its back, over its front shoulders, and curved beneath its body, where it wove between its four limbs and their ferocious talons.

"Shit," Sam said as she closed the door. "It's a bit creepy. That thing's real?"

"God, I hope not," I said.

Sam glanced at me, then back to the painting. I saw a shiver run down her spine.

Dad stepped out of Zola's car and moved the seat forward to let Edgar out. I blinked, surprised to see Edgar in the back seat.

The fairies grew, drawing swords and forming a triangle around our group.

"Something up?" I asked.

Foster shook his head. "This is not a safe area. Things that should not be walk the earth here."

"Have something to do with that massive ball of power?" I said as I hitched my thumb toward the cavern entrance.

"Keep your Sight locked down, boy," Zola said. "To look on a being like the Piasa Bird—"

Edgar cleared his throat. Zola stared him down.

"It would be unwise," she said.

"And unlikely to prolong your sanity," Edgar said.

Dad pulled his shotgun off the floorboard of the Chevy.

"You will not need that here," Aideen said. She pulled her coif down and let it pool around her neck. The tips of her pointed ears poked out from beneath her platinum hair.

"Leave it, Dimitry," Cara said. "It will do you no good in this place."

He hesitated only a moment before easing the gun back to the floor and closing the door.

"Fine," he said, biting off the word as he turned back to the group.

Edgar moved and gently turned Dad by his elbow. "Honestly, we need you to create an imbalance, a need for sympathy."

"You have the tact of demons, Amon," Cara said flatly.

"What?" Dad asked as he jerked his elbow away.

"Dimitry, stop," Zola said. "Do not be angered by this. The fight that is coming, we need help. Philip has allied himself with powers you cannot imagine."

He glanced at Sam, and then at me. "My kids, are they in danger?"

Zola let out a hollow laugh. "They are always in danger. This will help. Ah promise you."

His eyes trailed back to Sam and he nodded once.

Edgar glanced at Cara and narrowed his eyes, ever so slightly, adjusted the bowler on his head, and started walking toward the cavern entrance.

The entrance loomed large. An enormous arch opened into the bluff wall, a thirty- by fifty-foot space, split in two by a wide, rough column of stone. More columns shone dimly from within the darkness, all wider at the ceiling, obscuring what lay beyond.

Loose rock, from pebbles to boulders, littered the ground, rolling and twisting unexpectedly in attempts to snap our ankles or worse. I slid and cursed, kicking a sharp rock deeper into the cavern. The hollow sound of its impact echoed around us.

Cara led, with Edgar at her side. A dull blue light floated above his left shoulder, illuminating the passage ahead. Zola and Dad followed. Sam and I stayed a few paces behind, flanked by Foster and Aideen.

We moved forward slowly, keeping our formation as best we could. Nothing moved in the dim blue light. I looked behind us and saw the bright sockets of the entrance were fading, leading daylight away and bringing shadows close enough to touch.

Dad cursed as something large shifted deeper in the cave. The sound of lightning and a thunder crack in the distance rumbled up from the darkness.

"I have a bad feeling about—" Sam started.

"Shut up," I said, but I couldn't completely restrain my smile.

Edgar whispered something, and I could have sworn it was "My brother." My eyebrows drew down in thought as I wondered what he was talking about before something else caught my attention. A wall, slightly off to our right, shimmered and vanished. A flash of white, which emitted no luminescence, became Cassie, running forward to embrace Cara, and then Zola.

The fairy was armed to the teeth. Golden mail with intricate Celtic designs was draped over Cassie's shoulders and wrapped around her torso and legs. Her armor gleamed in the bluish light, a sword sheathed on either leg, with another hilt sticking up between her gray wings.

"You are here," she said to Zola with a hand on my master's shoulder. Her voice was light and more musical than those of the other fairies.

"You are safe," Zola said. I could hear the satisfaction in her voice, made even clearer as her accent deepened and her words came out quickly. "Ah'm sorry we did not come sooner."

"Do not apologize," Cassie said. "This is more important than any one of us. If Philip or Ezekiel claim the Blessing, the fight is done."

"If that happens, the world is done," Cara said.

"What of the Piasa Bird?" Edgar said, his gaze never leaving the cavern's depths.

"It stirs, Amon," Cassie said. "Since you arrived here I would call it restless."

Edgar's eyes focused on Dad for a moment and then returned to the darkness. "Enough delays," he said as he took one step into the shadow.

The avian cry shattered my senses. The cry of an eagle, magnified a thousandfold, rattled the walls and sent everyone to their knees, hands over ears. Except for Edgar, who laughed and almost jogged forward as pebbles and rocks crashed to the earth around us.

"Don't open your Sight," Zola said through gritted teeth.

I nodded and struggled to my feet with Sam's help. The ley lines battered my senses. I was drowning in their power, flying in it as I walked beneath a raging tsunami, torrents of power swirling and pushing and pulling.

"Christ," I said, my left arm outstretched in a vain physical effort to fight off a metaphysical storm.

Foster put a hand on my shoulder. "This is far older than Christ, Damian. Older than any human religion."

"I've never felt anything like this."

Sam put her shoulder under me and pushed forward. Dad helped Zola through the invisible storm as we followed Edgar deeper and deeper. The path sloped down and narrowed further in before a sharp bend to the north. We turned the corner behind Edgar and stopped dead.

I stared, slack jawed, at the beautiful monster hidden inside.

Talons like the blackest obsidian gripped the floor near our feet. Towering twenty feet above them stood an eagle. Brilliant gold feathers glowed across its entirety, etched with black highlights running to a brilliant white ring of fine feathers at its neck. Silver feathers gleamed like broadswords at the tip of its wings.

The behemoth cocked its head to the side, the movement too fast to follow. It blinked and a chain of lightning erupted from its eyes, blackening and scarring the cavern above it. Its head cocked to the other side and it bent close to Dad, its left eye only a foot or two away, above a black beak large enough to swallow a small car. A storm swirled where the eye should have been.

"Where is the Blessing, Cassie?" Edgar said.

"Tell him," Zola said without hesitation.

Cassie glanced at Cara, who gave her a smile and a small nod. "It is in Boonville."

Edgar turned back to the Piasa Bird. "Guard the town. We'll come in the hour of the sun. One of the Seals is upon us."

"Seal?" I asked as quietly as I could. I almost hoped no one answered, because the only Seals I could think of were ancient things I'd only read about. Old stories made them out as barriers between our realm and a host of places you really didn't want to go.

Zola shook her head slightly, and I took the hint. No more questions.

The bird regarded Edgar for a moment before shuffling to the side. It walked around us, keeping its eyes on Edgar as it moved to another passage I hadn't noticed. The creature paused and shook out its feathers like a normal bird. It hunkered down for a brief moment, then launched itself out of a narrow opening in the top of the cavern without moving its wings. The thunder-clap that followed shook the earth once more.

Edgar laughed and turned to the group. "Isn't he magnifi-cent?"

Zola rapped her cane on the ground and snarled. "You didn't tell us we were sending Cassie to live with a Thunderbird!"

CHAPTER FOUR

"Zola, it's okay. Thunderbirds have never acted against the Fae," Cassie said, her hands out in a placating gesture.

"And if we had come to find you?" Zola asked. "If we had set foot here without Amon and the bird decided *we* were an imbalance?"

Cassie's hands fell and she turned toward Edgar. "Would he destroy them?"

Edgar shrugged. "It is unlikely. The old Fae legends are much more severe than a living Thunderbird. There is far more evil in the world than there are things trying to destroy it."

We all stared at Edgar. A shiver ran down my spine. For all his talk and disdain for all necromancers, he'd just said—out loud—we aren't all evil.

Edgar laughed, pulled his bowler off, and bowed slightly. "Don't take that the wrong way. You still irritate me to no end."

"That's a relief," I said. "Thought my world was ending there for a second."

"Not yet," Edgar said as he started back up through the cavern.

I scooted closer to Zola as Edgar became a shadow in front of the cavern entrance. "What the hell is going on with him?"

"He has hidden himself from the world for many years," she said. "Not many people have been betrayed as badly as Amon. Those that violated his trust the worst were necromancers."

"Betrayal leaves a mark," Cassie said as she came up behind us, picking her way around the debris on the floor of the cavern. "Most of us were surprised when he joined the Watchers. He'd been all but a hermit before that."

"So what's the Thunderbird like?" Foster said to Cassie as he landed on my shoulder. I guess he'd decided the risk was over for the moment.

I caught Cassie's frown as the sunlight temporarily blinded us.

"It is … different," she said. "I understand it thrives on balance, but I don't think it is always balance as we see it."

"Gods rarely see things the same way we do," Zola said.

"A god?" I slid on a patch of loose rocks as I contemplated what that could possibly mean. "Thunderbirds are Old Gods?"

"Shit," Sam said. "You mean that thing is a god?"

"Oh yes," Zola said.

"What's an Old God?" Dad asked.

"Some things you are better off not knowing," Zola said as she patted Sam's arm.

"Bullshit." Dad turned to face us in the entryway, somehow seeming to block the entire cavern entrance. "You let this man drag me down here as bait, bait for some kind of god that's sensitive to the fact I just lost my fucking wife! You think there're worse things I don't need to know? Things I can't deal with? I'll tear this world in half to get her back!" His chest heaved and a vein throbbed at his temple.

Zola folded her hands gently over her cane and sighed. "Ah meant no disrespect Dimitry. Would you not do this to keep your children safe, to help find your wife?"

Dad narrowed his eyes.

"It seems our guest is early," Zola said as she turned her head.

A gray phantom caught the corner of my eye. I jerked a little when the shadow waved and laughed a low rhythmic sound, almost a giggle. "Oh shit," I said quietly.

"That's my cue," a voice said from the deeps of the cavern ceiling. A man dropped in a flash of blackened red flame. Stone powdered and billowed into thin clouds as he crushed it flat upon landing.

Sam blipped out of existence and pounced onto Mike the Demon, crushing him in a bear hug.

"You're kind of ruining the dramatic entrance," Mike said as he smiled and patted her back with a few good whacks.

Edgar watched the exchange briefly before walking closer to the cars. Mike dwarfed Sam, standing almost seven feet tall. His black hair was still closely cropped, and his hands were blackened, with trails of darkness leading up his arms like abstract tattoos.

"Damian, is this your father?"

I nodded.

"I have a gift for you, Dimitry," Mike said as he pulled at a strap secured diagonally across his barrel chest. "It will aid you with the powers you face."

Before my dad could even respond, I asked, "How did you know anything had happened? How did you know my dad was here? How did you know *we* were here?"

Mike held up his index finger. "One, Nixie called me after Glenn told her and she couldn't reach you with the Wasser-Münzen."

My hand instantly moved to my back pocket. Nothing. I must have left the damn thing back at the shop. "Oh," I said, annoyed with myself for forgetting to bring my best means of communication with Nixie.

Mike added his middle finger. "Two, Frank."

Sam blushed. "He, uh, wasn't supposed to say anything."

"Samantha Vesik," Zola snapped as her old New Orleans accent thickened. "Did you call Frank? Did you tell him where we were going even after Ah said not to?"

"I ... maybe I mentioned something." By the time she finished the sentence, I could barely hear her muttered words.

Mike extended his ring finger. "And before you ask the third, the gun is from your master, Zola."

Zola's mouth snapped shut and she glared at Mike.

Foster and Aideen snickered from their new resting spot on Sam's shoulder.

"There is no taint on this weapon," he said as he lifted the strap over his head. "It does not bind or obligate you to me in any way." As he finished speaking, Mike turned his head toward Dad.

"Bind or obligate?" he said.

"He's a demon," Zola said flatly.

Dad's eyes flashed wide and he took a hesitant step away from Mike.

The demon sighed and held out the cannon-sized gun in his arms. "I suppose I deserved that," he said with a small smile.

"Take the gun, Dimitry," Zola said. "He's a friend."

"Do not touch the fairies with this," Mike said.

Dad's about six feet tall, five inches shorter than me. When Mike placed the gun in his hands, it looked like it was going to pull him over. The stock was open. Where you expected wood it was a hollow and rounded triangle. A few inches up the stock, the trigger rested in a spacious guard with the hammer above. The barrel shot out from there, octagonal at first, but it broke into a cylinder in another six inches or so. The gun almost looked like a musket, but the entire weapon, even the ramrod, devoured light like cast iron, until the runes on the side began to glow. I recognized some. The sharp angles of Kaun looked like a mathematical less-than symbol, and Uruz bore a shape much like a sharp-angled lowercase n, runes of strength and fire.

"What is this thing?" Dad said, admiration obvious in his voice. "The barrel has to be two feet long. An elephant gun?"

"No, it's twenty-one inches," Mike said. "It's based on a whaling gun. The runes are a little something extra. They'll only activate in the hands of a mortal man."

"Truly?" Zola asked.

Mike nodded.

"Brilliant," she said as she leaned in a little. "Can a mage even fire it?"

"No, and neither can a necromancer, so don't try it. These wards at the end," he said as he pointed to a circular ring of squiggles, "will paralyze any magic user that pulls the trigger."

"What kind of rounds does it fire?" Dad asked.

"These." Mike reached behind him and unhooked a large leather pouch. He pulled out what looked like a small rocket. "It's called a bomb lance. Load it into the front end of the gun and ram it down." With one bomb lance still in-hand, Mike held out the leather satchel.

Dad reached for the pouch and grunted as he slung it over his shoulder. The weight was obvious. Mike held out the last lance and kept his grip as Dad started to pull it away.

"Don't point these at anything *near* anything or anyone you don't want dead." He let the lance slide out of his hand as Dad nodded. It was then I noticed the hammer in Mike's belt. It looked innocuous, with more substance at the front of the head than the back, and powerful as all hell—the Smith's Hammer.

"You got it back?" I said.

Mike's hand brushed the hammer and he smiled at Zola. "It was given back. I have been helping the Harrowers."

"They grow strong," said a small voice from the edge of the cavern. The little necromancer, ghost for almost two centuries, girlfriend to a demon for ages, sidled up beside Mike. He put his arm around her as easily as if she wore flesh and blood. Mike had grown attached to the girl when she was still alive. He'd watched her die in the Civil War, unable to save one of the very few people he cared about. She stared at my dad for a moment and then looked up at me. "You made them strong, Damian."

"I hope it was the right thing to do," I said. "I didn't know what I was doing."

"It was," Mike said. "Hell flees before the Ghost Pack."

"This is not the time to speak of it," Zola said. "Call Frank and Ashley." She paused and rubbed her chin. "If Philip's necromancers are in Boonville, and the Piasa Bird is heading there … never mind. We'll meet at the shop. Edgar, follow that damn bird and make sure it doesn't try to devour Boonville." If it was a request, there was no hint of it in her voice.

"I need to clean up the house," Dad said to himself as he stared off toward the river. "Andi won't be happy when she comes home to that mess."

I didn't miss Dad's use of 'when' instead of 'if.' Sam didn't either, if the small frown on her face had anything to say about it.

"Do not worry about your home," Edgar said. "It is done." He nodded when Dad thanked him, but Edgar didn't elaborate on why or how he knew it was done. I don't know if he didn't feel the need to tell Dad about the lengths Watchers go to while hiding our world, or if he just assumed Dad already knew because of me and Sam. Edgar turned to the fairies. "Cassie, Cara, would you care for a ride?"

The two fairies nodded and started forward before flashing into their smaller sizes and fluttering to either of Edgar's shoulders. The Watcher adjusted his bowler, cocked his arm at a ninety-degree angle in front of his stomach, and began to float into the sky.

"He's flying," Dad said, nowhere near as much shock in his voice as there should have been.

I heard a small chuckle as Cassie waved from Edgar's shoulder.

Zola turned back toward the rest of us. "Let's go."

Sam and I glanced at each other before we both nodded.

"Alright, you still want to stop by the farmer's market on the way out of town?" I asked Sam.

She nodded.

"I'm going to ride with Zola," Dad said.

"I'll join you if you have room, Damian," Mike said.

"Sure thing. Zola, you want us to meet you back at the Double D?"

"No, boy," Zola said as we reached the cars. "We'll join you at the market."

"Alright, see you there."

***

"I can't believe Cara went with Edgar," I said. "Maybe the world really is ending."

Mike laughed behind me, his gruff voice filling the car. "There are worse things in the land right now than tickets from the Watchers. Cara is a smart woman. She knows a powerful ally when she sees one."

"If Philip is coming for all of us ..." Sam said, her eyes on the road as we started back in to the city. "What about Frank, Ashley, the wolves?"

I smiled. "Frank has two badass cu siths trailing him everywhere he goes. Anything short of that damn bird would be a snack for Bubbles and Peanut." Sam grinned at that. "Ashley is no helpless witch, sis. Have you seen what she can do with those runes now? She is rising, even Cara thinks so."

"But what if it's Philip, or Ezekiel?"

"Ezekiel?" Mike asked. "I don't think I could defeat him at my best. His powers are too great."

I shuddered at the thought of Ezekiel. Philip scared me, but Zola said Ezekiel was unfathomably more powerful than Philip. She still hadn't figured out why he's tagging along with a weaker necromancer. I dread the day we find out.

"Best not to think about that now," I said. "As for the wolves?"

Sam gave me a sideways glance. "Yeah, never mind. Werewolves."

"Stubborn creatures," Mike said. "But they are valiant, even honorable, in the right situation."

I nodded in agreement.

"How are you doing without Nixie?" Sam asked.

I blinked at the complete logic leap of the conversation. "Where did that come from?"

"The werewolves. I was thinking about Hugh, which made me think of Haka and how Nixie saved him, and then how she's been gone for a few months now. Obviously."

I blinked again.

She swatted at me with her right hand. "Well? Did she call lately?"

"Call?" I said. "That's funny. I guess it's kind of a call, but seriously? You're going to bring this up in front of Mike?"

Mike laughed. "She is a good person, for a water witch. It is natural to pine for your lover." Mike looked at Sam, and a slow smile crept over his face. "Besides, the water witch did call me when you did not answer her call."

I groaned and rubbed my face while Sam laughed outright. "Yeah, anyhow, I'm due for a call today."

Sam pulled in to park and turned off the engine. Zola's Chevy stopped beside us. I stepped out and stretched for a moment, sending a flash of blackness and stars across my vision. Once my eyes started to clear I fumbled for the seat release and shifted it forward so Mike could climb out.

"A Scarborough Fair," the demon said with a smile.

"Not exactly," I said.

"A what?" Sam said. "Isn't that a song?"

Mike began to explain what the fairs were like in his time: merchants and entertainers gathered from lands far and wide, when spices were valuable enough a pound of cloves could buy a small herd of sheep. I looked over the market. Four rows of white tents lined the parking lot, nestled between two fairly modern brick buildings. I took a deep breath. The scent of rosemary from an herb dealer mingled with hickory smoke, fresh popped kettle corn, and the distant smell of the river.

"I am seriously hungry," I said.

"I am seriously shocked," Sam said as she rabbit punched me lightly in the arm.

Mike chuckled and strolled over to a homemade sausage vendor. A huge black smoker built into the back of a trailer sent a steady billowing stream of smoke into the air. The wind shifted toward us and I picked up the pace.

"Afternoon," the man beside the smoker said. A heavy flannel shirt hung down over his jeans, the collar obscured at the top by a long and neatly trimmed beard.

"Hi," Sam said.

"Do I smell smoked bologna?" Mike asked.

The man's eyes widened a bit before he nodded and smiled. He pulled the top of the smoker up and pointed to four huge links on the leftmost side. "Yes, but I'm surprised you could pick out the scent with all the cooking here today."

"I'll take a link," Mike said.

"A whole one?"

"Indeed sir."

"You going to eat all that?" I asked.

"I'll let you try a bite. Of course, you'll probably want one of your own. I tend to work up an appetite battling the forces of evil."

Sam snickered and I heard Zola snort from the next stall over. She leaned over to Foster and Aideen, and I assume she relayed Mike's comment because they both laughed.

"That looks like some very fresh jerky there too," Dad said.

The vendor pulled a strip off and handed it to him. "Enjoy. If you boys, and girl," he said with a nod to Sam, "are buying a whole link, I'll pack some more up, no charge."

Dad took a bite and nodded. "That's fantastic. Thank you."

We wandered around the market for a few minutes. Sam stopped and bought a set of hand-blown glass earrings and a stuffed toy, ferret. I was pretty sure the ferret would end up taunting Vik in some dastardly manner.

Mike passed out some chunks of his bologna log. It took all of two bites for everyone to become converts to the glory of smoked bologna.

"Holy crap, that's good," I said around a mouthful of soft, smoky, deliciousness.

"Natural casing," Dad said. "Adds an extra snap."

Sam grimaced and took another bite. "Let's just say it tastes good. I don't want to think about the *snap*."

"It is good," Mike said. "There's a butcher in Hermann." He took another bite and swallowed. "He makes black pudding. I think you call it blood sausage. That takes me back," he said with a smile.

"Nasty," Sam said.

"Whatever, sis. I recall seeing you at a sushi bar one time."

"Oh, not this again," Sam said under her breath.

You're scared of a little blood sausage? I've seen you take down raw octopus."

"That's different."

"No," Mike said, "*That* is nasty."

We turned the corner and started back up the last row tents, bantering all the way. I'm sure I wasn't the only one whose mind was stuck on Mom, but I trusted Zola. If she thought we needed to delay our arrival in Boonville, I wouldn't question it, no matter how much I wanted to kick in the front door guns blazing. My hand instinctively moved to the pepperbox under my jacket.

"Here they are," Foster said as he swooped back and landed on my shoulder.

Zola stepped up to the second booth from the end.

I slid in next to her, Foster leaning on my neck for a second as he caught his balance. The booth was full of tiles. Some baskets were filled with small white squares and rectangles, others black or red or any color you can think off. Some had holes drilled in them and sat beside a display of cords to make bracelets or necklaces.

"What did you need here?" I said, honestly curious.

"Dragon bones," Zola said, reaching out for a basket in the back row. She picked up a few large scales, which looked like a cross between a fish and a crocodile.

"By the ..." Mike's words trailed off as he reached into the basket too, coming up with a handful of scales. "These aren't just bones, Addanaya."

"Fellow practitioners, I see," said the small woman behind the table. Her voice was quiet and a little scratchy. She adjusted the afghan around her shoulders and smiled at the group.

"Where did you find these?" Mike asked.

"That is a secret long held by my family," the vendor said.

Mike nodded. "Guard it well. It is a treasure to be sure. What is your price?"

"For each? Two hundred dollars."

I choked on the water I was drinking. Sam's jaw almost hit the pavement. Dad just gnawed on some jerky.

"That's a good price," Aideen said.

"We need some rune tiles as well," Zola said. "Black and white."

"Black?" the woman raised her eyebrows as she spoke.

"Yes," Zola said, without inflection.

"Very well."

"What is your price for all of them?" Mike asked.

"All?" the old woman perked up. "I have two hundred scales." She stood up and leaned over the booth toward Mike. "That's forty thousand."

Mike nodded. "Throw in all your rune tiles and I'll pay you thirty."

"Thirty? Dear, you're adorable, but I can't take less than thirty-seven fifty."

"Thirty-five, in gold, right now." Mike reached around his back and pulled out a sack I swear hadn't been there a moment before. He dropped it on the table top to the chime of dozens of coins. "I'll come back in six months and buy more after your dragon sheds again."

The woman blinked at Mike, her mouth forming a little O. She glanced at the hammer on his belt and said, "You are well traveled for a blacksmith."

"You have no idea," Mike said.

She opened the sack of coins, glanced at them without counting, and nodded. "They're all yours."

"Thank you, lady," Mike said. "May we keep the baskets?"

"Oh yes, I think I can afford to replace them now," she said with a small smile.

We picked up three baskets with hundreds of tiles and the smaller basket of scales. I waited until we were away from the booth and closer to the car before I opened my mouth.

"Are those real?" I asked.

"Yes," Mike, Zola, Aideen, and Foster said at once.

"What are you going to do with all these?" I asked as Zola opened her trunk and we set the baskets down.

"I assume the rune tiles are going to the green witch, your friend Ashley," Mike said. "I will share the dragon scales with your master, as she most likely wants to destroy them."

Zola flashed him a smile.

"I will not, however, let you destroy them all," Mike said.

"Why destroy them?" I asked.

"They are too powerful," Zola said. "If Ashley uses a dragon scale as a rune tile, her spell will be magnified a hundredfold."

"Or more," Aideen said. "Dragons are almost pure ley energy. We can't really know what it will do."

"A scale in the hands of our enemies is unthinkable. Ah have seen firsthand what dark menace they can bring." She looked up at Mike. "As have you."

He nodded, but didn't respond.

"What do you want them for, Mike?" Foster asked. There was an eagerness to his voice. Guessing by the smile on the demon's face, Mike heard it too.

"I am not sure yet. Armor perhaps, or a weapon of some sort. I will think on it."

"You two have some interesting friends," Dad said as he glanced between me and Sam.

"You should meet Aeros." Sam smiled as she gave Dad a sideways glance.

"I think I've had enough surprises for today, but thank you." He returned her smile with a smaller one.

"Yes," Zola said. "Ah agree. Let's get your wife back, Dimitry."

CHAPTER FIVE

We pulled into the parking lot behind the shop. Sam jumped out and dashed across the cobblestones for the back door. The deadbolt saw her coming.

"No, no, no, no!" the little face squealed a moment before Sam's boot connected with a resounding thud. The deadbolt snapped open and Sam pushed her way through. The other, non-Fae deadbolt, usually stayed unlocked while the store was open.

Mike put a basket over each arm and started for the door with Zola and Dad close behind.

I was behind them all when I said, "Oh, hold on a sec. Dad, did you hear something? Could you check the door for me?"

"What?" he asked as he took a few steps out in front of us and looked toward the open door. "Why?"

A chain of barks echoed like a train whistle as Bubbles and Peanut shot out the door, bearing down on Dad. He cursed and braced himself against the green and black blur of overexcited pups. The cu siths—or possibly ponies, depending on your age and their temperament—stood up to my waist now. Their bristly green fur had softened along with their braided tails since the battle at Stones River, but that's all secondary when a hundred-and-fifty-pound pooch tries to kneecap you. Dad stumbled back only to be pushed forward by Peanut. Bubbles licked his face with her outrageously long tongue and then panted. She snapped at Peanut, led him on a wild chase around the parking lot, and then disappeared into the shop again.

"I thought those were a lot smaller when you told me about them," Dad said as he wiped his face on his shirt. "They got big."

"That's just a matter of perspective," Foster said. "Some cu siths have been known to—"

I held up my hand. "I don't want to know."

I heard Aideen laugh as she glided through the door.

"You keep a strange home, necromancer," Mike said, and there was nothing snide or negative in his words.

"I try."

The demon followed Zola through the door.

We made our way down a few steps and through the back room, past the pantry, also known as the junk closet. I heard the tick of the fairies' grandfather clock before we passed the old Formica table. I pushed through the saloon doors behind Dad. Sam giggled, and I looked up to see why. Frank was reaching for a sizable crystal on a shelf above the counter and my sister's hand was firmly attached to his ass.

"Samantha," Dad said in a perfect echo of our teenage years.

Frank jerked on the step ladder and fumbled the crystal in surprise. I closed my eyes as it started to fall.

"It didn't break," Mike whispered in my ear.

I cracked an eye and saw the crystal in Sam's hands. "Oh good, that looked expensive."

Frank climbed down and wiped his forehead as he turned around. All he had on was jeans and a muscle shirt. My jaw almost hit the floor.

Sam caught me gaping. "I know, right?!"

"Frank," Zola said. "You look great."

Frank grinned and reached for the shirt he had laid over the counter. The man was ripped. The pudgy bald man I was occasionally fond of had been replaced. His head was shaved down to a thin covering of gray hair. Lean muscles slid and bulged in his arms as he pulled his shirt on. While I couldn't tell if he was sporting abs, his paunch was gone.

"Frank," I said. "Good god man, all I recognize anymore is your eyebrows."

"Yeah, Sam won't let me trim them."

She smiled and plucked at the furry caterpillars over his eyes.

"Hear anything about your mom?" Frank asked.

Sam's smile slipped and she shook her head.

I walked toward the back of the store again while Sam and Foster got Frank up to speed. Sam hadn't been the same since she'd become a vampire. I knew she'd had trouble adjusting to her new life, despite her vampire family, but now she seemed more like the Sam I used to know. Frank was changing something in her, and it was a hell of a lot more subtle than what she'd been changing in him.

I started up the stairs, turned at the landing, and jogged the rest of the way up. A few steps creaked and moaned, but they'd held up pretty well for being centuries old. Zola swore she'd never replaced them when the shop had been hers.

I slowed my stride a bit as I started down the thick gray carpet of the second floor. The center aisle was encased on either side by monolithic bookshelves and I took a deep breath, savoring the slightly dusty scent before stopping at the back wall. The small shelves behind the walnut table were enclosed like a barrister bookcase, and held my favored books and possessions.

I knelt beside the old leather chair and pulled an ancient chest out of a small recess. Its surface was covered in ornate wards that kept the chest hidden from prying eyes. The hinges were quiet as I opened the top and stared at the contents. A key of the dead was hidden there, given to me by Gwynn ap Nudd himself. There was also a bloodstone. A demon, Tessrian, was trapped in that green and red rock. I frowned, knowing we'd have to deal with her eventually, but for now I pulled out a thin, blue obsidian disc. It had originally been a coin used by undines in times long past. Now it was essentially a phone to Faery.

I closed the trunk and stopped to look at the stack of books on the table. Frank had picked up a few new ones. An old grimoire caught my eye. It seemed to have the same graphic etched into it as the manuscript I'd studied to create an aural blade, but that would have to wait. There was even an old Hemingway in the stack. I raised my eyebrows a bit. Sometimes Frank surprised me. Sometimes Frank surprised me a lot. I was pretty sure he hadn't picked that one up for me to sell, which most likely meant it was for him. Definitely not for Sam. She hates Hemingway, but she loves Steinbeck. Whatever. Vampires are strange.

I came back downstairs and glanced around the store. "Ashley not here yet?"

Frank shook his head.

Zola sighed. "You have time boy. Go ahead."

I nodded. "Alright, I have to make a call."

***

I crouched in the edge of the river with the dark blue Wasser-Münzen clutched in my hands, just beneath the rushing water. The icy cold swirling around my fingers couldn't stop my smile as Nixie's face pushed out of the water's surface. Even in a water sending, where her image stayed translucent, her eyes sparkled with crystalline greens and blues, and the scent of the sea washed over me.

"Hello, Damian." Her voice was musical, but I knew her singing voice was murderous.

"You look bald," I said.

She narrowed her eyes and pouted at me, lips pursing in blatant sensuality. Her eyes closed for a moment and the water moving around her image took on the vague impression of her pale hair, complete with ears poking out the edges, which she damn well knew drove me nuts. She'd cut her hair since the last time I'd seen her. It was only down to the top of her hips now as the water piled beneath her and swelled to form her body.

"Better?" she asked.

"Nice ears." I let my hands slide away from the blue obsidian. Now that the sending was established, I didn't need to hold on to the Wasser-Münzen.

"I thought you'd like them." She grinned at me.

I wanted to reach out and hug her, but that would get me nothing but cold and wet. I rubbed my hand over my face. "So, when you coming back?"

"You miss me?"

"No, not at all."

"You're a terrible liar, Damian."

I flashed her a smile of my own. "You look all clothed and stuff. Seems awkward."

She looked around. "It's daylight."

"And?" I asked.

"You'll be embarrassed long before me," she said as her watery hand slipped into one of my jean pockets.

I yelped and hopped backwards as she started laughing. Now it was me who looked around, mortified my friends and family might walk up behind us. "Okay, okay. You're right, dammit."

She giggled and pulled back, briefly allowing the waters to solidify, giving me a peek at a translucent, completely nude Nixie.

"You are so evil."

"You love it."

I groaned as she let her sending sink back into the water.

"Mike told me some of what's happening there," she said. "Do you need me to come?"

I shook my head, but not without hesitation. "How's the Queen?"

Her smile faded. "Talks are breaking down. I don't think she's willing to accept the change that's coming. She's not willing to step down either."

I frowned and crossed my arms. "She can't force you all to kill. It's wrong. What happens when neither side can agree?"

"War, though I fear to say it. War is what will happen. And all war is …"

"Is more killing," I said.

She nodded and looked behind me. "A friend is coming."

"Alright, stay safe. You know if you need help the fairies will be there in a flash."

"And you?"

I grinned. "Maybe, guess you'll just have to see."

"You need their help more than I right now," she said as her image rippled in the wake of a small bass boat.

"Damian," said a voice from behind me and a little to the left. I had a good idea what angle I'd need to point my pepperbox to bring any conflict to an abrupt end, but I recognized the voice and let my arms unfold.

I glanced behind me and found Ashley. "Damn, are you following Frank's exercise regimen? You look great!" She usually came into the shop with her cloak on, but today she wore a tight-fitting green leather vest and dark brown leather slacks. Her compact frame was slim, but even with the weight loss she bore an impressive chest. A series of pouches hung from a white rope belt at her waist along with a wicked-looking nine tails capped with intricately etched silver gray blades of Magrasnetto crowned each flail. Ashley sniffed and rubbed her slightly upturned nose before running a hand through her blonde hair to push it back over her right ear. It showed off dark leather vambraces that matched the greaves on her legs, all bearing a tree of life. She flashed a short smile. It didn't reach her blazing green eyes.

"Thank you. I was followed."

I glanced at Nixie. "You didn't mention that part."

"Call the others," she said. "They must be masked. I still don't sense them."

"Necromancers," I said with a grumble. Nixie snickered at the negative use of my own title as I nodded and reached for the phone in my pocket. I casually texted Sam and Frank to fill them in. "We're coming," came back almost immediately.

"Gotta run Nix," I said as I blew her a two-fingered kiss.

"We'll meet again soon." She smiled and her image vanished.

I heard the van's doors first as I pocketed the Wasser-Münzen. One, two, and then the hiss of a hydraulic door. I glanced up and my eyes widened. One of those carpool vans was unloading less than a quarter mile away, and I was pretty damn sure every single thing getting off was a zombie. The last man off was human, and obviously a necromancer, dressed in a passé solid black cloak and hood.

It was his turn to stare in shock as Bubbles trotted down Adams Street and crossed a parking lot, carrying my staff in her jaws. I started to laugh until I saw the tourists. They were pointing at Bubbles, then at Peanut, and started wandering toward the zombies. Bloody hell, they must've thought it was a show. Ever since Stones River, commoners could see Bubbles and Peanut. We still weren't sure why, but people seemed to make assumptions about them being a rare breed. I didn't argue. Mike, Sam, and Frank were close behind the cu siths.

"Get the hell out of here!" Mike's voice boomed as he yelled at the people on the street. He raised his hand and shot a geyser of flame into the air, billowing out in a yellow orange fireball. Some of them took the hint, and others applauded, but I'm afraid all it really did was gather even more attention.

I started walking back toward Main Street, meeting Bubbles and the others halfway. One of the men stepped forward, tall and imposing in a black trench coat and thin sunglasses. "Hand over the Blessing and this all goes away."

"Hey handsome," Sam said. "How about you get the fuck out of here and you won't go away in pieces."

The slide of Frank's shotgun pump was jarring in the silence that followed. Then everything went to shit.

Trench coat had guns in his hands before I could even blink. We scattered. Frank dove behind a car in the lot, Ashley behind a low shelf in the riverbank, and I angled for a shrub before I realized it was just a shrub. Bubbles followed me and I pulled my staff out of the cu sith's mouth instead of seeking cover. My vision was distorted slightly as a shield sprang to life, the flowing glassy dome sheltering me and Bubbles.

"Assassins?" Mike asked before he burst out with a rumbling laugh. "You didn't get paid enough for this." Three shots rang out in quick succession. Mike grunted as the rounds hit him in the chest. Then he growled. Fire erupted from his outstretched arm and Trench coat screamed as his arm turned to cinders. The fire demon was on him in a flash. The scream died with a horrible crack as the man's head came loose and sailed into the river.

"Stay away from that one!" another man yelled. Black robes, another necromancer, came out from behind another car on the street, trailing another gunman. He muttered something else and held out a staff. A thick beam of water shot out at Mike. He dodged and the liquid cut a hole six inches wide through the car behind him.

"Black mage!" Foster yelled as he blossomed into being above the man. The mage cursed and dodged a swipe from the fairy's sword.

"Blood mage, insect," the man spat as an athame sliced into his arm. He ran his fingers through the bright red blood. His hand curled into a claw and a sigil of flame appeared in front of him for a split second before a fiery wall of force sent Foster spiraling through a glass storefront to the northeast.

Our group was scattered. Ashley, Bubbles and I were closer to the river than anyone else, and the zombies reached us first. Gunfire erupted across the front of the shop in the distance. I saw Aideen and Zola dive back inside.

Frank unleashed three rounds from the shotgun. Two zombies went down in pieces and one of the gunmen caught a face full of shot as I picked off what zombies I could without using my necromancy. Sam ran past Frank, charging into the cluster of zombies, tearing them apart as someone began to attack them from a distance with concentrated bursts of fire. I looked toward the source of the flames and found Zola and Aideen outside the shop, closing on our attackers.

"Enough!" Ashley screamed, and her scream was intense enough to startle me. Peanut was at her side. I could only guess he'd been there since the start. "Sam, run!" My sister removed herself from the line of fire in a flash as Ashley tossed a handful of runes into the air. The nine tails lashed out, cracking like thunder as it shattered the bone-colored tiles.

I could see Foster picking himself out of the window. When he saw what was coming, he dove back into the storefront.

Black clouds roiled out from the broken tiles like a hurricane. They swallowed everything in a flash of blue lightning and flame-etched shadows. Mike cursed and leapt away from a zombie he was dismembering as the storm rushed in. The smoky clouds swelled and then collapsed in on themselves as fast as they'd appeared.

When the smoke cleared, the power of the runes was undeniable. Pieces of the cars were missing, exposed to the world like cutaway models. One had lost enough mass that the remaining half crashed to the ground in a screech of metal. Part of the street was gone and dirt showed where cobblestones should have been. I thought it had started to rain until I realized a fire hydrant was showering the entire scene in an icy wash, its upper half disintegrated. Zombies were gone, necromancers were gone, bodies were gone other than a few bits the cloud hadn't devoured.

Foster tentatively poked his head out of the shattered window. He stepped out and circled around the northern edge of the destruction until he was beside Ashley.

The blood mage stood with a single gunman behind his flickering shield, water splattering a few inches from his face. I didn't think his shield had saved him. Judging by the ground in front of him, Ashley's cloud of doom had missed him by a couple feet. His surprised expression faded to rage. He dropped his shield and slashed his arm again with the athame.

A boom and a hiss like a rocket taking off rattled my head. I glanced backwards at the source of the noise.

Dad. He'd gone around the back of the shops on Main Street and come up the riverbank behind us. Good thing the gunmen hadn't thought of that. The cannon Mike had given him was propped up against his shoulder and a trail of smoke was rising.

"*Impadda!*" the blood mage cried. His shield sprang up and then shattered into a billowing electric blue cloud as the bomb lance simply dissipated it. He screamed and stared at the hissing projectile lodged in his chest, pinning him to the wall. It was the last thing he ever did.

The explosion killed the gunman beside him in a deadly storm of blood and bones. The last of the zombies fell, lifeless once more, cut off from their master. The few remaining passersby no longer thought it was a show. Their cries bled with terror and they ran like hell was at their heels.

"It worked," Mike said, a smug grin splitting his face as he pulled a chunk of blood mage off his shoulder.

Aideen ran to Foster, watching carefully for any stragglers along the way. He leaned against her while she tried to look over his wings.

"Mike, what the hell?" I said.

"Well done," Zola said as she walked across the remnants of the street. "Did you add runes to the lances?"

"Wards, actually," Mike said. "I can't take all the credit. An old friend did assist me. They should break anything short of a shielded circle."

Zola tapped her foot and raised her eyebrow.

Mike's eyes shifted back and forth and his lips quirked up in a slow smile. "Of course, they can only be fired by someone with no connection to the arts. Even a latent ability could render them useless."

"Except for the exploding part?" I asked.

Mike paused and scratched his head. "Indeed, I believe they would still explode."

I started to smile, but my lips fell as I stared at the damage and destruction around us. It'd never been this bad in the city. Not even close. The bystanders had already run screaming. The Watchers would have to track them all down. It was right about then I saw the kid with the phone pointed at us. He saw me looking, hopped in his car, and squealed his tires as he sped recklessly across the cobblestones.

"We are so fucked."

CHAPTER SIX

"Edgar, it's Zola. We were attacked near the shop." She paused and listened for a moment. Her cell phone was clenched against her right ear. "It's a clusterfuck. Buildings are damaged, parts of the road are missing. Several witnesses have already fled. Both sides threw strong arts. Mike thinks the men that came for us were mercenaries."

The phone squawked in an unpleasant way and Zola pulled it away from her ear.

"Okay," she said as she held the phone out and put it on speaker.

"All of you, listen to me closely." Edgar's voice was hushed, metallic, and hurried. "Ezekiel is in Missouri, which means Philip is probably here too. The Cleaners, or what's left of them, are on their way. Get the hell out of there. You don't need to get caught up further in that godforsaken train wreck."

"There's more," he said before hesitating. "Get to Boonville. We're going after the Blessing. If Philip or his men get the Blessing before us, they're not going to need a live hostage. I've only spent a couple hours in the taverns here and the locals are buzzing about the influx of outsiders. Get here fast."

I could tell he was going to hang up so I just spat it out. "Edgar, wait. I saw a kid with a phone. He was either taking pictures or maybe video. He jumped in a white sedan and took off as soon as he noticed me watching."

"How much did he see?" Edgar asked through a growl.

"I didn't see him until the fight was over."

The cursing exploding from the phone was enough to make a demon blush. Even Zola's eyebrows rose.

"Noted," Edgar said. "We don't have the men to deal with that right now. Ezekiel has killed too many. Get the fuck out here." The line went dead, and even the faint click sounded angry.

"Ezekiel?" I said. My voice trailed off as the implications of Edgar's words spawned a thousand horrific scenarios in my mind.

"Frank, we have to move." Zola said. "You need to stay with the shop."

"No," Sam said. "I'm not leaving him here alone to deal with Watchers."

Frank smiled and put an arm around Sam, balancing the shotgun on his toe. "Sam, it's fine. The battle wasn't in the shop. I can play dumb just fine."

No one took the easy shot.

"Are you sure?" Sam asked.

He nodded.

"I'll stay with Frank," Ashley said.

Zola turned slowly toward the priestess and cleared her throat in an attention-getting stutter. "Girl, Ah am not entirely certain what the hell it was you unleashed, but Ah suggest you hide those runes."

Ashley nodded.

"Mind you, keep them handy, but out of sight."

"And don't vaporize the shop," I said. "Thank you very much."

Ashley flashed me a weak smile.

Foster ambled up beside us with his arm around Aideen. He groaned and then stretched. "Ow," he said as he winced. "You can set the runes inside the clock, Ashley."

Aideen nodded. "The power from the nexus will mask just about anything, including the potential energy in those runes."

"I don't want to sound ungrateful," Dad said, "but can we please get moving? I'd really like to find my wife and get her the hell away from Philip and his mercs."

"Mercenaries," Zola spat. "Ah hate mercenaries. The only good thing about them is there's always more to kill."

***

We loaded the cars with road food and weapons in minutes.

"Where are we headed?" I said as I opened the driver's side door to get in.

"Rivercene," Zola said. "Dimitry is riding with me."

"Any particular reason?" I asked.

Zola glanced up at me, and then turned her attention to straightening her gray cloak. "Have you not seen how unsettled Sam is around him, boy?"

"It's …" I paused and really thought about it. "It's better than it used to be."

"Ah think you would do well to keep your sister close. Talk to her when you have the chance. Ah thought Dimitry and Andi would have gotten over their prejudice well before now. Obviously they haven't." There was a bite to her words.

I stopped and watched as Zola hefted a backpack into the trunk. She looked eighty, but she moved better than I did. She scratched at the scar on her wrist, briefly attacking the line of smooth tissue where it met her darker, wrinkled skin.

"What?" she asked without looking at me.

"Eyes in the back of your head," I said as I stifled a laugh.

"That happens when you live too long." She slammed the trunk. "Out with it."

"What's the deal with Edgar?" I asked. "We've never been on great terms with him, and now you seem friendly, sort of. He pretty much hates anyone with a hint of necromancy."

"He has his reasons for that, boy." She crossed her arms and leaned against the back of the trunk.

"That's it? That's your answer?"

"Yes, it is. Now let's go."

"We're not done with this," I said as she climbed into her car. I swear I caught the hint of a frown on her face.

"Just drop it, D," Foster said. I glanced down and found him and Aideen steaming in my electric coffee mug, now their hot tub. I noticed the pile of armor beside the mug next.

"Are you two … naked?" I asked, unable to keep the surprise from my voice.

"Oh yeah," Sam said from the passenger seat.

"Indubitably," Mike said from the backseat.

"Oh, get over it and just pass the hat up here, Mike," Aideen said. She sank down to her neck and motioned to Foster. He bounced his eyebrows a couple times and slid around the oversized cup.

"Bloody hell," I said as Mike passed an old green bowler up from the backseat. I remembered getting that hat on an ill-fated trip downtown. Frank was convinced he'd found evidence of a "real" vampire. He still didn't really know about the supernatural world back then. The trip ended up with Frank almost getting eaten. I covered the cup and reached for the radio. "Loud music, anyone?" I said as I cranked the volume up.

I stole a few glances at Sam as she channel surfed. She was almost as bad with the radio as she was with the TV. We jumped from modern rock to classics to Barry White (which got rousing applause from the coffee cup) and finally landed on some accessible metal. I fought off a frown as I turned my attention fully back on the road. She did seem more relaxed now.

"I do like the music of these times," Mike said. "Wasn't long ago you were lucky to catch a minstrel along the road or performing at an inn. Any man with a lute was a rock star back then."

"Back when?" Sam asked. "How old are you?"

I caught Mike's smile in the rearview mirror. "I was alive long before the Old Man brought Rome to its knees, before the pharaohs built their tombs and the Gods of Light and Shadow waged their war in the Abyss."

"So … older than Zola." Sam said.

Mike let out a slow laugh. "Yes, much older than Zola."

I glanced at Sam. She seemed to be taking that in stride. I wasn't sure if she knew the legends of the Abyss or not. Hell, I was rusty on them, but I knew the Abyss was said to be a realm between ours and the Burning Lands. There was a passage in a very old tome I'd read some years ago.

For nothing wanders the Abyss where the Old Gods lie dormant. Nothing exists but death, and a pathway into insanity.

That book was one of the Pit's oldest possessions. Warded against decay, it didn't show its age. Vik had told me it was 7,000 years old.

Close to an hour passed in relative silence.

"Why couldn't we take the Ways out there?" Sam asked.

A put upon sigh came from the vicinity of the coffee cup and Foster lifted the hat off.

"Foster!" Aideen squeaked. She wasn't quite dressed yet, and he'd briefly exposed her topless form to the rest of the car. Foster slowly lowered the hat as he stepped outside the cup, a wicked grin etched onto his face.

"What?" he asked. "We've known everyone in this car long enough to go au natural. Except maybe Mike, but he's a demon, so what's the problem?"

"Perhaps a little warning next time so I'm aware you've made that decision for the both of us," Aideen said. "Not that you're wrong, you just surprised me."

"Sorry, dear."

"Oh, you will be," she grumbled.

"Are those real?" I asked casually.

Sam swatted my arm, but not before she snorted a laugh and then covered her mouth, trying not to laugh harder.

"You're going to get me killed," Foster said.

"I'm quite sure you did that yourself," Mike said, rolling his gaze away from the window and letting it fall on the fairy.

"I … I … never mind," Foster said as he wiped his plastered hair out of his eyes. "Look, Sam, we can't take the Warded Ways because there aren't any around Rivercene. The closest jump would be thirty minutes away, and then we'd need to rent a car or something."

"Or fly," I said.

"Of course, if we could fly, we wouldn't have had to drive," Mike said, his voice bare of sarcasm.

"Thank you, Captain Obvious," Sam said under her breath.

I caught Mike's smile in the rearview.

"Now, now, children. We're almost there," I said. "We're already past Columbia."

The landscape rolled by. Green forested hills were lit by the fading sun, and the river valley was cast into shadows by the same. In the daytime you could see more hills, colors faded by the distance. At night the darkness swelled and surged along the river, impenetrable and altogether threatening.

I flicked the signal on and merged off the highway. We passed a gas station, hotels, and a Wal-Mart Supercenter. Those monstrosities seemed to be a staple in every small town. It wasn't long before the road narrowed into two lanes. Old homes began to crop up on either side of the road until full-blown subdivisions were suddenly flanking us on all sides.

A few chain restaurants and strip malls rolled by before we hit a surprising amount of traffic in downtown Boonville. While the cars stopped and started, I watched the old streetlights and brick buildings do the same. Boonville was another old town, close to the same age as Alton, but ravaged by the terror and brutality of the Civil War. An oppressive, dark energy settled on me as we bore deeper into the streets.

"This is a dark place," Mike said from the backseat.

"No, it only has a dark past," Aideen said. "There are many places that have overcome their pasts and risen beyond them."

"I feel it," I said. "We're surrounded here. War, death, fear. I can feel the lost all around us."

"The lost?" Mike asked.

"The souls that are left behind," I said.

He nodded in the rearview. "It's a good name."

A small voice changed from a whisper into a shout as Foster said, "Irish Pub!"

I glanced to the left, in the direction of his pointing hops and grinned. A neon stein, bubbling over with suds, lit the entrance set in the old brick building's green façade.

"I believe we found dinner," Mike said.

Foster and Aideen huddled together, speaking quickly and flapping their wings in excitement.

"What's up with you two?" Sam said, taking the words right out of my mouth.

"We're trying to remember who owns the pub," Aideen said.

"I think it's one of Glenn's friends," Foster said.

"Great," I muttered. Glenn was the nickname of Gwynn ap Nudd, the Fae King.

"Glenn has done nothing but help us," Sam said as Foster and Aideen coughed back laughs.

"I would sooner trust a demon," Mike spat from the backseat. I raised an eyebrow and glanced at him in the mirror a second before he frowned slightly. "Forget I said that."

The rest of the car burst into laughter.

"Glenn's okay," Foster said as the chuckling died off. "Just don't get in his way."

On that cheery note, we continued our stop-and-go journey toward the bridge that would take us across the Missouri River.

The buildings grew more modern at the corner of East Spring Street, and then immediately returned to solid blocks of storefronts and brick. Antiquated streetlights adorned the curbs alongside historical markers, dormant trees, and a total lack of parking spaces.

The bridge was in view by the time we reached the next block, and when the signal changed, we started the incline up over the Missouri River.

"That's an eyesore," Sam said as she looked out to the west.

"What?" Foster asked. "The casino or the rusty old bridge?"

Aideen punched him in the arm. "Idiot. Of course the casino."

"It is better than letting the town wither away, year after year," Mike said. "A little sin can go a long way."

"First you say you'd trust a demon," Sam said as she held up a finger. "Now you're telling us the benefits of sin?"

"To support a local economy?" Mike said. "Yes, there are many benefits."

"Just stop," Foster said. "I am going to hurl if I have to listen to you two debate economics. I'd rather talk about the rusty old bridge."

"Sometimes I can't believe I married you," Aideen said. "That bridge is a living history, a testament to mankind's ingenuity. MKT used that line—"

"MKT?" Sam asked.

"Missouri-Kansas-Texas railroad," Aideen said. "They used it to complete a route between Hannibal and Texas in the 1870s, and this town boomed because of it, and because of the river, of course."

"Why do you even know that?" Foster asked.

Aideen glared at him.

"So," I said, rapidly changing the topic. "Zola is older than that historically important bridge."

Silence filled the car for a moment before it exploded into laughter.

By the time we finished laughing, I turned the signal on and pulled the car onto a gravel road. We bounced onto County Road 463, gravel pinging off the wheel wells as we passed an industrial site of some sort. Its white silos and conveyor belts were silent.

Zola's taillights brightened a little ways ahead of us and I followed her into the far side of Rivercene's driveway. My foot eased off the accelerator and I gaped at the old Victorian mansion nestled among a few ancient, bare trees. Alex, one of the ghosts that frequented my shop to chat, tended to ramble about Victorian architecture and I immediately thought of him and his lingo. Two stories of brick topped with a third story, adorned in gray-green hexagonal shingles and half-sunken bay windows sat beneath a mansard roof with an elevated center. Dentils hung from the portico and from the base of the third floor. A short brick tower on the east side rose about halfway up the second story. Parts of the shingles and some of the woodwork showed wear, but the overall effect was inviting. I couldn't wait to go inside.

"It's kind of creepy," Sam said.

"What?" I said, disbelief obvious in my voice.

"It's alright," Foster said as his gaze swept from one end of the mansion to the other. Aideen stood beside him with a small frown on her face.

"I'm going to have to agree with Sam," Mike said.

"Oh, whatever," I said as I parked beside Zola on the other side of the walkway. There was another building beside us, and

I could only imagine it had been a guest house at some point in time.

Twilight sank over Rivercene in the time it took us to unload the trunks and start up the brick walkway to the front door. I walked beside Zola and we both turned our gazes to the sky. There was still light pollution here, but the Milky Way was plain to see. It was a glorious band of light, sprawled out across the heavens.

"It is better here," Zola said. "Better here than in town. The spirits are restless around Boonville."

Something large and winged streaked across the disc of the moon.

"I'd say they have a right to be," I said as we walked up the short flight of stairs to the mansion, shivering from the cold as much as the unseen eyes watching our arrival.

"Your mother would love it here," Dad said, his eyes distant as he picked up his old green suitcase.

Mom.

Philip was going to die.

CHAPTER SEVEN

I reached out for the doorbell and then paused with my hand outstretched. The bell was mounted in wood trim that was shaped like a rope. The detail was beautiful, but the bell was strange. It stuck out like a key, with no button to push.

"You twist it," Zola said, with a slight edge of impatience.

I grabbed the cold metal and did just that. I could hear a bell clanging inside in time to the speed of my turns.

"That is so cool," Sam said.

I nodded. "Yes it is."

"You two are easily amused," Mike said from behind us. He was standing back on the large, wooden porch with the rest of our group. Footsteps echoed inside the house.

The hinges creaked and one of the huge doors swung inward. A short woman with round glasses and frizzy brown hair peered around the edge. Her eyes swept over us and then shot up to the fairies hovering above my shoulder.

"Adannaya, I presume." Her voice was throaty and gruff, but a hint of kindness bled through.

Zola nodded.

"You look the same as your pictures. Come in." As she stepped to the side, I could see she was comfortably overweight and likely less than fifty years old.

"Hello, what's your name?" I asked as I extended my hand.

She narrowed her eyes. "It's nothing you need to know, and I don't need to know yours. Too many people asking about folk we don't know. I'd prefer to keep it that way."

I let my hand fall as I pondered the logic of that rambling. Then my eyes tracked the rest of the group as they gawked at the mansion's interior. A grand staircase flowed up to the second floor, carved from mahogany and walnut, and flanked by a wide banister on the left and only the wall on the right.

Past the staircase I could make out a hallway, hung with aged portraits. Beige Victorian chairs and an intricately detailed couch sat below the lighted paintings. A curio lay beyond those, lit from within to display a small ocean of treasures.

Foster and Aideen flitted from one room to the next. Mike leaned on the doorway to the left and let out a low whistle.

"That is quite a piano," he said as he admired the ancient grand inside the room.

"It doesn't work," the innkeeper snapped.

Mike let out a low chuckle. "You and I both know that is not true. It may not play music, but I believe it 'works' just fine."

Surprise flickered over the woman's face and then her mask settled back in. "I will show you to your rooms."

We followed her up to the second floor. I kept one hand on the old, wide banister as I slung some luggage over my back. I caught a glimpse of an old wheelchair and a riverboat captain's uniform out on display before we started up the next staircase.

"Watch your step. These old stairs get a little narrow," the innkeeper said. "Not made for big feet." She eyed me and Mike. I gave her a dazzling smile, to which she rolled her eyes.

I jumped as something landed on my shoulder.

"You should see the kitchen!" Foster said.

"It's truly a sight," Aideen echoed from my other shoulder.

"A little warning next time, guys?" I said.

They ignored me and prattled on about the incredible fireplace and how they could have cooked for dozens of people, even back in the 1800s. I smiled as I balanced on the balls of my feet and navigated the narrow stairwell. The echo of our footsteps was deadened as we climbed higher and carpeted floors replaced the spread of hardwood outside the staircase.

The ceilings were just as imposing on the second floor and again on the third. The third floor felt homey despite the elevated ceilings. The far end of the hall had a short coffee table surrounded by a blue, wood-framed couch and chairs. The bay window sat behind those, though I wasn't sure if it was really a bay now that I was standing on the other side. It was up off the floor a bit, but sunk into the wall like a bay window. Below the window, a few modest bookshelves were filled to bursting with old tomes. I stared at that plain hallway for moment, trying to figure out what was wrong.

One thing bothered me, and it made my skin crawl.

"There aren't any ghosts here," I said.

"Oh, I assure you there are," the innkeeper said.

I closed my eyes and pushed my senses out. Nothing. No spirits, no impressions, only a vacant space of calm.

"Don't bother." I heard Edgar's voice before I opened my eyes and saw the man standing before the window at the end of the hallway. He started walking towards us as he spoke. "This place has been shielded for over a century, as much to protect the old ghosts here as to keep hostile spirits out."

"I always wondered why they wanted the piano here," Mike said. "It would make sense."

The innkeeper looked up at the demon, surprise obvious on her face once again. "How could you possibly know anything about that?"

"Drop it," Edgar said. "If you truly wish to keep yourself separated from us, you don't want to know how he knows."

The innkeeper nodded and said no more.

"Anything else around we should know about?" I asked as my gaze wandered to Sam and back to Edgar. "Anything Sam should be wary of?"

"Vassili has already been here," Edgar said.

Sam perked up. "What? Why?"

"To make sure it's safe for you, I assume." Edgar rubbed his hands together slowly and frowned. "I can only guess he sees you as leverage in case he royally pisses off Damian one day."

I shrugged. "Not a bad move on his part. Where is he now?"

"He'll meet us at the Fae pub later tonight with Cassie and Cara."

"Whose pub is it?" Foster asked. "I can't remember."

"Cassie's brother," Zola said.

"Glenn's nephew," Edgar said. "I believe that is the fact you are trying to remember."

"You mean Cassie is Glenn's niece?" I said after a moment's hesitation.

Edgar nodded.

"Bloody hell," I muttered. "Glad she likes us."

"Does her brother have the …" Mike paused and glanced at the innkeeper before saying, "… item?"

"Hell, no," Zola snapped. "What kind of idiot do you take me for?"

Mike laughed quietly. "I meant no disrespect."

"Enough talk. Take your rooms. We leave in a half hour." Edgar continued past us and started down the stairs. There was a thin creak and then the clack of his heels on the wooden stairs faded.

"Strange company you keep," the innkeeper said with a small shake of her head.

"Enough, woman," Zola said. "Show us the rooms."

I caught a brief smile on the innkeeper's face as she moved forward.

"Adannaya, you're in the Twilight room here," she said as she pulled a ring of brass keys off her hip to unlock the door. The keys were aged. Elaborate, oversized teeth sang against the metal as she eased the key into the lock. There was a loud click, and the door swung open.

Zola placed her bags beside a small twin bed off to the side of the pink-tinted room.

"Take the queen, Sam," she said as she gestured at the larger, dark-framed bed in the center of the room.

Sam nodded and tossed her duffel bag onto the queen from the doorway.

Zola joined us in the hallway again.

"Demon, you're in Angela's Lookout," she said as she unlocked the next door.

Mike and I both stepped forward, then glanced at each other.

"Who do you mean?" I asked, not sure if she was referring to Mike or my nickname.

"I mean the fire demon," the innkeeper said. "Apparently the fire demon that forged the core of the wardstone within our piano."

I stared at the innkeeper, and then at Mike.

He nodded. "Well, she's not wrong." He smiled as he started into the room and glanced around. It was also home to two beds, though the room was smaller than Sam and Zola's. Mike set his ancient leather bag beside the larger bed and turned around.

"How did you know?" he asked, an open curiosity in his voice.

"Edgar says many things without saying anything at all," the innkeeper said.

Foster and Aideen groaned.

"He's a pompous do-good on a power trip," Foster said as he glided from Zola's shoulder over to mine. "More trouble than he's worth."

The innkeeper raised her eyebrows and then barked out a laugh. She started down the hall again. "That leaves you in the Nile," she said to me.

My first impression of the room was blue. Lots of blue, from the comforter on the canopied brass bed, to the area rug over the dark hardwood, the walls were a deep blue, and even the small porcelain hats laid out across the bench at the foot of the bed were a light blue. The painted parts of the wall were covered in drywall, but every few feet a section of old brick was exposed and trimmed in wood. The effect was stunning.

"This is huge," I said.

"It was the last room we had available," the innkeeper said.

Aideen glided past me and settled on a small armoire set against the wall beside the door. Further into the room, a table with two leaves folded down sat beneath a brass chandelier. I tossed my bag down by the vanity on the far wall and glanced at the bathroom.

"Holy crap," Foster said as he swooped by. "That's a whirlpool tub. Oh, sweet, sweet whirlpool. You're sharing, right?"

"We'll talk," I said as I made my way back to the hall.

"What about Dad?" Sam whispered to me. Christ, I felt like an idiot.

"Uh, Dimitry?" I said, trying out Dad's real name for a change.

He smiled and winked at me. "Yes?"

"Where are you staying?"

"He is welcome to stay with me," Mike said. "Of course I will understand if my nature makes you uncomfortable."

"Take my room," I said. "I can grab the couch."

The innkeeper sighed. "No, that room is for you, and you alone. I have another room I can open. I didn't want to clean an extra set of sheets if it wasn't necessary. It's the first room on the second floor. I'll have it ready for you."

"Thank you," Dad said with a nod to the innkeeper.

"Feel free to explore the mansion on your own," she said, "but I warn you to stay out of the basement. I'll not be cleaning up the mess if one of you decides not to listen.

"I'm sure Edgar is in the kitchen, if you care to join him." With that, she nodded and started to walk away.

"We don't have keys," I said.

She didn't bother to turn around. "Your rooms know you now. No one outside your party can enter." As if on cue, all three doors slammed shut and the locks clicked in rapid succession.

I blinked and looked at Sam.

"It's a little creepy," she said with a smile.

I sighed and slowly started for the stairs. I let everyone go ahead before I pulled on Sam's shoulder to slow her down.

"Are you okay?" I asked. "You seem … off. Is it Mom?"

She glanced down the hallway at the others.

"You know what Dad said to me?" she asked as her voice grew quiet. "Do you?"

I shook my head.

"They felt like *I* abandoned *them*. Like I walked out of their lives when I joined the Pit. Like I was already dead."

"They're wrong," I said.

Sam's lip trembled before she gathered herself. "That's what Dad said to me at the house. After I helped him fight off those necromancers."

"He what?" I stared at Sam until she looked up and met my eyes. She still seemed like the kid I grew up with sometimes, but I could feel her aura shifting when she stared back. Her vampire instincts were always hunting and prodding their surroundings for a potential meal.

"That's why they always asked what could be done about my *condition*." Sam reached out and grabbed my hand. "Mom always thought if I was human again, I'd be around more." A tiny note cracked in her voice. I wouldn't have even noticed it if I hadn't known Sam so long. Her words came out in a whisper. "He said he was sorry."

I turned my gaze back down the hallway. Our party had already descended the stairs, but I pictured our father there, apologizing. To say it was unlike him would be the understatement of the century.

Sam's grip on my hand tightened, and when I turned back to face her, that little girl I knew and loved was carefully hidden away once more. "If I don't get the chance to talk to Mom about this, Damian … If we lose her, and I never get to tell her … I'm going to kill so many people."

"We're going to do that anyway," I said. "We'll get her back."

Sam wrapped me up in a rib-cracking hug before she started down the hallway. I almost hit the ground with my face when she grabbed my hand and yanked me forward with her.

I laughed as I regained my balance. "Alright, I'm coming, I'm coming."

"Boy," Zola said as we reached the stairs.

I nodded. Sam released my hand and continued on ahead by herself.

I watched her go for a moment before turning back to Zola. "You've been here before?"

Zola nodded. "The captain who built this house was a good man. Gave shelter to anyone in need, especially anyone gifted." She put a hand on my arm as I reached the bottom of the staircase.

A tall, gold frame caught my eye in the little alcove to our right. It held a huge patchwork quilt, a miasma of patterns and colors laid out into twenty squares and held within a shiny, red fabric border. The entire quilt was behind glass in the thin, traditional frame.

"Last time I was here, they'd just finished that quilt."

I bent down to read the date in the corner. "1884?"

Zola nodded. "Come, let's meet up with the others."

I followed her, watching her small form shuffle and lean with her cane like you'd expect of someone her age. Her braids tinkled as the silver-gray charms of Magrassnetto swayed into each other as she lurched along. It was all an act. She made it look so natural. I wondered how long she'd been practicing the deception. For that matter, how much had she really seen? How many people must she have known, or at least met? Here, in the middle of nowhere Missouri, she had known a family wealthy enough to build a mansion soon after the Civil War.

We came to the bottom of the main staircase and started down the hall toward the kitchen. Dim light came from either end of the hall, but the center was unnervingly dark. I had an urge to stop, but followed Zola through the shadows anyway.

"You felt that?" Zola asked.

"Yeah, what was it?" I rubbed the goosebumps on my arm.

"Old magic. Old enough Ah doubt many would recognize it."

"How old?" I said, adding a little intensity to the question. "Aeros old?"

"Yes, perhaps older. It's also why you should stay out of the basement."

"Done and done," I said as we passed an upright piano tucked beneath the stairs. A little further on, a closer glance at the curio showed me a treasure trove of antiques and old photographs, even a weathered journal. I wanted to stop and take it in, but we had more pressing concerns.

I slowed as we entered the kitchen. Dark hardwood stretched out to modern cabinets and electric appliances. Small saloon doors separated the kitchen from the dining room off to the west, but my attention was all for the enormous fireplace nestled in the middle of the room.

I was fairly sure I could lay down in it, aside from the roaring flames currently occupying the space. Ancient and ornate fireplace cranes adorned either side of the gaping maw, two holding cast iron Dutch ovens in the flames, and the rest pulled forward, away from the heat.

The innkeeper deftly pulled one of the cranes out of the fire with a long metal implement, lifted the lid with a covered hand, and frowned at the contents. A cloud of something that smelled rich and salty filled the air. She let the lid fall with a clang and swung the squeaky assembly back into the heat before walking over to the microwave and pulling out two green mugs. She handed one to Edgar at the small kitchen table beside the refrigerator, and another to Mike. They both thanked her and sipped the brew.

"Coffee?" I asked with more than a bit of hope.

The innkeeper nodded. "You want a mug?" she said to Zola as she pulled out three more.

"Yes, thank you."

Foster and Aideen settled on an ancient five-shelf spice rack with jars the size of the coffee mugs as Zola seated herself in a rocking chair at the table beside Edgar. Sam was leaning against a small island between the two parties, so I pulled up a stool closer to her and the spice rack. Dad hung back, just on the other side of the island.

"I want you all to be prepared before we approach the pub tonight," Edgar said as he sipped his coffee and then set it down. "Our friendly innkeeper has informed me there are at least three necromancers in the city. Two have tried to enter Rivercene, but this is a fortress against our enemies.

"I don't know if Philip is with them," he said with a glance toward Zola.

"It doesn't matter," she said as she took a cup from our host.

The innkeeper handed me a steaming mug and I thanked her for it. She offered a brief smile and left the room. I sipped the coffee and sighed at the slightly bitter warmth. It was damn good coffee.

"What about the Thunderbird?" Sam asked.

Edgar shrugged. "It may help us. It may try to destroy us. It may do nothing. It is an unpredictable creature."

"Super," Foster muttered from the spice rack.

"Finish your coffee," Edgar said. "We go armed. Anything you brought, wear it."

Does anyone need to get their weapons?"

We all looked at each other and shook our heads.

"You learn quick," he said with a small, humorless smile.

CHAPTER EIGHT

We lucked out with a parking spot a few doors away from the pub. My breath fogged in the crisp, night air, and I was glad I had a leather bomber jacket in the trunk. Everyone was in their winter gear. Zola wore an ancient leather trench coat almost worn to the same pale brown as her knobby old cane. She adjusted a light blue fabric hat snuggly pulled over her head. Makeshift earflaps made from the same material hung down on either side of her head, and a similar flap covered the back of her neck.

Sam had on a puffy black coat, with Foster and Aideen peeking out of either pocket on her chest. Dad followed close behind in an antique leather jacket with some obvious signs of wear. Mom hated that thing.

"Mom may tell you to leave her with the kidnappers if she sees you in that," I said.

Sam snorted a laugh and Dad's face lifted into a small smile.

Mike held the door open, a padded vest pulled over his usual coarse, unbleached linen shirt and jeans as we all filed past him.

The old music hit me first as it wove its way through the aged bar, seeming to bring the lengthy stretch of dark wood to life. It was timeless but structured and flowing like an ocean. Two women sat on the low stage with lutes cradled in their arms. Their pale fingers danced, shifting into different positions with inhuman speed and grace. I barely noticed the other patrons, seated at tables along the left wall, opposite the bar. I didn't have to know what the song was to know I was hearing something few men had ever heard.

And then they sang. It was all I could do to stay on my feet. It bore a power and grace and beauty matched only by their slender forms. I shivered in the glory of the music, so insubstantial a thing. I would have thrown myself into the seas for such magnificence as it whispered and pulled at my soul.

Something tickled the back of my brain about that being wrong, but it felt so right.

The lutes quieted and the audience released a collective sigh. An explosion of applause broke the spell, bringing me back to my senses as I focused on the antique beer signs in the dim yellow light. I caught a glimpse of Cassie talking to Zola. Cara was beside them, waving to me from a corner table. A pale man leaned back in the shadows. He nodded to me and I nodded back as I realized it was Vassili, his white hair fiery in the dim orange glow.

One of the women on stage leaned forward with a smile on her face. "Thank you," echoed quietly around the room from the PA speakers. "We don't often play Nudd's Damnation. Thank you."

Her accent was thick. Spain perhaps? Some blend of Mediterranean countries? I wasn't sure, but as we moved toward a table in the back and they exited the stage in our direction, her eyes flashed in the spotlights. Ice blue and a crystalline green.

"You're water witches!" I blurted out unceremoniously. Edgar said something under his breath, shook his head, and started back to the corner table where the group was waiting.

The witches stopped and looked at each other before nodding to me. "That must be him," they said simultaneously.

The black haired woman extended her hand. "I am Alexandra, Damian."

I shook her hand and before I could put my arm down the other woman grabbed it. Her eyes were very close to Nixie's, and though her hair was shorter, it was very much the same otherwise. "I am called Euphemia."

"Why are you here?" I asked as I tried to think of a casual way to ask the next question. "Are you here to support the queen?"

The raven-haired witch's face cracked into a huge smile. "A wise phrasing for a dangerous question. I see why she likes you."

I frowned, which made Alexandra laugh.

"Oh, yes," she said in agreement.

"What?" I said.

Foster landed on my shoulder. "Hey, clueless, you figure it out yet?"

"They know Nixie, Demon," Sam said, calling me by my nickname. "You sure that song has worn off?"

I narrowed my eyes at Sam.

"Just saying," she said.

"We fight," Euphemia said as she shifted the lute case on her shoulder. "If we wanted, we could have had this entire audience tonight."

I saw Mike stiffen.

Alexandra reached out and put a hand on his arm. "Peace, burning man. We were told of your exploits with our sister, and we witnessed your actions at Stones River."

Mike relaxed a fraction and nodded.

"I was there," Euphemia said. She took a step closer to Mike and whispered in his ear. "I saw you wield the hammer. The forge of Hephaestus is not cold yet." She planted a chaste kiss on his cheek.

Mike's hand flexed around the hammer and I swear his chest swelled up just a little. The ghost we knew only as the little necromancer suddenly appeared beside Mike and glared at the water witch.

"I'd like to shove that flaming hammer right up her—"

Mike burst into laughter and ushered the ghost toward the back of the bar.

The rest of the party started trickling back to the table. I waited until they were gone.

"You were at Stones River with Nixie?"

Euphemia nodded. "I am sorry we could not help your wolves. The man, Carter, and his wife."

"Maggie," I said with a small nod.

"They were very brave."

"Yes, but … it's complicated," I said.

Euphemia frowned and then shrugged.

"What was that all about? What you said to Mike, I mean."

The witches exchanged a look. Alexandra leaned closer to me, the scent of the ocean rolling off her made my heart lurch for Nixie. "He *is* the fallen smith. Do you understand?"

"He's a god?" I whispered back.

"Once, in ages long past, before his pact with the under-world."

"Speak no more of this," Euphemia said. "He is a good man, no matter what he's been."

Alexandra started to open her mouth, but Euphemia silenced her with a glance.

"Call if you need us. There are enemies all around you here."

"How do I call you?" I said.

Euphemia laughed and held out a napkin with a number written in a graceful hand. "Use the phone."

"Ah. Right."

I watched them go, bundling up in matching aqua blue parkas. They briefly nodded and waved to a few tables and then took an envelope from the bartender. He held the door for them as they left.

I walked to the back as I took my jacket off. There weren't any open hooks at the rear coatrack, so I smothered Sam's with mine and then sat down near one end of the oval table beside

Dad and Zola. Sam was flanked by Vassili and Dad with Mike and Zola seated across from them. Edgar was at the opposite end of the table, leaning over and whispering to Vassili. The fairies were all gathered in the center of the table, a miniature version of our own, complete with a tiny flower arrangement.

"Damian, you have to meet my brother," Cassie said. She waved at another table and a bulky fairy glided over to stand beside her.

"Angus, you already met everyone else, but this is Damian."

"Nice to meet you," I said.

"Let me give you a proper greeting," he said. His accent was light, just a hint of Irish left in it. He jumped off the table and flashed into his larger form. My jaw dropped a little as I craned my neck to look up at the behemoth.

He extended his hand with a grin and almost yanked me out of my seat on brute strength alone. Even standing, I still looked up at him. He had to be at least seven and a half feet tall, muscled like a werewolf and armed with two enormous silver-hilted claymores crossed over his back.

All of his armor was silver, not golden like Foster's and Aideen's. I'm sure there was some meaning to it, but I couldn't do more than gawk at the enormous grin on his face. His teeth were sharp. They were far sharper than any fairy I'd met before, and the effect was somewhat unsettling.

"Bartender! Round of the good stuff," he shouted as he ran his finger in a circle around our table. "Right then," he said as he flashed back into his normal size. "Enjoy the food, and try to enjoy the company, though I know that's tough with Cassie around."

He waved and glided back to another table as Cassie laughed and cursed at him without any real conviction.

"Enough," Vassili said as he waved Edgar off. "We don't know who the necromancers all are, *da*? We don't know who their allies are. We cannot fight what we do not know."

"They can't be allies," Edgar said with a small frown.

"What would you have us do?" Vassili's voice fell to a whisper again. "Kill the innocent, 'in case' they are an enemy?"

"No," Edgar said, a hard edge to his voice. "That's not what I meant."

Dad shifted the bundle leaning against the wall beside him. I was fairly certain it was the cannon Mike had given him. I caught myself moving my hand toward the pepperbox under my arm, and instead redirected it to the innocuous looking hilt at my right hip.

The bartender dropped a tray of dark ale in the center of the table. He leaned over and placed a shot glass filled with a golden liquid in front of Dad. "Thought you might prefer this."

Dad summoned a smile and a quick nod for the bartender.

"Philip is getting desperate," Edgar said. "There's no other reason for him to make a move for the Blessing."

"Or he makes a distraction, *da*? The wolves have always been good at distraction. A silver wolf in particular." The table was silent for a breath before Vassili continued. "What will Philip do with such a thing?"

"After Stones River," Zola said. She closed her eyes and looked away as she took a deep breath. I was surprised to catch a small frown on Edgar's face, something resembling compassion. "After that," she said, "he cannot be left alive."

"Agreed," Vassili said as we all pulled a glass off the tray. "If he is allowed to live, he will become something more."

"Something worse," Mike said before his words dropped off to a near mumble. "We don't need another crazed half god running around this world."

Zola flashed Edgar a huge grin.

The Watcher didn't smile, only gave a slight shake his head.

"What?" I asked.

"Nothing, boy," Zola said. "Just an old joke."

"Cassie?" Mike said. "Where is the Blessing?"

Vassili glanced around the room, staring down anyone who turned their attention toward us.

"It's okay," Cassie said. "We're safe to talk here. Everyone here knows if they cross us, they cross the king."

Vassili's gaze fell on Cassie. "I think there is something you have not told me?"

"She's Glenn's niece," I said.

"Shit," Vassili said with a grunt. "We are friends, *da*?"

Most of the table chuckled. I took a drink of the ale and almost melted. Yeast and hops with a slight sweetness that didn't turn into a thick syrupy mess. "What the hell is this?"

"It's good," Sam said.

"Gulden Draak," Foster said with a smile. "He did pull up the good stuff."

"Amazing," Dad said as he looked at the little shot glass in his hand. He took another sip and set it down.

"So where is the Blessing?" Mike asked.

"It is hidden within the Ways," Cassie said.

"There are no gateways here," Mike said. "Boonville and all the surrounding area has been cut off for over a century." He paused. "Maybe closer to two centuries."

"There are no unguarded gateways here," Cara said from beside Cassie. "Rest assured, there are still Ways."

"Like the path into the Thunderbird's lair?" I said. "Yeah, that sounds fun."

Cassie walked across the table to Mike and motioned to us all to lean in. "The Blessing is hidden beneath Rivercene. The Guardian there is formidable."

"Understatement," Zola muttered.

"Only someone of our bloodline can retrieve it. All others will die."

"There is always a loophole," Zola said. "There are men on this earth with power enough to battle the Guardian."

"Yes," Cassie said quietly. "But the Guardian watches two paths. There are two gateways beneath Rivercene."

"The second's an escape hatch," Foster said. "Drops you in Hermann. An old German town not far from here. Good wine."

The little necromancer misted into view behind Sam. "Damian, there are other ghosts at Rivercene looking for you, from the Ghost Pack. They say it's important and you should just 'raise your damn Sight.' They're kind of annoying sometimes."

"Tell them we'll be there soon. I don't want them wandering around town without us if Philip is here."

"One's kind of cute."

Mike frowned.

"Hey, flame boy, you're the one who kissed a water witch," the little ghost snapped. Then she vanished.

"That's not exactly what happened," Mike said. His voice was quiet, but the grumble was unmistakable.

"She's certainly chatty these days," I said. "So, what do you get a two-century-old ghost as a makeup present?"

Sam leaned across Dad and punched me in the arm. "Leave the poor fire demon alone."

"It is a strange group that considers a demon in need," Vassili said. I wasn't sure he was joking until the corners of his mouth raised just a hair.

A wave of timid laughter circled the table.

"Back to task," Zola said as the humor faded. "We know where the Blessing is, but do any of us really know what it can do?

Cara cleared her throat. "Even though it's a modern crafting, it still has many of the same issues as the oldest Fae artifacts."

"Modern?" I said. "It's as old as this country."

Cara snorted. "Yes, it's modern, child."

I hesitated, and then asked, "What do you mean by *issues*?"

"It can bestow great gifts on its wielder, great things on all who follow them. But if the wielder wishes only the best for his people, and the best for his people is for him to die, then he will die."

"Fate will fall to favor the wielder in all he endeavors," Cassie said. "But that is not always what he intends."

"That's why it was hammered into Independence Hall," Aideen said. "The will of the entire country became the wielder. In the hands of one man, well …"

"Yeah," I said. "Cassie's told us some horror stories. End of the world and all that."

Cassie let out a small laugh. "That is very unlikely."

"End of a civilization?" I said with a cocked eyebrow.

"That is a more reasonable estimate."

Vassili said something in Russian, and I'm fairly certain it was unpleasant. Edgar took a sip of ale as he watched Vassili.

"Why so quiet, Edgar?" Foster asked. "Seems like five minutes ago you were acting like our leader."

Edgar glanced at Zola and Vassili, and then turned his gaze on Foster. "I am not the leader here. Protecting the Blessing is our priority. I may have suggestions, but I will not lead you all blindly into this conflict. Vassili is a long-lived and cunning strategist. The vampires will follow him into the Abyss if he asks it of them. The rest of you will follow Zola."

Foster stared at Edgar, slack-jawed.

"Edgar is wiser than you may think," Zola said as she gave Foster a tight smile.

"If I give you an order as I would one of my Watchers," Edgar said, "just know it is in the madness of conflict and I believe it best for our entire group."

I tapped my fingers on my glass of ale and watched a thin bead of cold water roll down its surface. Edgar sounded downright reasonable, which really made me wonder what made him tick. I knew he'd been betrayed by necromancers in the past, but was that really why he seemed to despise me all these years?

"So why are we here and not in Hermann?" Dad asked. It was a good question.

"Because everything thinks the Blessing is here," Zola said.

"You mean every*one*?" I asked.

Zola shot me a look. "No, Ah mean every*thing*."

"We've dropped breadcrumbs into the rumor mill for the better part of a year," Edgar said as he set his ale down. "Anyone with knowledge of the Blessing believes it is below Rivercene, and they dare not venture there." Edgar shook his head. "I never imagined you would have hidden it anywhere nearby."

Cassie just smiled.

The bartender dropped off a very un-Irish appetizer of toasted ravioli. Several hands shot out at once and a small battle for the parmesan cheese ensued. Sam won. Sam always wins when parmesan is on the line. I flashed her a smile and she narrowed her eyes.

Edgar swallowed a toasted rav and chased it with some ale before continuing.

"They'll all come here. We'll be waiting for them."

"Us?" Dad asked. "Just us? How many could show up? We don't have the numbers to engage more than a handful."

"It's not just us, Dimitry," Zola said. "There are three more Watchers in this bar. You may have missed the vampires on the roof."

Sam glanced up at Zola and then at Vassili.

Vassili's eyebrows were raised. "You are observant."

"Ah'm not senile yet," Zola said.

Vassili smiled and gave Zola a silent toast before taking a drink.

"The Thunderbird is here—" Zola started to say.

"Yeah, that has no chance of backfiring in fantastic and horrifying ways," Foster muttered.

Zola's eyes moved to the fairy as she finished. "—and is our easiest path if Ezekiel comes. The Guardian is here, and an old friend should be meeting us soon."

Edgar's eyes flicked to Zola and then to Foster. "I'm not sure I want to know."

"You don't," Zola said.

A busboy, or girl in this case, picked up our appetizer plates and the bartender set down a tableful of steaming food. I took a deep breath and almost drooled on the bread.

"Oh man," Foster and I said together.

"Bacon and cabbage, wheaten bread, and poundies," the bartender said. "Enjoy."

"Poundies?" I asked as he walked away. "Looks like mashed potatoes."

"Yeah, until you taste it," Foster said.

So I did. It was creamier than most American mashed potatoes and the scallions added a sharp, onion flavor. "You're right."

"Bacon and cabbage, what more can you say?" Dad said as he scooped up a mouthful.

"I can say give me bread," Sam said as she tore a piece in half and almost groaned.

Silence reigned for a while after that, as it often does when good food abounds. When we wrapped up, Mike leaned back in his chair and stretched.

"So what do we do now?" the demon asked.

"Walk the streets," Edgar said.

"Umm, no?" Sam said with a smirk.

Cassie and Aideen snickered. Vassili choked on his ale as he fought back a laugh.

"That is not what he meant, *da*?"

Edgar ignored them. "We make it known we're here. They'll come after us. If Philip or Zachariah, or anyone under their orders sees us, they'll bring everything they have in the area to bear. We'll engage them at Rivercene, away from the city. They'll show their hand before they know ours."

I wasn't sure if Edgar was a genius, or suicidal, or a suicidal genius. I was fairly certain the night wouldn't be dull.

CHAPTER NINE

"**F**oster, is it just me or does this seem like a really shitty plan," I said as we bundled up and followed the group to the front of the bar.

"I don't know," Foster said. "Edgar can be a pretty devious bastard. I don't think he'd put his own people at risk if he wasn't confident."

I nodded and walked out into an icy breeze.

Foster mumbled a string of curses, but all I caught was "Bloody cold as a witch's tits out here."

"In my experience—" I said.

"Stop, just stop. I don't want to hear about you and my cousin and what new horrific things you've found to do to each other."

I grinned as Foster scooted his legs under the edge of my jacket's collar.

Sam turned toward us. "You're a pervert, Demon."

"What?" Mike said with a frown. "What was that for?"

Aideen giggled from the pocket of Sam's coat. "She meant Damian."

"Oh," Mike said. "Can't argue that."

I gave them a little bow from the waist. "I try. Although, in my defense, I haven't violated any coffee mugs."

Sam flashed her fangs at me and turned around with a little laugh while Foster muttered obscenities from my shoulder. We walked past the cars, angling for the old Butternut Bread building past Chestnut. A shadow flitted by in my periphery, drawing my eye up and down the long structure while we waited for the signal to change. The building was all brick, and it looked like it could have been a repair shop at some point, but now the bays were bricked up. There was no sign of the shadow. I didn't know if the building was home to a bakery or what, but the name sounded tasty.

I glanced at the roof as we crossed, catching movement in one of the deeper shadows. I raised my Sight and looked again. The ley lines all throughout the area were a mess, possibly scrambled by the Guardian or perhaps the presence of the Thunderbird. The lines leapt and dove from the ground, and as I traced one particularly high arc, I found the source of the shadow I'd glimpsed earlier. Another necromancer, and I was pretty damn sure he had been tracking us.

I looked away casually and sidled up beside the rest of the group as they waited to cross the street again.

"Necromancer on the roof," I whispered. "The vampires all have amulets?"

Zola had gifted Vassili's vampires amulets to protect them from necromancy. It was a risk, granting them power like that, but their alliance had already helped save our asses.

Vassili nodded. "Of course. This would not be a fight for vampires otherwise, my friend." He held up his bronze amulet. It was still on the black silk cord Zola had given him. Runes blazed on either side. Deep red, yellow, and violet lines twisting around each rune, penetrating the amulet and forming a delicate-looking braid.

As I let my Sight fade, I began to notice pale gray forms all around us. I couldn't suppress a shiver. A hell of a lot of ghosts were gathering, probably drawn to whatever art the necromancers were warming up around us.

I caught a glimpse of dark hair and a weak chin beneath a black hood as it vanished around the next corner. Sam blurred into motion. She stuck her head around the edge of the building, low to the ground. She nodded to Vassili and came back in a hurry.

"It's him," she said. "Zachariah's here."

"Good," Edgar said. "I didn't think it would take long to bring them out. Get back to the cars. We meet at Rivercene. If they attack, I don't want civilians in harm's way."

Good was not exactly a word I normally associated with Zachariah.

We split up, Edgar and Zola took the fairies in her car. They pulled out before we piled into my car and I swear the shadows hopped and slithered along behind them, following the car across the bridge. One had a shock of white hair. Vassili.

"Hurry," Mike said. "They do not need to be alone for this."

Sam, Mike, Dad, and I climbed into my old '32 Ford. I started the car and flipped a questionably legal U-turn. Though there were still few parking spaces, traffic was gone. We hit the signals just right and started over the bridge.

"That's no riverboat," Mike said as he leaned toward the window. "Military?"

I glanced out the window and saw the small black craft near the casino.

Dad leaned over Mike to look. "Gunboat. Looks old."

The city went black. The casino's lights were extinguished in a heartbeat. Streetlights died, and the only luminescence I could see for miles was headlights.

"Christ, I can't see shit behind us." I floored the pedal and shot across the rest of the bridge. I could see Zola's brake lights off to the east.

"Hurry," Sam said. The stress in her voice ratcheted up the anxiety in the car.

We slid on the gravel as I took the turn faster than I should have and rocketed toward Rivercene's driveway. Zola had gone past the house.

"Lights are still on in the mansion," Dad said.

"Follow Zola," Mike said.

She cut her lights and pulled behind a small cluster of very large trees. I did the same and drove the last quarter mile by moonlight.

"What the hell is a gunboat doing here?" Dad asked.

"Mercenaries," Mike said as we started to climb out of the car. "Disposable men."

We closed the doors as quietly as possible and regrouped, with everyone between the cars. Edgar and Vassili were nowhere to be seen. Combined with the stand of trees, the cars made a crappy shield, but it was better than nothing.

"Ah did not anticipate so many more mercenaries here," Zola said, her voice barely a whisper. "That boat may hold a dozen."

"Don't worry about them," Dad said as he unwrapped the whaling gun. "Be careful Sam, Damian. I love you both." With that he turned and slunk away into the shadows toward the river.

"Dad?" I hissed. "What the hell are you doing?"

"I can get him," Sam said.

Mike shook his head and gently put his arm out to stop Sam. "He's a military man. He knows what he's doing. He knows the risk."

"Dammit," Sam said.

I ran my hand through my hair. "We can't lose them both."

"We haven't lost either one," Sam said. "We'll get Mom back."

"Enough," Zola said as she put a hand on either of our shoulders. "Focus."

"I'll follow him," Aideen said. "Nothing will harm him."

She hugged Foster and took to the air.

Quiet footsteps came up behind us. I turned with my pepperbox drawn. Edgar stood there with two other Watchers.

"Why are we helping Vesik?" the short blonde woman asked. She wore a suit much like Edgar's.

"Do not argue, Mindy," Edgar said. "They are here to help, and we shall do the same."

"She has a point," The other Watcher said as he adjusted his black bowler. He was big, and I waited for his suit to tear when he moved his arms. "We've lost too many men to be out here babysitting a goddamned necromancer."

Edgar didn't even flinch. He didn't even seem annoyed at being questioned. "You have your orders."

"Fine," the larger Watcher said. "So long as we see some action."

"Do not be casual," Edgar said. "We face many this night."

I heard the hiss of Dad's whaling gun followed by a clang and screams. A thunder followed the orange glow of an explosion through the shadowy branches of the southern trees.

"The mercenaries have lost," Mike said, his teeth gleaming in the moonlight.

There was another hiss, but no screams were heard as a second fireball erupted behind the tree line. The ground shook as the explosion expanded, roared, and slowly died out.

"You two," Edgar said to the Watchers, "flank the house. Foster, move into the trees. Stay out of sight as best you can. Zola, we'll follow the path Dimitry and Aideen took. Vassili is already scouting ahead. You three," Edgar said as he pointed at me, Mike, and Sam, "hole up in the shell of that guest house."

The other Watchers left with a nod.

"Sorry," Edgar whispered. "They have to believe you all listen to me."

Zola's face pulled up in a wrinkly smile. "For now, we'll survive."

We scattered into the night.

"Go behind Rivercene," Mike whispered. "We don't know what's between us and the river."

Sam nodded and we followed him to the back of the mansion. Sam scouted ahead and peeked around the edge of the covered wraparound porch. She held a finger up and we froze. Sam crouched and leapt lightly to the roof above the wooden porch before disappearing in silence. A few seconds later she landed on the ground beside us.

"Clear."

We moved forward again, staying low and hugging the side of the structure. At the next corner I could see the old guest house a short way off, a squat brick structure barely lit by the moonlight. Our path looked clear, but we waited for a moment while silence reigned in the darkness. Every step in the brittle grass seemed like a tree splintering in the stillness.

Mike pointed toward the edge of the roof and crouched. Sam leaned forward, and I could see her squinting before she shook her head. Mike nodded and led us along the main house and up to the gravel drive in near silence before we slipped into the black rectangle that was once the front door.

The loudest sound was my own heartbeat until another small explosion echoed up from the river.

"Leftovers?" I whispered.

Mike shrugged and then froze. A lance of adrenaline stiffened my spine as something thudded against the roof. I pulled the pepperbox out of its holster and slid around the corner into a hallway. Mike shook his head and held his index finger over his lips. Quiet.

I nodded.

The first man to walk by the door died in utter silence as Mike's blackened forearms reached out and snapped his neck like a sapling. He handed the body to Sam and she gently laid it in the corner.

It. Christ, it's a he. The man didn't look evil. Hell, he looked like he probably had a wife and kids and paid his taxes on time.

Sam grabbed my shirt and put her face next to my ear. "I know what you're thinking. Stop. These bastards took Mom, they might kill Dad, and they're trying to kill our friends."

"You're right." I nodded rapidly.

Someone started shouting in the distance. A few quick bursts of gunfire cut through the silence before something landed on the roof.

There was a short, brutal exchange above us. I half expected the ceiling to collapse. The next person to come by the door was the little blonde Watcher. Only it wasn't all of her. Her head fell into the doorway and rolled to a stop at Mike's feet. Something metal glistened in the dim light.

"Oh, fuck. Grenade!" he yelled.

As Mike and I tried to scramble away, Sam picked the head up and threw it in the blink of an eye at a shadow across the yard. My vision was night-adjusted enough to make out a spray of gore where the head smashed into another body. Someone else cursed and then the grenade detonated.

"Picked up the spare," Mike said with approval obvious in his voice. "How did they get behind us?" He stared out the door, across the driveway for a moment, and then stepped away from the vacant doorway.

"Let's move, out the back," I said.

Mike nodded and we headed down the hallway to the back door.

I heard the click behind us and instinct took over.

"*Impadda!*" I said as I pushed myself in front of Mike. The shield's glassy surface sprang to life between us and our would-be assassin. A hail of bullets shredded the walls around us. Puffs of ancient dust clouded the air and choked us as the walls took the brunt of the attack. Explosions of electric blue lightning sprang from the shield when some of the bullets found their targets. I could see our attacker plainly as he continued firing. Each round sent a yellow-orange burst of flame into the night.

As soon as the clip ran out, I dropped the shield and blew his fucking head off.

I slammed an extra round into the pepperbox. "Don't know what the hell I was thinking, Sam. Almost forgot who we were dealing with." The kah-chunk of a shotgun pump whispered through the wall.

"Step aside please," Mike said as he ushered Sam away from the door. He took one small hop and kicked the top of the door. Hard. The heavy steel door clanged as the hinges snapped out of the wall and flattened whoever was behind it. The end of a shotgun barrel was sticking out the side of the fallen metal along with an unattractive mush.

Mike drew the hammer from his belt. "These are pawns. They're fishing for our positions. Let's move."

A flash of lightning burst through the trees to the southwest along the river. Branches shattered and burned as a focused spiral of flame blossomed in response. The ring of steel on steel echoed through the thunder and fire.

I felt a shift in the ley lines before I saw the necromancer. He appeared in a burst of black smoke near a clearing to the southwest, arm extended and a snarl on his lips. Zachariah.

"*Tyranno Eversiotto!*" Lightning stormed from his hand, burrowing into the ground in arcing blasts. It cast debris up between us and obscured our view.

"*Impadda!*" The incantation sprang up and Zachariah's spell landed a glancing blow. It knocked me back a few steps and my shield flickered as a burst of ozone filled my nostrils, joining the heavy scent of burnt gunpowder.

I caught movement in my peripheral vision. Something weaved slowly through a copse of trees near Zachariah, but my eyes were all for the necromancer.

"Zombies!" Sam shouted as she blurred into motion. She took two down before I could even respond. I focused my Sight and could see the lines of power leading back up to Zachariah.

Christ, he'd cast a spell that strong while animating twelve zombies?

No hesitation. Mike moved toward the necromancer. I pulled the hilt of the focus out of my belt and channeled an aural blade through it. My vision dimmed for a moment as my aura was ripped through the focus and blazed into a pulsing red blade, but all I needed was momentum. The slash cut through Zachariah's necromancy.

He stumbled backwards as Mike leapt into the air. The Smith's Hammer exploded in his hands, coming to life as an enormous war hammer. Flames licked the dual-headed weapon and Mike brought it down hard.

Zachariah threw himself backwards with a shout and vanished in another burst of black smoke. Mike's hammer was embedded a foot into the ground. He jerked it out of the dirt and slipped back inside the guest house as his eyes scanned the shadows around us.

The far-off crack of gunfire echoed in the darkness. Then nothing.

CHAPTER TEN

"There's no way this is over," I said.

Mike nodded his agreement. "Give it time. Wait for a message, or an attack."

We stayed there in the edge of the shadows, Sam barely breathing behind my right shoulder. I wiped the sweat from my palm and squeezed the trigger guard on the pepperbox.

Minutes passed before I spotted one of the fairies moving in the trees to the south. As the figure swooped down toward us a moment later, I could see it was Foster. Blood saturated his face and the front of his armor. It was starting to dry, but still shone in the moonlight. The grin told me it wasn't anyone we'd miss.

"Edgar's calling us back to the house. He doesn't think they expected this level of resistance."

"Where's he been?" I asked.

"Two necromancers attacked them," Foster said. "We helped." His smile was terrible.

"Dead?" Sam asked.

Foster nodded. "Zola incinerated one of them."

"Philip?" I asked.

Foster shook his head. "Edgar saw what you did to the mercenary who killed Mindy," he said as he landed on Sam's shoulder. "He may never thank you for it, but I know he appreciates it."

"Don't get that on my parka," Sam said with a sideways glance at Foster.

Foster wiped his face and started to lean forward with a glob of blood on his hand.

"Dammit, bug!" Sam growled.

The fairy burst into laughter and fluttered over to Mike's shoulder.

"Did we only lose one?" Mike asked.

"So far," Foster said. "But the battle hasn't really started, has it?"

Mike shook his head. "Let's move back to the house."

The demon turned and led us back to the hollow doorway at the front of the guest house. Foster flew out and waved us over once he thought it was clear. We ran, hunched low to the ground, with our boots and shoes crunching on the gravel until we hit the wooden steps with a rhythmic series of thumps.

For a moment I questioned the intelligence of walking back in through the front door. Then a vertical bar of yellow light appeared as the heavy walnut door cracked open and we slipped in, joining our allies, who were spread between the hall and the living room. I nodded to the innkeeper as we walked by. Aideen was on the grand piano in her small form. She had her chainmail armor across her lap, carefully cleaning blood from it with a needle and thread. Each run through the loops dyed the white thread with blood. Zola had a hand on Edgar's shoulder as he sat on the bench.

"You couldn't have done a thing," my master said, her old world New Orleans accent in full swing after the adrenaline rush of the fight.

"You know that's not true," Edgar whispered. "We've lost so many. If I'd just let it go, if I just—"

"Hush, it is done."

He nodded and looked up at the rest of the room. Vassili stood nearby, beside an ornately carved marble fireplace. He picked up an old fireplace poker and eyed the handle. A small smile flitted over his face before he set it down. Dad sat in a chair beside Vassili. Dad nodded and I returned the gesture.

"Nice shooting?" I said dryly.

"Quite so chap," he said, just as dryly.

The large Watcher standing beside him exhaled loudly.

"Sorry about Mindy," I said.

He cocked his head to the side and then looked away. Either he didn't give a crap about Mindy, or he really didn't like me. Or maybe both.

At the same time I realized who the wall of muscle standing next to him was, Sam squealed.

"Dominic!" The hug would have crushed any mortal man. And the thump he gave her on the back would have crushed any mortal woman.

Dominic was a monster, one of the Pit's enforcers, and he was hella handy when shit went bad. He was still sporting an ultra-short blond crew cut. His eyes were black as pitch in the orange light, even though I knew they were a dark brown.

Once Sam released him, I extended my arm and traded grips.

"Good to see you, Damian."

"You too, Dom," I gritted out in mild agony.

He raised his eyebrows, glanced at my arm, and said, "Oh, sorry. Sometimes I forget. After all, you survived your sister."

"So far," I said as I rubbed my arm.

Mike had no such issues. He smacked Dominic on the back hard enough to send him stumbling forward three steps.

"Good to see you, Smith," the vampire said as he extended his arm. They shook hands like we had, hands to elbows.

"We should meet on better terms some day," Mike said. "Haven't seen you since the battle with Prosperine."

"Hardly a battle," Dominic said. "Damian chewed her up and spit her out, and all he had to fight with was a shiny tooth-pick."

Zola snorted and Edgar seemed to be making an effort not to listen.

For a moment, I thought I felt the other Watcher staring at me. When I looked up, his focus was on Edgar, but his lips were in a tight line.

Edgar stood up and all the attention in the room trailed to him. Even Vassili seemed to be respecting the Watcher, which made me curious if nothing else. Vassili had been around a long, long time, which made him patient, calculating, and utterly terrifying. But he was damn good at making you forget all three. His motivations were beyond me.

"I don't think they'll come at us again tonight," Edgar said. "The resistance they met had to be more than expected. They may come at dawn, when the vampires will be weakest, or they may come tomorrow night when the darkest arts will be strongest. We have scouts out now. Cassie and Cara are in the woods and Vassili has two vampires on the roof. We sleep in shifts—"

Damian! My head snapped up and I looked around. Nothing was there, but I'd heard the shout.

"Did uh, did anyone else hear that?" I asked.

"Don't schiz out on us now," Sam said.

"—I want four scouts awake at all times," Edgar said, ignoring my interruption and drawing my attention back to his strategies.

Most of the group nodded or grunted in agreement.

"I know it's unlikely so soon after a battle, but let's try to get some rest."

We mingled briefly and said our goodbyes for the night before Sam, Dad, and I started up the stairs.

"This is crazy," Dad said. "This is your job?"

Sam and I glanced at each other. I wasn't sure if he meant me, or her, or both.

"My other job's a bit stranger," I said.

"The store?"

I shook my head. "Genealogy."

"Genealo-what?!" Dad said. "Are you joking?"

Sam laughed softly. "It's more than he makes it out to be, Dad. He talks to ghosts, ancestors of living families. He helps them confirm rumors or family secrets."

"And occasionally I just plug some holes in a family tree."

"And they believe you?" Dad said as we approached the staircase to the third floor.

I grinned. "It takes a special sort."

Sam reached out and hugged Dad. I did the same.

"We'll see you soon," she said.

Dad nodded and closed the door to his room behind him.

"You didn't tell him about Koda," Sam said.

"Tell him about my friendly neighborhood ghost that likes to help assemble family trees when he's not researching forbidden magic and the history of demon-kind?"

Sam put on an impressive scowl.

"No," I said. "I didn't."

"I'm so not getting any sleep," Sam said as we climbed the stairs again.

"I hear you. Maybe I'll try out the whirlpool tub."

"Bastard," Sam muttered.

"I beg to differ. I believe we just parted ways with my father."

She snorted a laugh and started down the hallway on the third floor as Foster and Aideen swooped past us.

"You want to share some of that sweet whirlpool action?" Foster asked.

"Eh, sure," I said.

Sam scooped me up in a hug and it felt like my ribs were shattering. "Urck!" I squeaked.

"Goodnight, Demon," She said as she let me go and walked over to her door. "Don't scar him too bad Foster. He's delicate." She sounded out each syllable as though she was talking to a child. The lock clicked and the ancient wood swung into the room as Sam disappeared in a muffled fit of giggling.

"I think she's adopted," I said as I padded down to my room, the Nile, and just like Sam's room, the locks clicked and the door swung in.

"Okay," I said. "I admit that's a little creepy."

Foster and Aideen glided into the dark room. I flipped the lights on and strolled over to the bathroom.

"Remember the Roman bath houses?" Aideen asked as she settled on the back of the sink.

Foster nodded. "I still think Greece was better."

"My favorite was the Onsen in Japan," Aideen said. "Hot springs in the outdoors, there is nothing like it."

"I've never been to Japan," I said. "Hell, I've never even been to Canada."

"You should go to Japan some time," Aideen said with a smile. "It is a beautiful place with a rich history."

"Now you're making it sound boring," Foster said.

I chuckled, leaned over, and turned the water on with the modern brass handles on the tub. It was huge, and it was going to take a while to fill. I dropped the drain cover and stood up.

"You two want to get the blood off in the sink?"

"Way ahead of you," Foster said as he leaned against the faucet handles to start the water flowing. He kicked the little white rubber stopper into the sink and jumped in after it to position it over the drain.

"I'll leave you alone for a bit," I said as I added a healthy dose of bubble bath to the tub. I stepped out of the room and started to close the door.

"Leave it open," Foster said. "I don't think the exhaust fan is going to keep up with the steam."

I frowned slightly, started to say something about steamy fairies, and then thought better of it.

I slid my black boots off and hung my holster on the chair by the vanity. My shirt followed, covering the pepperbox and focus. I rolled up the black leather belt with the bulky gray buckle and set it on the vanity.

I had one leg out of my pants and boxers and was balancing to pull them off the other foot when something flickered beside me.

"Damian!" the shout was deep and booming.

I squealed like a teenage girl and fell over sideways. Foster and Aideen streaked into the room, quite literally, with swords drawn.

My eyes glanced past Foster, though I still noticed the man looked like he'd been chiseled from marble, and fell on Aideen.

I couldn't help but stare at Aideen, even though she was still small. She was pale, like Nixie, and everything was perky. Oh my god, did I ever miss Nixie.

I didn't know how much longer Nixie would be away. How long *does* it take to incite a revolution among immortal water Fae?

I slowly turned my head and then peeled my eyes away from Aideen to stare up at the dead werewolf.

"Carter," I said. "You have impeccable timing."

He was the old Alpha of the River Pack, though it hadn't been known as the River Pack while he still breathed. He was still five eight or nine with a light covering of beard and a strong chin. His eyes had once blazed with a huge sunburst iris rimmed in black, but now were shades of gray with the faint yellow glow of his soul. He'd been killed in battle with the Destroyer, but when I'd used his soul and the soul of his wife as a weapon, there were unanticipated consequences.

"How have you been ignoring me?" Carter asked. "You've never been able to do that before." He sounded impressed, and looked annoyed.

"Carter!" Foster said. "It's good to see you."

"Nice pants," said another familiar voice.

I looked up from the floor and found Maggie perched on the bed. I am fairly certain I turned several shades of red. Maggie was petite, with short gray hair that had been silver in life. Her once-green wolf eyes now stared out in grays and blacks. I sighed and kicked my pants off the rest of the way.

Maggie let out a little chuckle.

"So?" Carter said. "How?"

"Zola taught me a meditation trick, cuts off the ghosts for a bit. It's not usually that effective. It probably has something to do with this place." I held up my hand as I said, "Speaking of how, how did you two just appear in here? This place is guarded against ghosts."

"Not exactly," Carter said. "There are still many ghosts here, but it's more like they are guarded from you, from necromancers."

I picked myself up and walked toward the bathroom door all dignified-like.

Maggie gave me a little wolf whistle and I felt a blush crawl over my face again.

The tub was just about full, so I dumped in a little extra bubble bath and then slid into the hot water. I was relieved to have a nice covering of bubbles. I heard Maggie and Aideen laughing about something in the bedroom before both the fairies glided into the bathroom. Foster landed on the right side of me and Aideen settled on the edge of the tub to my left. I kept my focus squarely on Carter.

"To what do we owe the honor?" I asked.

"We can help," Carter said.

I shook my head. "No. Philip's here. Maybe Ezekiel."

"Not to mention a slew of other necromancers," Foster said.

"We already fought a blood mage, in downtown Saint Charles," Aideen said. "Who knows what they'll bring here."

"Shit," Carter said. "I understand your concern, but the Ghost Pack won't stand by and do nothing."

"Nothing?" I said. "How many pack members have you already dragged out of the Burning Lands?" Hugh had told me of the raids into the realm of fire. Something was attacking the dead wolves, dragging them into other planes of existence where they should never set foot. "I've heard the demons of the Burning Lands fear you."

"They damn well should," Maggie growled as her aura flared into a golden light. "They've crossed the line, stealing the pure, damning the innocent. That's not how it's supposed to be."

"It's getting worse?" I asked.

Carter nodded. "They've been taking kids. We found a six-year-old girl in the caves of the eighth circle this week."

"No," Aideen said, and that one word held a terrible fury. A fury to match my own. The demons had taken to calling their prisons 'circles.'

"Why?" I asked. "Why would they do that? They killed her?"

Maggie nodded. "Vicky annihilated the demon that did it. It was a minor demon, but she destroyed it utterly."

"Vicky?!" I said. "What the hell was Vicky doing there? How did she …? I mean, bloody hell!" I'd read many things about the Burning Lands. The Society of Flame thought it was the realm hell was based on in so many religions. So much so its inhabitants were labelled demons, monsters the Fae used in their own children's tales. It was no place for Vicky to be. It was no place for any of us to be.

"Is she okay?" Foster asked, the concern bare in his voice.

"You know she's changed," Carter said.

"She's been changing since we saved her," Foster said quietly.

"We didn't save her," I growled. "We were too late for that."

"You did as much as anyone could have possibly done," Aideen said.

I took a deep breath and stared at the ceiling. "But what is she becoming? I feel like she's my responsibility, but Happy and Aeros take care of her. I should be doing more, guiding her somehow." My thoughts turned to one of the only secrets I've ever kept from Sam. Zola thought Happy and Aeros had both given Vicky powers, enhanced whatever gifts she would have had in life.

"She's a wrecking crew," Carter said. "Maybe she'll be a new Guardian, like Aeros?"

I nodded, but what I was really thinking was that Aeros isn't a Guardian. He's an Old God. What the hell happens when Old Gods grant powers to mortal ghosts?

"Bloody hell," I muttered.

Foster cursed in agreement and then slipped into the water. He propped himself up on a little ledge a few inches down the side of the tub, his arms thrown back along the top edge. The bubbles came up to his chest. He motioned to Aideen, and I was thankful she decided to walk behind me, and not glide across my field of view.

"You can use us," Carter said. "The soulsword can slay a demon, not banish it, but kill it. It should be more than enough to kill a few necromancers."

"No, I'm not doing that to you again. We don't know what it does to you two. Against Prosperine, yes. But now? We don't even know what you are."

Carter shrugged. "Does it matter? If we are mortal or not, we can still be killed by demons, and we can still fight back."

"I do wonder if you are mortal," Aideen said as Foster wrapped his arm around her. "I wouldn't think so, but I've never heard of souls being forged with so much power. We don't know if you're aging or not."

"She has a point," I said. "I can't even tell if you have any more gray hair now."

"I'm a ghost," Carter said. "All my hair is gray."

Maggie grinned and sat down on the closed toilet seat near the tub. "Damian, Carter and I are together. How many people can say that after getting murdered by an immortal demon?"

"Two?" I said nonchalantly. "Although the demon doesn't seem very immortal now."

She smiled. "You've given us more than we ever thought possible. Dying did not change who we are, we still fight for the River Pack. Even if something were to happen to us now, we know how lucky we've been to be together for a little while longer."

"Well, when you put it that way," I said. "No."

Foster and Aideen both laughed.

"He's pretty stubborn," Foster said.

"Fine," Carter said, "but promise me you'll talk to Zola and Edgar. Find a way for us to help."

"I will."

Carter nodded and held his hand out to Maggie. He pulled her up and they walked out through the doorway.

"Still using doors?" I asked.

"Occasionally," Carter said. He whispered to Maggie and then they both leapt through the outer wall, three stories above the ground.

"Okay," I said. "I have to admit that's pretty cool." I yawned and wiped a line of sweat from my forehead.

Foster slid out into the currents of the whirlpool jets. He was flat on his back, wings cutting through the water as the ripples and whorls spun him around the tub and sent him careening into a bank of bubbles. He was upside down when he briefly resurfaced on the other side of the tub before vanishing once more in the torrent of water.

Aideen sighed as she watched Foster come spinning out of the bubbles like a white water rafter. "It's getting warm."

Before I could fully register what had happened, Aideen flopped onto my shoulder. I locked my gaze on the light switch across the room and didn't move my eyes. Water sprayed my face as she beat her wings to get them dry. She readjusted herself and began casually wringing the water from her hair.

"It is warm," Foster said as he climbed out of the water and took up residence on my other shoulder.

"Are there tiny balls on my shoulder? Seriously?"

Foster and Aideen both stopped shaking the water from their wings.

"Damian Valdis Vesik," Foster said as he stood up on my shoulder. "Fae cannot abide such dire insults. I accept your challenge. Aideen, bring me my sword!"

"Umm, Foster?" I said as I leaned my head away from the naked, enraged fairy.

Aideen broke down in a fit of muffled hysterics and I cast her a sideways glance. She was laughing so hard she could barely breathe.

I turned my head back to Foster. "Pfff, tiny."

"You thought he was serious," Aideen said when she finally caught her breath. "You should have seen your face!" She flashed Foster a huge smile and started braiding her hair.

"Okay," I said as I turned my head toward Foster. "I'm out. It's getting late and I'm actually tired."

"That's good," Foster said as they both climbed off my shoulders. "Maybe you can get a little sleep before your shift comes up."

"Sounds nice," I said. "Is that your subtle cue for me to get out?" I stood up slowly, deliberately sticking my ass out toward the fairies.

"Nudd blind me!" Foster shouted.

"Now where'd that towel go," I said as I slowly scooped up a folded terrycloth towel and wrapped it around my waist. "You two enjoy the tub. I'm going to get some sleep." I turned and started to walk away.

"Damian?" Aideen said.

"Yup?"

"Nice ass."

I shook my head as Foster burst into laughter and cannon-balled back into the water. I walked over to my luggage and pulled out some clean boxers and a Double D t-shirt, Frank's idea. I turned off the lamp, dove into the bed, and was shocked at how comfortable it was. It was my last thought before sleep rose up to take me. It didn't last nearly long enough.

CHAPTER ELEVEN

"Hey, Demon. Wake up!"

I cracked my eye and was ready to reduce my sister to a sparking mass of rubble, the most common fate for irritating alarm clocks in my life.

"How did you get in here?" I mumbled.

"Don't know. The door opened up for me. Cool, huh?"

"Super," I said as I buried my head in my pillow. "I love you Sam, but I have to kill you now."

"That's cute, are you wearing clothes?"

"Yes, why?" The why trailed off into a yelp as Sam picked me up under my arms and stood me beside the bed. She held on until I managed to get my legs halfway stable. I groaned as the room spun and stars swam in my vision. "I hate you."

"The innkeeper made breakfast. Let's get some food before we take our shift."

"You're taking a day shift?" I said as I pulled my jeans on.

"Yes, Vassili wants at least one vampire on watch during the day. I'll still have better eyes than you, even in the sun."

I shrugged as I tied my boots. "Not arguing. Need coffee."

"How in the hell does your hair look that good right out of bed?"

I flashed Sam a grin and leaned over to look in the mirror. A bit scruffy, but my black hair stood up in artful clumps. The circles under my eyes were surprisingly small, but they still stood out over the pale skin.

Sam put her hand out toward the diagonal line of four slashes a vampire had given me, ripped across my left bicep. It trailed down my chest and over my stomach. Foster had offered to heal the burned skin of my right shoulder, but I'd declined. His idea was to cut all the scar tissue off and heal it again. Thanks, but no.

I sighed and pulled my black shirt on before strapping the pepperbox holster back to my chest and covering that with a black fleece.

"Going all Johnny Cash today?" Sam asked.

"Don't I always?"

"I guess your jeans are a bit more charcoal than black," Sam said, and her voice seemed almost gleeful in my coffee-deprived state.

"Shut up," I said with a small smile as I led her into the hall.

"Morning," Mike said as he closed his door and joined us.

"Don't talk to him yet. No coffee," Sam said in a loud whisper.

I narrowed my eyes in a vain attempt to stop her giggling. "Did you see Foster and Aideen when you came in?"

"Yep, I hear you had problems staring at Aideen's tits."

I groaned and hung my head as we clumped down the stairs.

"Don't feel bad," Sam said. "I wanted to jump Foster something fierce the first time I saw him naked."

"Ah," Mike said. "I'm not sure where this conversation is going, but I might like to be elsewhere."

"Sam," I said, ignoring Mike for the moment. "Yeah, she's attractive and all—"

"Attractive?" Sam said with a snort. "Do you find Nixie *attractive*? Please, the Fae are effing hot."

Mike and I both burst into laughter.

"Touché," I said. "Well played, madam."

"I speak the truth."

I gave Mike a quick glance. He grinned. Not a little grin, but a full on demon full of mischief grin. I laughed and walked into the dining room shaking my head.

"Laughter before coffee?" Zola said as she sipped at her own mug. "These people are obviously a bad influence on you." She gestured to the seat beside her at the table for four, and I almost pounced on the oversized black mug. It was more like a soup bowl.

I sipped at it, winced as I burned my lips, and then sipped at it some more before setting it down on the white lace table cloth and looking around. I watched Mike as he took another mug from the innkeeper and walked past another marble fireplace adorning the north wall. White wooden trim outlined the windows and formed the baseboards. A hutch set into the wall beside the doorway to the kitchen rattled as the fire demon passed it. It was filled with old glasses protected behind a sliding glass door.

"About time," the innkeeper said as she followed Mike in from the kitchen. "I've been keeping this warm for you three."

"Is Dad not on our shift?" Sam asked as she pulled out the chair opposite Zola.

Mike sat down across from me.

"Dimitry is on no one's shift," Zola said. "As long as he sleeps, we leave him be."

"He'll be grumpy if you don't wake him up," I said.

She smiled. "Ah'll take my chances."

The innkeeper set three trays into a lit buffet warmer in the center of the table. "Breakfast soufflé, goetta sausage, and bread pudding," she said as she pulled the lid off each steaming vessel.

"Soufflé looks a little flat," Zola said.

The innkeeper laughed. "You said the same thing last time you were here." She walked the lids back into the kitchen.

"Admitting you've been here that long now?" Zola asked. "Long enough to know more than a photograph? Ah assumed you'd keep a greater distance."

The innkeeper spared Zola a glance, but said no more.

"She's a bit older than she looks, isn't she?" Mike asked.

"Ah haven't been here since 1884," Zola said.

"You both look pretty good for being over a century."

"A century?" the innkeeper said as she came back into the room with a pitcher swathed in a fabric napkin. "I am well over three, thank you very much."

Mike gawked as she poured orange juice from the silver pitcher. "But you are no necromancer, are you?"

"No, demon, I am not. We'll leave it there for now. It's nothing you need to know. I've already learned half your names. As Adannaya insinuated so subtly, I do not wish you to know mine."

Mike looked at his plate and took a bite of bread pudding. His eyes widened. "Madam, if you continue to bring me bread pudding like this, I shall ask nothing else of you."

"Fair enough," she said as she started to walk away. She paused and looked back. "You're somewhat social for a demon."

Mike laid his fork down and swallowed another bite of bread pudding. He laced his fingers together and took a slow breath, his eyes never leaving his plate. "One mistake does not define a man, but it may damn him."

"The damned can always be redeemed," she said as she disappeared into the kitchen.

"Were that only true," Mike said. He stayed silent for a moment and then shook himself. "You really need to try this bread pudding."

Sam opened her mouth wide for a forkful of soufflé and said, "Nuh-uh." She chewed and swallowed. "Soufflé, so good, oh so good."

I watched Mike for a moment, wondering what I didn't know about the man, wondering what—other than the little necromancer—drove him. I took a bite of soufflé and understood Sam's reaction. The eggs were perfect. Throw in the cheese, and sausage, and a bite of goetta, and it was a heavenly affair.

"That's good," I mumbled around a mouthful of food, forgoing the coffee.

Mike shook his head. "Bread pudding."

"Ah'm with Mike," Zola said.

I stabbed some bread pudding. My teeth sank into it and my taste buds exploded. "Pudding. Like bread, with sweet goo, oh god."

"An apt description, boy," Zola said with a chuckle. "Finish up. We need to take over the watch. We're pulling a long shift, so most of the group will be well rested tonight."

A clatter of knives, forks, and lip smacking eventually led to the end of a stellar meal.

***

I shivered in the crisp morning air and leaned on my staff as we stood at the base of the steps outside Rivercene. A few flurries fell from the gray skies and the naked tree branches struck each other like drumsticks in the wind.

"We're going to be out here how long?" Sam muttered as she wrapped a crocheted Hello Kitty scarf tightly around her neck, covering the darker patch of donor skin on her neck. Sometimes I could see that scar and think nothing of it. Other times it took me back to the night my sister died and I had to piece her back together. The night she'd become a vampire.

I breathed into my hands and then slid some thin leather driving gloves on. Better than nothing. "I have a question."

Sam, Zola, and Mike all looked at me.

"We know Philip has the hand of the dead Fae king. Couldn't he just pop in here at any time? Zachariah could pop in and out. Why not Philip? Is keeping watch really doing us any good?"

"Do you not listen, boy?" Zola said. "If anyone comes through the Warded Ways, the Guardian here will destroy them."

"Even through a new portal?" Mike asked.

"Yes, even then."

Mike eyed Zola. "What guards this place?"

Zola gave him a flat look. "Darkness. Pray you don't learn more." Her eyes shifted to me. "Damian, before you even ask, the spell Zachariah and the others use let them move briefly through a chain of dead auras. They can't use it over long distances, and it's still a risk even at short distances." She rubbed her wrist and looked up toward one of the taller trees. "Let's relieve our friends."

There weren't many necromantic texts that had survived the trials of time, but I'd read mentions of teleportation by necromancy. The two times I'd read of it, in the Black Book and in an old manuscript from the Society of Flame, it was considered suicide.

We hadn't taken three steps when Cassie swooped down from the trees and landed on Zola's shoulder. She hugged Zola's neck and sighed.

"We get to go inside?"

"Yes, how was the cold?' Zola asked.

"Nothing Cara's thermals can't beat," Cassie said as she pulled the edge of a white bodysuit out from under her armor.

"I need to ask Cara for one of those," Sam said through her scarf.

"Christmas is coming up pretty quick," Cara said as she glided in and settled on Sam.

Sam grinned.

"Where's Vassili?" Sam asked.

"He's around," Cara said.

"Yes, I am," Vassili said, and I jumped. He nodded as I turned around and found him perched on the portico roof, crouched with his right hand on the edge of the trim.

"Anything interesting happen?" I asked.

"*Nyet*, Cara saw Volund's bald head, but that is it."

"If Volund and Zachariah are here, Philip is too," Zola said.

A black blur moved across the roof above Vassili and leapt. I shifted away on instinct, but there was no reason to run. Vik landed on the brick with a whumpf, his knee-length coat soaring in the breeze behind him. He was still wearing his raven-black hair cropped close to his head. Just looking at his sharp cheekbones in the frigid air made me shiver.

"Vik!" Sam said as she gave the old vampire a hug.

"Samantha, it is good to see you." He turned and held out his hand to me, we traded grips. "Sorry about your mother."

"Thanks," I said.

"I trailed Zachariah," Vik said. "It was a near thing, but he vanished again."

Vassili nodded and jumped down from the roof. "They are slippery. We need one alive."

"Yes," Zola said. "We have to find out where they're keeping Andi. Ah doubt they'd hurt her if they don't have the Blessing, but Ah cannot be sure."

I pulled out the pepperbox, broke it open, checked for six rounds, and snapped it closed. "At least we only need one of them alive."

"I can get on board with that," Sam said.

"Be careful," Mike said. "We fought three of them at Stone's River. We failed to kill them, and capturing them may be more difficult."

"We will rest," Vassili said. "The demon is correct, use caution. Come." He made a quick gesture to Vik. Cara and Cassie followed suit, migrating to either of Vik's shoulders.

"Ah thought there was another vampire with you, no?" Zola asked.

"*Da*, Mary. I sent her to Columbia. We have many friends there. I want backup if it is needed."

"You always were a bastard at chess," Mike said.

The old white-haired vampire nodded as the group slipped into the mansion.

"Alright," Zola said. "Damian, Mike, walk the river. Sam, you're with me. We'll make a quick round before we split up."

Mike and I started south, down the brick walkway as the snow started to fall a little heavier. Trees in the distance turned to a pale mass as the snowflakes obscured our view. I glanced back to see Sam and Zola disappear behind the mansion. The brick path ended and we crossed a stretch of grass and then the gravel road.

"Last time I was here, this is where the river was," Mike said as he paused beside two stone columns. Each was only a few feet high and topped with a stone sphere, gray and weather-worn.

I glanced back at the house. "That's insane. Why would someone build so close to the river?"

"Only a riverboat captain would be so bold," Mike said as he led the way down a short incline into a stand of trees. "I hear he researched the highest flood markers and then built the mansion just a little higher."

"Gutsy." I followed behind the demon, his bare arms exposed to the cold, as I tried to watch my footing and keep an eye on our surroundings at the same time. At one time it may have been the river, but now we were in a thick stand of trees and the river was a whisper over another rise.

"Why isn't the river still in the same place?" I asked.

"Man, and his inability to leave nature alone," Mike said. "I don't know, I think it was the Army Corps or some such thing. I don't remember why."

We passed through the trees and skirted the incline beside the river. The quiet rush of the water in the winter air was calming. I took a deep breath and watched the river wash along the banks and swallow the falling snow. The fields across the water were flat and even, and I guessed it was a farm. As I looked into the distance, I shivered, and it wasn't from the cold.

"The First Battle of Boonville was over there," Mike said as he pointed across the river. Right at the area I was staring at.

"Bad?" I asked.

"In my experience, war is never good," he said. "In this case though, not too bad. I believe less than a hundred men died."

I focused my Sight and looked again. A familiar gray and black mask settled over the world, bringing the dead to bear. Only a few men were left standing here. Soul fragments in Union uniforms and clusters of Confederate dead in the distance. None of them were looking at us, but they were all looking at something. Off to the west.

"Can you see them?" I asked.

"Yes," Mike said. "I don't have the benefit of hiding them from my vision. I always see them, always see the ley lines."

"They're looking at something."

Mike cursed and pulled me to my knees, his voice falling to a whisper. "We move slow, back into the trees. They focus on necromancers. If they're not looking at you, they're probably looking at Philip's men."

"Or Philip himself."

"Let us hope that is not the case."

I nodded in agreement as I pushed a branch to the side.

"It will be easier to catch a servant than their master. Come, faster." Mike pushed ahead and began a quick trot in a low crouch. I followed him, surprised how easily we slipped through the close-knit branches. Mike found paths in seconds that would have taken me a minute of searching to break through the dense weave of branches in the dormant under-brush.

"Mike, stop," I hissed.

He froze and looked back at me. "What?"

"Across the river. Black cloak on the higher bank."

His eyes trailed across the river. "I see it. Whoever it is, they aren't looking this way."

I could barely see the black cloak ripple in the breeze, but Mike could see which way it was facing? "Okay, eagle eye."

He flashed a small smile and moved forward. I followed.

"If he's a lookout, we might get lucky," Mike said. "They'll have to fly, or cross the bridge. I'm gambling on the bridge."

Moving out without the others may not have been the brightest idea, but if it gave us a chance to catch one of Philip's men unaware, I was all for it. Sam and Zola would be on watch if anything went bad.

Mike accelerated his pace, and I followed suit. We came to the edge of the trees, closing in on the industrial silos and heavy equipment. The bridge was on the other side, but we didn't need to go that far. Volund was talking to another necromancer beside one of the huge cylinders. His cloak was pulled tight with a series of ropes crisscrossing his chest and waist. Steam rose from his head and his face was scrunched, like someone had smacked him with a two-by-four.

The other necromancer nodded and Volund said something I couldn't make out at such a distance. He pulled his hood up and walked away, leaving the unknown man alone. The straggler leaned against the silo and a shaky hand pulled out a pack of cigarettes. Sam used to smoke those, and I'm glad she'd quit young, not like it really mattered anymore, though.

"I was never one for guard duty," Mike said, "but I must admit this has been entertaining."

"You want me to paralyze him?" I said as my hand shifted up my staff. "Or just take a cheap shot?"

"Oh no," Mike said. "Leave him to me."

The demon reached vampiric speeds as he leapt out of the woods. By the time the necromancer realized something was coming, he didn't have a chance. His cigarette and lighter were falling to the ground as he fumbled for something in his cloak. Mike swung an elbow and the man's head snapped back, his body falling into a heap. Mike hoisted the limp form over his shoulder and jogged back to the tree line as though he was carrying a light sack of potatoes.

"Let's move," I said. "Zola's going to want to have a chat with him. For that matter, *I'd* like to have a chat with him." I matched Mike's pace and we jogged toward Rivercene.

"I have noticed something," Mike said.

"What's that?" The cold started to burn my lungs as our pace increased to a run.

"It seems your chats end with dead people."

"Only people I don't like," I said between breaths.

Mike laughed. "That doesn't bode well for this man."

CHAPTER TWELVE

Zola and Sam squatted on either side of the unconscious man. His hair was short and sandy, the left side of his face already blossoming into a red, swollen bruise. Zola turned his head to the left, and then back to the right.

"He's alive, but you broke some bones."

Mike shrugged. "Gives you something to work with."

Zola let out a dark chuckle and wiped a snowflake from her eyebrow. Her gray cloak was beginning to darken where the snow was melting.

"He knows where Mom is?" Sam asked.

"Maybe, maybe not," I said. "We won't know until he's awake."

"I want to kill him." My sister leaned down and her fangs flicked out. Her voice fell to a dark place. "I will kill him."

"Not yet," Mike said, as if there was no question Sam would eventually kill him.

The man's eyelids flickered.

"Do it," Zola said.

I nodded and set the edge of my staff in the faint circle we'd carved around him, my fingers wrapped around the smooth gray Magrassnetto inlays. "*Orbis Tego.*"

The man's eyes snapped open as his body was completely cut off from the ley lines, his necromancy confined to a simple circle shield. His dark eyes flicked from me, and then to Sam before they finally settled on Zola. The sheer terror that took root in those eyes told me he knew who she was.

"Killing me now?" he asked, blood weeping through his closed teeth as he struggled not to move his broken jaw.

"You should be so lucky," Zola said as she placed her hand on Mike's shoulder. "This is a demon of the ancient circle."

The man almost whimpered.

"But he would not dare cross the vampire beside you. Understand this, you kidnapped her mother."

"Oh god," the man whispered as he began to hyperventilate. Blood ran from the corners of his mouth.

"Tell us what we want to know," Mike said. "Where is the woman you took?"

"I didn't!" the man said. He winced, and almost reached up to touch his swelling jaw. "I didn't take her!" He was getting harder to understand.

"You didn't stop them," Sam whispered. "They came into our home. They tried to kill me. Tried to kill our parents." Her eyes glazed over into black pits. "Drop the shield, brother mine."

The man's eyes locked on me and his whisper was almost a cry. "Vesik? Oh, god help me. God help me!" I couldn't tell if his muffled scream was from the pain, or his increased understanding of his situation.

I let the shield fall. Sam ripped the pinky off his left hand and lanced the severed digit with her fangs.

It took a second for the man to realize what had happened, for his body to tell him pieces were missing, and then he screamed. Blood flowed from his shattered jaw, and the scream rose in pitch. Some part of me, some small part, felt a pang of sympathy for the bastard. The rest of me knew he wouldn't suffer long.

Sam spat the finger onto the ground, a thin line of blood leaking down her chin. "You're tasty."

"Where's our mother?" I asked.

"I can't tell you! I don't know!"

"That's two different answers," I said as I held his gaze. His beady eyes reminded me of Philip, reminded me of the man who took our mother. "Sam."

Two more fingers came off. The slurping sounds were enough to churn my stomach, and the thin arterial spray didn't help.

Mike leaned down to the bloody stumps. "Can't have you bleed to death." He cupped his hand and a bloody orange flame burst into existence, consuming the necromancer's hand down to the wrist. "There now, all better."

The screams of agony cut off into hiccups of shock.

"Where?" Zola said as she laid her cane against the man's eye. "Ah'm not nearly so kind as my students." The promise in her voice sent shivers down my spine.

"Chesterfield, Chesterfield Mall."

"Is Ezekiel here?" Zola asked.

"We do not speak his name!" he said as his eyes rolled wildly from one side to the other.

"When is Philip coming?"

"I don't know." I could barely understand him now. Between the blood and his broken jaw, it was like he had a mouthful of marbles. "I don't know."

"It will be soon," Zola said as she lifted her cane. "He'll know we have you. We're done here."

Sam grabbed his head and bit into his throat in the blink of an eye. He flailed uselessly for a few seconds and then Sam ripped his throat out in one vicious strike. She bent his neck back further and drank again from the gaping maw.

I watched his aura fade into a flowing, black-and-white ribbon. It no longer pulsed and shifted like a living aura. It traveled around his body in the slow rhythm of the dead. A white mist formed from the snow behind the corpse, and a moment later Carter stood beside the dead man. Carter reached out and grabbed the aura. The entire ribbon exploded in golden light and the necromancer's ghost was suddenly standing in the werewolf's grip.

"No! What is this?" The ghost was screaming, utterly hysterical. "No! You already killed me!"

Carter's lips peeled back. "You hurt our family. Those under the protection of our pack. I'm here to escort you to hell. Mike," he said with a nod to the demon.

The demon's hand stuttered and seized in a complex series of movements before a sickly orange flame leapt from his palm and swelled into a pillar of fire. When the flames died, the ghosts were gone. Mike's arm lowered slowly as he heaved a series of deep breaths.

My aura felt heavy, dirty, like some great filth had crawled across it and nothing would ever wash it clean again. An acrid stench hung in the air. "What was that?" I asked.

"Hellfire," Zola said. "A portal for some, a death sentence for others."

I shivered, just a little, before I changed the topic. "Chesterfield Mall," I said. Nothing good had happened there for me in the recent past. I had fond childhood memories of time spent in the arcades and food court when I wasn't training with Zola, but now all those memories were tainted by Vicky.

The murdered child. The rising Guardian. The unstoppable harrower.

I ground my teeth together.

"We need to get to that mall," Sam said as she wiped her mouth on the dead necromancer's cloak.

"We can't leave yet," I said.

"What?" Sam stood up. "Are you crazy? We know where she is!"

"The boy is right," Zola said. "We need you here to protect the Blessing. A battle comes soon. It's finally time Philip met his doom."

"Are you sure?" I asked. "That's … it's not going to be easy."

"It should never be easy to kill someone you once loved." Zola rapped her cane on the dead man's head. "Strap this one up on the tree stump," she said as she pointed to a massive y-shaped stump. "Let Philip and his cult know we're ready."

"I'll do it," Mike said as he pulled a length of rope from between the porch railing supports. He dragged the body by the ankle to the old stump. I watched him for a bit, tying a limb up and securing it with one hand before he moved on to the next.

"Why was there rope on the porch?" I asked, but the thought left me as I watched Mike work. "Looks like you've done that before."

Mike glanced up, but said nothing.

"Cheery thought," Sam said. Her face was pulled into a scowl. She wasn't happy about waiting to get Mom. I wasn't happy about it either, but I didn't want to get everyone killed by leaving. That would punch a hole in the defenses at Rivercene. A big hole.

"Bloody hell," I said.

Zola looked away from Mike and up at me. "What?"

"Do you think Philip planted him? Tried to get some of us to leave and chase after Mom?"

"It would be a strong ploy." Her gnarled fingers wrapped tightly around her cane and squeezed. "It seems possible."

"Seems likely," Mike said as he rejoined us. "That man was fodder and Philip damn well knew it. What now? Wake the others?"

Zola shook her head. "Give them another hour to rest. Then we wake Edgar."

Mike nodded. "Give Vassili and the first watch time to rest while we plan."

"Yes," Zola said.

"Zola, why don't we move our cars over to that cornfield?" I asked as I pointed off to the east. "I think they'll be less likely to get scratched."

"Scratched?' she said with a snort. "If all they got was scratched, Ah would count myself lucky. Let's go."

***

We stood outside as evening approached, well fed by another of the innkeeper's meals and bundled up with gloves, scarves, and coats.

Edgar stared at the man strung up on the ancient tree stump. It was odd to see Edgar in a trench coat in addition to his suit. "I thought I knew all of them, but him I do not recognize. Volund, Zachariah, Jamin, Smith, Cutter, Lensher. Who were you?" he said as he reached toward the body. His hand stopped and he rubbed his fingers together. "Hellfire?"

"Yes," Mike said. "He had an appointment to keep."

Edgar sighed. "You risk too much in the open."

"Come now, Amon," Zola said. "We are hidden quite well here."

He looked at Zola and gave her a half-hearted grimace. "Still."

"I doubt you will be so concerned when they come for your head," Mike said.

"We shall see," Edgar said. "You've made quite a signpost for them. I rather doubt they'll try to scout us anymore. It's more likely their entire group will come at us at once."

"When?" Foster asked from his perch beside Aideen on my shoulder. The snow was beginning to pick up, leaving a thin layer of white across the grass.

"Twilight or nightfall, if they have a blood mage." Edgar turned toward the river and tensed. He relaxed a moment later.

Apparently whatever had spooked him was gone. "The darker arts of the blood are stronger then."

"How did you learn anything of the blood magi?" Zola said. "They are more secretive than us."

"They are more taboo than you," Cara said from Sam's pocket. Cassie nodded her agreement beside her.

"Pots and cauldrons," Edgar said. "We have a blood mage in the Watchers now."

"Things do change," Mike said.

Edgar's sandy face pulled up in a small smile. "Yes, they do at that. Not long ago we would have killed a blood mage on sight."

"There was a time you'd have done the same to a necromancer," Zola said.

Edgar looked away, his eyes angled up toward the trees before he nodded. "That was our mistake, my friends. Judging an entire people for the actions of a few was wrong. Even a demon can be a good man if he is so inclined."

I didn't miss the smile on Mike's face.

Edgar. Watcher. Friend? Maybe the world really was ending.

The front door slammed and Dad walked out onto the porch. He hadn't taken the news well when we told him we knew where Mom was, but weren't yet going to get her. He'd finally calmed down when he smashed a very expensive vase, scattering the pieces across the hardwood. The innkeeper had muttered something about touchy humans and then vanished down the hallway.

"I'm sorry," he said. "You're right, Zola. Andi would never forgive me if I left our friends to die." He adjusted the strap over his shoulder, the whaling gun swinging out past his hip as he turned.

"Do not apologize," Zola said. "Ah know it doesn't compare to your own, but this is not an easy decision for any of us."

"What's the plan?" Dad asked.

Dominic appeared beside Edgar, a thin trail of snowflakes filling the void he left behind him. "Lord!" he shouted.

"*Da?*" Vassili said from the edge of the roof.

Dominic nodded.

The white-haired vampire leapt from the top of the three-story mansion and came down hard enough to crack one of the flagstones. He blinked and shifted his foot to the side. "I shall pay for that. I do not wish to anger the innkeeper further."

Dad's eyes flicked to the side and he scuffed his shoe through the snow. I stifled a laugh.

"They are coming," Dominic said. "A large force moves in from the west. At least fifteen necromancers, each controlling several zombies."

"Fifteen," Edgar said. "That's half of Philip's cult."

Vik jogged up behind us. "Volund and Zachariah come from the east and north. Each has ten necromancers in tow, nearly a horde of zombies between the two. Some are moving fast. I'm afraid they may have vampiric zombies too."

I cursed. "I hate those things."

"Is Ezekiel with them?" Zola asked.

"No, I didn't see anyone else with a complexion like Edgar's."

"That's how you told them to recognize Ezekiel?" Edgar said with a laugh.

Zola shrugged.

The big Watcher with the bowler joined us, floating in from the northwest. "Edgar, this is madness. You cannot hope to oppose Philip's army with this rabble."

"James," Edgar said as he shook his head. "You haven't seen how big a mess this rabble can make."

"James?" I said. "I guess I don't have to call you Bowler."

James spared me a glance and then turned his attention back to Edgar. "Orders?"

"You'll push ahead with me," Edgar said. "We'll handle the western front. Cara, it would please me to fight with you."

"You will fight with us all," Foster said.

Edgar nodded. "Take up positions in the trees. Stay hidden until the necromancers can be put down. Mike, Damian, Zola, take the north and eastern fronts. We will join you as soon as we inflict significant casualties on our front.

"Vassili, divide your people as you see fit."

"Sam, roof," Vassili said as he pointed to the mansion. "Dominic, the roof of the guest house. Vik, stay on Damian." Vik nodded and took a step towards me. "I will help who needs it."

"And me?" Dad asked.

"What can you do against this?" James said. "This is no fight for a commoner."

Dad dropped a bomb lance into the barrel of his cannon, flicked the ramrod out, rammed the lance home, and slid the ramrod back in place in a series of quick motions.

"They took my wife. They violated my home, threatened my children. I'll go through you to get to them."

James's eyes widened and he took a step back.

I caught the hint of a smile on Edgar's face.

"I would recommend the roof," Vassili said. "You will have excellent view of targets."

We heard the moans first as the zombies grew closer. The unnatural groans and grunts of the undead began to filter through the distance.

"Move," Edgar said. "We're out of time."

CHAPTER THIRTEEN

They struck when the dying sun set the skies on fire, turning snow to cinders on a canvas of silhouetted branches.

"Now it begins," Mike said as he pulled the hammer from his belt.

Shadows snarled and leapt as fire and lightning struck all across the roof. The dim flash of fairies growing and shrinking, slashing and blocking, danced across the back-lit structure.

"Vampires?" Sam asked. "Why are they with Philip?"

"It's likely not by choice," Mike said.

"I'm going up," Sam said as she gestured at the roof. "Get to the north side."

"If things go wrong, get to the basement," Mike said.

"What about the 'Don't go in the basement' thing?" I said as I quoted the air with my fingers.

Mike looked at the sky and took a deep breath.

Sam's lips quirked up in a tiny smile. "He's just, well, you know."

"I know," Mike said with a chuckle. "Be careful, all of you."

Sam nodded and blurred into motion.

Zola was out ahead of us, her cloak disappearing around the corner as Mike and I followed. I spared one last glance at Sam as she tore into someone on the roof before I turned and jogged away. Vik had gone on ahead. He should already be on the north side. I turned at the mansion's southeast corner, right behind Mike. Vik and Zola were at the next corner, pointing off into the distance.

" —almost here," Vik said as we approached.

The groaning and shuffling of the undead signaled their arrival on the northern and eastern fronts. My pepperbox practically leapt into my hand. Six shots, five zombies down. I cracked the gun open, dumped the shells, and slammed a speed loader home. My tactical vest was emblazoned with "Cub" and adorned with two dozen conveniently placed speed loaders. Even if I didn't miss a shot, it wouldn't be enough to take down the sea of zombies.

"Why aren't there vampires here?" I asked as we started to fan out.

"They must be engaged with Vassili and the others," Vik said. "Keep the trees between you and the necromancers." I saw his hand move and drop the bronze amulet around his neck into his vest. His hand lashed out and a zombie's head exploded. Vik took two steps back and looked at his fingers. "What in the name of?"

"What's wrong?" Zola shouted as she baited a zombie toward me.

I raised my Sight, opening my senses to both worlds. The seething mass of undead was all tied to one man, maybe two, but something was different. The currents of necromancy weren't dim and gray in my Sight. They burned with a brighter blue light, like a ley line. My eyebrows drew down in thought as I shot down four more zombies with six bullets. There wasn't as much blood as there should have been. Too few chunks exploded from their overripe heads.

"Something's wrong," I said.

"Agreed," Zola said. "They're too slow."

"There's no blood on my hands," Vik said as he tore another zombie in half.

Mike stepped forward and put his fist through one of the zombies. He stared at his own hand. "Vik's right. It's like they're sawdust."

The blazing trail of a bomb lance lit the night above us as it streamed from the mansion's roof toward the heart of the on-coming force.

A fireball lit up the field and the bluish lines of power dissi-pated. Half the eastern front vanished in the blink of an eye. There was nothing. No trace of power, no substance, everything was just, gone.

"What the fuck?!" Mike said as he took a hesitant step back.

"It's a ruse!" Zola said. "They're a goddamn illusion. Find the mages, kill them."

With that she bolted forward, running through zombies like they weren't even there, because they weren't really there. Bod-ies exploded and gore flashed into the air like each had been hit by a cannon shot every time we touched one, but nothing stuck to us, nothing slicked the ground beneath our feet.

I followed the lines toward the back of the horde. The bas-tards had to know we were on to them, but they didn't make a move.

"Mike, red!" Vik shouted from off to my left. I caught the flicker of a dark red cloak as Mike moved.

The Smith's Hammer blazed to life and came down with a thunderous crack. A bloody red cloak flapped at the edge of the fires that raged around the hammer. Another quarter of the zombies disappeared. The lines closest to me all drew in on one man. He stood with his eyes closed, his lips constantly moving, fueling the illusion. Waves of ley line energy pulsed out from his hands.

"Bloody hell, they're fodder," I said as Zola pulled up beside me.

"We still have to kill him. He could hide much within these illusions."

I raised my gun and shot him in the head. He fell. His remaining eye stared blankly at the clouds above. Another huge swath of the horde vanished.

"If this entire front is a ruse, what the hell is coming at us on the other side?" I asked.

Zola muttered a string of curses. "Get back! Regroup at the house!"

Vik made a vicious twisting motion. There was a meaty snap and the last of the zombies vanished. The entire field of wandering undead was gone. Nothing but an icy breeze filled the area as we turned back to the house, the faint sounds of battle echoed around the mansion.

Another bomb lance streaked from the rooftop. I saw it strike in the distance as we came back to the front of the mansion. The blue flash of a shield falling was followed by a scream a moment before dirt and debris shot skyward in a shadowy fireball. Our feet pounded across the grass and flagstones as I watched a handful of zombies fall over near the guest house. Real, not an illusion.

Vassili was suddenly at my side, pacing us. "Vampire zombies, *da*." He shouted a string of what I can only guess were curses. A patch of light near the mansion showed me the blood in Vassili's hair, and the deep gash below his right eye. "Hurry my friends. We are strong, but they are many." With that, he blurred into motion, racing toward the nearby silos off to the west.

"Vampiric zombies?" I said to Zola.

"Christ, puppets again?" Vik said.

Zola shook her head, her wrinkled body keeping pace with us just fine. "No, not puppets. There are true necromancers here. Not a demon …" Her voice trailed off and Mike cursed.

"That's the ruse," the demon said. "That's the goddamned ruse, they're going after the mass grave. It's on the other side of town."

"Let's get back to the cars," I said as I started to slow. Zola grabbed my arm and pulled me into a run.

"No, boy, we have to clear the grounds."

"Some of us should go ahead," Vik said.

"No! Use your addlepated brain, vampire! That's what he wants. To separate us."

"Pick us off in small groups," Mike said.

"Bloody hell," I said as I drew in deeper breaths of icy air. "He planned this too well."

A huge spread of black and gray wings came running at us. Shadowed stretches of blood were smeared across them, and splashes fell in runnels from Foster's shoulders to his feet.

"Zola, this is too complex for Philip," Foster said. "He's never sacrificed this many men before."

"Pilot Knob," she said.

Recollections of that damned town floated back to the surface of my memory as I ran. The entire population had been murdered and set to rise, a trap for anyone seeking Philip's implements. He'd hidden a document describing a key of the dead, and a Magrasnetto sheet Cara had used to create two dark bottles, inside an ancient book. Philip had brought the demon Prosperine onto our plane using soul in a trapped in those very dark bottles. The demon killed Carter and Maggie. I killed the demon.

Carter. I thought the name. "Carter!" I said out loud.

The wolf was there in moments. I couldn't help the relief that flooded me.

"Think of something useful for us to do?" he asked with only a mild hint of impatience.

"The graveyard on the other side of town," I said.

"We think Philip is going to raise another demon," Mike said.

Any trace of irritation fell away from Carter's voice. "What can we do?"

"We'll be there as fast as we can, but scout it out, see what's happening," I said.

He nodded.

"Be careful, Wolf," Zola said. "These men are not to be trifled with."

Carter nodded and vanished.

"Unnerving," Vik said. "I know you are speaking to Carter, but I cannot see him."

"Don't worry. He's gone now," I said with a bright smile.

Vik nodded and then slowed as we reached the trees beside the construction yard. Foster ran on ahead, jumping back into the fray beside Aideen and Cassie. I couldn't see Cara or Sam, but there was enough chaos strewn across the gravel yard to hide anyone.

The Watchers came in from the west.

"Edgar?" Zola said. "How did all these zombies get behind him?"

From the look of rage etched across Edgar's face, the slash and blood on his suit, I was guessing it wasn't quietly.

"*Solis Incendo!*" Edgar growled. His voice boomed above the shouts of the fairies and necromancers. A needle of fiery yellow orange light bore down from the heavens, lancing through the skull of a bald necromancer. I realized a moment later it was Volund, shock and terror scrawled across his face. Every sound in the vicinity drowned as the crescendo of a rushing train roared and the needle of light exploded into a column of golden flame as thick as the silo beside him.

Volund died in terror and fire.

"Edgar's pissed," Zola said.

"Let's move!" Mike said as he dashed forward. Vik circled around behind the silo with Zola, and I followed Mike.

"Help them," Mike said as he pointed to a fast moving ball of chaos. He broke off to the south and laughed as a mage sent a torrent of flames toward him. Mike inhaled the maelstrom and the Smith's Hammer flared brighter.

I finally caught a glimpse of Sam in the snow-obscured scene. She was back-to-back with Cara as they fought off four of the vampiric zombies in a constant, dizzying motion. They were losing ground. Cara winced as one of the zombies reached past her flickering blade and tore into her left wing. It cost the zombie an arm, but the bastard didn't care. Sam lunged and punched through his head, but it left her back open. One of the others got an arm around her neck and started to bend her backwards. The vampiric zombie was damaged, and its aura was exposed. I'd seen enough.

I raised my arm and my necromancy flared out. It enveloped the zombie on Sam's back and I flinched as the flash of knowing began.

Ancient, he'd died in the black plague, or at least he should have. So many years past, lost, alone, a rogue vampire for almost three hundred years. So many dead lay in his wake, and he reveled in the destruction. He laughed as he stood on the rubble of a fallen castle. Years passed before a man found him. A man with a sandy complexion, round features, and dark, kind eyes. A demon in everything but body. He tore the vampire's soul away and replaced it with a demon's aura, birthing a vampiric zombie. Conscious of his surroundings, but unable to act, he just wanted to die.

I shuddered as the flash faded and my mind became my own again.

Ezekiel.

I'd been looking into the eyes of Ezekiel. I inhaled and tore the zombie's head off with a flick of my wrist and a blade of necromancy.

Sam spun to face her attacker as his grip loosened. Surprise showed for only an instant before she shoved the body away and dove at the zombie attacking Cara. She knocked its legs out and Cara removed its head before it hit the ground. The last backed away slowly. I can only guess its master was hesitating at sacrificing the last creature.

"Back!" Dad shouted from the edge of the trees. Sam and Cara both ran as another bomb lance screamed past them and lodged in the zombie's chest. The zombie stumbled from the impact and then kept backing up until it exploded. A hole opened in the side of one of the silos and the entire structure groaned.

Vik and Vassili charged into the clearing in pursuit of another vampire. Their prey was looking over his shoulder and didn't see the small Cajun woman step out from behind a silo.

Zola held her left hand up, fingers to the sky, and pinched all her fingertips together. The vampire stopped so suddenly I thought his eyeballs would pop out. Vassili's arm flashed out and stopped Vik from getting any closer. The vampire struggled against the force of Zola's necromancy, but he didn't have a chance in hell. She splayed her fingers in the space of a heartbeat and the vamp's body tore itself apart in an explosion of gore.

"Oh, nasty!" Foster shouted. I glanced over fast enough to see him pulling an internal organ of some sort off his already blood-soaked shoulder. It wiggled a little as it splatted at his feet.

"Was that the last one?" Cassie asked as she leapt down from one of the silos. She carried a head in her hand, her fingers wound within its hair. Her armor was almost as bloody as Foster's. Smears and scrapes adorned the surface and a nasty dent folded the light around her left temple. She dropped the head onto the gravel with a wet thud.

Aideen checked Cara's wing. Both of them bore flecks of blood across their armor and swords dripped red from their blades. A small flash of light gleamed as Aideen healed the tear and Cara nodded to her in thanks.

"We must move," Vassili said. "There are more on the bridge." He pointed into the distance. I could just make out a row of humanoid shapes across the concrete span.

"Shit, that's a car," I said as I watched a pair of headlights run down the road from the north.

"You allow more witnesses, Edgar?" James asked from somewhere off to my right.

"Shut up and move," Edgar said.

And we did.

CHAPTER FOURTEEN

Icy air tore at my lungs as we ran, our pace scattering the thin layer of fallen snow before us. The headlights were almost to the bridge. The car slowed as the driver must have realized there were people in front of him. A horn sounded, but none of the figures on the bridge moved. The driver laid on the horn, the sound a non-stop blare as the car moved ever closer.

"Idiot commoner," James said, and the Watcher didn't even sound out of breath as he ran.

I was about to tell James exactly where he could shove his commentary when a blinding white bolt of power shot through the car. The horn cut off immediately, smoke rising from the hood and windows. The little yellow compact rose into the air, teetering slowly back and forth as it floated toward the river.

"No!" Edgar said, but we were too far away to do anything.

My pace faltered, and I slowed as the scene unfolded before us.

A fireball rose to meet the car, engulfing its entirety in hellish flame. I swear I heard a short scream before the metal squealed and the car exploded in a hail of burning fragments. I could hear the hissing as the flames reached the river, could hear the splashes as larger pieces fell into the water.

"We need to look for survivors," Mike said. He took a step toward the river before Zola put a hand on his shoulder.

She shook her head. "There are no survivors. Ah can see the dead from here. A child and his father."

Mike's head fell and he slid the hammer back into his belt.

What happened next is something I will not soon forget. A cry tore through the heavens, piercing like an eagle, but a hundred, a thousand times louder. Wings whispered above us before the Thunderbird landed on the bridge with a crash. Concrete and steel groaned beneath its bulk. The Thunderbird leaned back, spread its wings toward the heavens, and lightning stormed from its eyes. One second, a crash of thunder and light, the next, silence.

The Thunderbird vanished as we continued to jog toward the bridge. There was no sign of the creature as we set foot onto the expanse. The river below us and our heavy breathing were the only sounds I could make out.

"Why did it do that?" James asked.

Edgar wandered forward, inspecting the incinerated corpses of the necromancers on the bridge as he went. Their bodies were strewn among scorched and exploded concrete. Vassili and Vik followed close behind Edgar. The rest of us trailed behind them.

"Balance, James," Edgar said. "Always balance. There are far more men here wishing to do the world harm than there are those of us trying to stop them."

"That doesn't mean they're stronger than us!" James said, his voice rising in pitch and volume. "What if it tried to balance the power instead? You're insane! That thing could have killed us just as readily as it killed those necromancers." His voice trailed off to a whisper as he apparently realized he was shouting.

"He does have a point, *da?*" Vassili said as he glanced over the edge of the bridge.

Edgar's mouth was in a flat line as he glanced back at the vampire, and then James.

"I meant no disrespect," James said as he squeezed his shoulder, sending a small avalanche of snow down his sleeve. "We've just lost so many Watchers."

"I know," Edgar said as he turned away. "Don't forget we need allies."

James frowned slightly, and then seemed to shake something off as he followed Edgar.

"Did you see that?" Vik asked as he pointed toward the darkened lot of the casino in the distance.

Vassili nodded. "There is movement. Four, maybe five running. Hard to tell."

"You can see that far?" Mike asked, sounding impressed. "I can't make anything out in this light."

Vassili nodded.

"Running for the cemetery," Zola said. "We need to move."

"We need to be careful," Mike said. "They've already had plenty of time to do whatever the distraction was meant to buy them time for. Having us rush headlong into it may be exactly what they plan."

Regardless, Mike stepped up his pace in time with Zola. We were moving at a slow jog as we reached the other side of the bridge. The old town was utterly unnerving in the silent, unlit night. The snow picked up, further obscuring our view as the wind whispered along the bricks.

Edgar held up his right hand, fist closed. He was silent until we crept up beside him.

"Next intersection, two men ran to the west, around to the right. Stick to the building."

I glanced to the right and saw six columns, blacker than the sky behind them. The war memorial wasn't very old, but it drew many ghosts. Gray forms huddled around the center column, which was crowned with a black eagle. One of the ghosts held its hand up and glided toward me, insubstantial legs seeming to hover across the ground as I opened my Sight.

"You can see me, yes?" the ghost asked.

I nodded. "You've seen necromancers before?"

He was a young man with square features. I think the uniform placed him in World War I. He cocked his head to the side and frowned. "Necro-what?"

"People like me, who can talk to the dead?"

He nodded. "The civvies, they're in an uproar, said someone's killing them at the cemetery." He shook his head. "That can't be right though. We're already dead. We can't die again, can we?"

I hesitated, and I saw his eyes widen.

"We're here to stop them."

He paused and then nodded slowly. "I … believe you." He nodded again, apparently convincing himself. "A man and his wife, strange folks, said they were wolves and we should trust the old woman and her whippersnapper."

A small chuckle from Zola briefly interrupted the ghost.

"There are two behind this block," the ghost said, indicating the building beside us. "There are two more on the roof.

"I've been told there are seven left in the cemetery. You killed the rest on the bridge. What was that light?"

"A Thunderbird," I said, too stressed to think of a cover story.

He crossed himself like a Catholic. "Like the old Indian legends?"

"Yes, exactly like that. Stay the hell away from it if you see it."

He nodded rapidly and began to drift back to the memorial, probably to warn the rest of the gathered spirits. "If those men can truly kill us again, please stop them."

"We will," I said.

"Two on the roof, two behind the building, seven in the cemetery," I said to Edgar.

He blinked, barely masking the surprise on his face. "You spoke to someone?"

I bared my teeth in a savage grin, "Or I lost my mind and started talking to myself. Take your pick."

"Leave the roof to us," Vik said.

Vassili nodded and leapt onto the brick wall. Sam and Vik scrambled up the brick wall behind him.

"Dimitry, come with us please," Edgar said as he motioned to James. Dad didn't argue, just followed them towards the back of the building.

The fairies split up, Cara going with the vampires, Cassie with the Watchers. Foster and Aideen stayed with us.

"Graveyard," Zola said. Mike and I picked up the pace and jogged along behind her.

Foster swooped down onto my shoulder, followed by Aideen. They both tucked themselves under the flap of my collar. It was a thin shield against the snow and cold, but better than nothing.

"Alright," Foster said, "So Carter was here. Where is he now?"

"I think we can guess," Aideen said. "Let's just hope he's okay."

We almost made it to South Street, running in relative silence, a thin layer of snow deadening our footfalls. Zola threw her hands out as we came to Sycamore Street. We were exposed, with an open lot to our left and a gas station looming just to our right. A torrent of flame erupted from the hill beside the pumps and widened into a wall of fire as it bore down on us, orange and red bursts bright enough to blind our night-adjusted vision.

"*Impadda!*" Zola and I cried at once. Both of our shields snapped into being, but it wouldn't be enough against the heat bearing down on us.

Foster cursed and then Mike leapt out in front of us, arms thrown wide. He opened his mouth, flexing his chest and drawing air in like some terrible, rasping machine. The wall of fire collapsed in on itself before it ever reached us, rotating and vanishing into Mike's open jaws with a snap and a fizzle. He belched and I half expected smoke to rise from his mouth.

"What the hell was that?" I said. I'd seen Zola throw some mean fire spells around, but she'd never unleashed anything close to the wall of flame we'd just witnessed. The frozen grass on the hill was on fire, defrosted and lit up in the span of a few seconds.

"Blood mage," she said. "He's going to be hurting after that."

"He's going to be dead," Foster said as he and Aideen shot ahead into the night.

Another series of blasts came. They missed the fairies by a mile.

"Run!" Mike yelled as he pulled me and Zola into a flat sprint despite our protests.

I realized why a moment later. The mage hadn't missed a goddamn thing. The streamers of fire tore away the gas pumps and asphalt and ignited the storage tanks beneath the earth. We were thrown to our knees a moment later as sharp, fiery bits pierced my skin and slapped against my leather jacket while the blinding fireball expanded and blackened and shook the ground like an earthquake.

"Foster!" I screamed as I scrambled to get up. "Aideen!"

"Damian, no!"

I heard Zola, but I didn't listen. My staff was in one hand and the pepperbox in the other as I circled around the exploded station. Fires were already spreading through the surrounding homes. People were in the streets now, more exposed, more at risk. Panicked and disorganized as their night worsened.

I glimpsed movement beyond the flames. A glint of orange as a sword reflected the inferno beside it. Aideen. Her left wing was burned. Bits and embers were still falling from it as she lunged and dodged the blood mage's attacks. Both the man's arms were christened in blood, his athame held ready to cut himself once more.

Foster was leaning against a tree, crumpled. His left arm was folded beneath him. I saw him move, just a little, and my pace picked up. I barely noticed the flames licking at my jeans. The pepperbox rose. I slowed my stride, inhaled, and squeezed the trigger as I exhaled. The explosion was only a pop next to the raging inferno. The blood mage's head jerked to the side as blood and bone left the opposite side of his skull. He fell, and I started to run to Aideen.

"Get me to Foster," she said. "Something hit him. Don't know how bad."

I got my shoulder under her arm and we shuffled toward Foster. I thought I saw the blood mage twitch, so I aimed the pepperbox and pulled the second trigger. The five remaining rounds riddled his upper body in one vicious boom.

People started screaming. I heard calls go out for an ambulance, calls for the police. Most people just ran.

I helped Aideen settle in beside Foster. Blood was pouring down his left arm as I turned him over.

"Hurts," he said through gritted teeth. "Won't stop."

I guessed he meant the blood. I hadn't bothered to drop my Sight, and when I looked at the gash running from his shoulder to his bicep I could see something in it. Short, its stubby body pulsed and writhed, flaring in a sickly black and red aura. It reminded me of the godforsaken thing we'd cut out of Carter not so long ago.

"What the fuck is that?" I asked.

"Move," Mike said. He reached out and grabbed the thing. It resisted as he tried to rip it out of Foster, but it tore away with chunks of flesh and blood. "Bloody leeches. Mage must have been insane to call one of these."

Foster grunted and fell backwards.

"Foster, Foster!" Aideen screamed as she jumped toward him. Her incantation lit up the night as soon as she landed beside him. "*Socius Sanation!*" The light was blinding and I looked away, toward Mike.

He frowned, disgust twisting his face as he pulled the hammer out and dropped the fat worm on the ground. Mike brought the hammer down immediately, smashing the gaping black hole at the front of the creature. It stiffened and then went still before dissipating in ribbons of black and red.

"What was that?" I asked as I turned away from the demon and started for the fairies.

"Later," Mike said as he raised his hand. Some of the flames that had found their way into the homes dimmed and seemed to rush toward the fire demon. Mike gasped and his shoulders slumped. "I can't put it all out. It's not natural."

"Do what you can," Zola said as she knelt beside the fairies, checking them both over.

"We're no good right now," Aideen muttered. "Too much energy."

Zola nodded. "Get in the trees, away from the fire. Get back to the mansion if you can."

"Kill him," Foster whispered.

"We will," Zola said as she stood up and started jogging toward the cemetery again. Mike and I followed in silence.

It wasn't long before we turned onto South Street, heading straight for the cemetery gates.

CHAPTER FIFTEEN

"We're just walking through the front door?" I asked as the arched, wrought iron gateway loomed into view.

"Yes, Ah intend to finish this," Zola said.

A flicker of gray caught my eye, and when I focused on it, Maggie materialized in a glow of golden light.

"She's a stubborn old bitch, isn't she?" Maggie said.

Mike muffled a laugh and Zola glanced back at him. Her eyes narrowed and he cut off immediately with a whisper-quiet cough.

"Maggie," Zola said. "Ah'm glad you're okay. Don't make me do bad things to you."

Maggie smiled as she said, "You were right. They tried to attack us but they couldn't touch me or Carter."

"What?" I hissed. "What are you talking about? I told you both to stay the hell away from them."

Maggie went on like I hadn't said a word. "We couldn't touch them either. I don't know what you ever saw in that cockless bastard Zola. I could kill him just to shut him up."

"The thought crossed my mind on occasion," Zola said.

"Why can't they touch each other?" I asked.

"Glad Foster's not here to respond to that," Mike said.

My lips started quirk of their own accord and Zola shook her head.

"Boy, it's because you bound your soul to them," Zola said. "Now it's spreading like the pox. Most of the Ghost Pack glows like a goddamned balefire in the dead of night."

I started to ask a question.

"Not now," she snapped. "Now we kill Philip. Later we worry about what in God's name you did to those ghosts." She stalked off through the gates.

My jaw snapped closed and I started after her.

"Wise choice," Mike said.

I sighed and quickened my steps to catch Maggie. "How many?"

"Three necromancers, maybe a dozen zombies," she said. "Also some of those vampiric half-breeds too. I don't like those."

"You and me both. You want to send up a signal flare, Mike?"

He pulled the Smith's Hammer from his belt and raised it to the sky. It grew, increasing in mass and presence as flames burst from the head and Mike supported it across his torso with two hands.

"Philip, dear," Zola said, projecting her voice. "Ah'm afraid we need to talk."

That laugh. That dark, stuttering, maniacal laugh. Philip.

"Dear, we do." Philip stepped out from behind a tree, the glassy surface of a shield flowing around him. His voice was rougher than the last time I'd heard it. The circles under his eyes were dark enough I could make them out in the shadows. His face was gaunt, drawn, filled out more by his beard than the plump roundness I'd seen at Stone's River. It must have been a hard year for the old bastard. Good.

He stared at me. "Still sleeping well, Vesik? Still wondering if you've crossed that line? I can tell you already have. Look at those—"

"Volund is dead," Zola said.

Philip shrugged. "He was weak."

"He was one of your best," Zola said. "Who is left? Jamin? Ezekiel?" she growled the last name. Philip flinched.

I could see the zombies moving towards us now, off to our right, shuffling past the caretaker's shack in the falling snow. Something shimmered in my peripheral vision, standing beside Philip, but it was nothing my Sight could reveal.

For someone who seemed to have a knack for villainous plots, I thought Philip would have had a defense prepared for the Watchers. Apparently not.

Edgar landed silently in the distance, amidst the dozen or so zombies. Three of the zombies tore away from the group and closed on him with ungodly speed. Edgar simply punched the first one in the throat. I could hear the crack of bone over the groans of the undead. As the first vampiric zombie hit the ground, Edgar raised his hand and the next went up in a burst of yellow-orange flames.

James started hacking through the other side of the zombies, making his way toward a necromancer who was only now starting to back away.

Philip glanced behind him and cursed as Mike ran to help the Watchers. He raised his hand and two vampiric zombies appeared from the shimmering shields beside him. They streaked across graves, shattering headstones as their legs moved through them almost unimpeded. Almost too fast to follow, but not as fast as a soulsword.

The focus was in my right hand and my left settled an instant later on the blade rune carved into the staff. A shimmering blade wrapped in blue and gold and silver filaments shot from the empty hilt. The blade sliced clean through the chest of the first vampiric zombie, severing Philip's power and the creature's mobility in one bloody swipe. I didn't have time to reset, so I raised the blade in an awkward backhanded motion.

The second zombie was just as fast. I didn't get the sword around in time. The zombie knocked the staff away with one quick strike. The blade vanished and I barely dodged the creature's follow through. I couldn't outrun it. I couldn't grab it with my necromancy because its aura was buried inside its body. I saw a blur pounce from the groundskeeper's shack. I realized it was Sam as she struck the zombie with a single brutal kick.

"Sam, move!" I said as the zombie started to fall forward. She jumped to the side as I angled a horizontal slash at the zombie and channeled an aural blade up through the focus. I lurched as the focus grabbed more than I could give, but the momentum took care of the rest. The golden glow of a soulart erupted from the hilt, severing the zombie's upper torso and head. Philip recoiled as he lost control of his creation.

"You still can't stop me," he snarled. His hand vanished into the shadows of his black cloak and the gnarled hand of the dead king came out with it. I saw Carter then, poised to strike at Philip, Maggie beside him. How in the hell did Philip not see them? Or did he really think they couldn't touch him? Bingo.

"Nice trick, but I have a new one too," I said.

He hesitated. It was all I needed.

I forced a torrent of necromancy through the focus, intertwining it with the soulart as it shot out across the field. Philip only had time for his eyes to widen as Carter and Maggie materialized beside him in a golden flash. Philip's wrist snapped as Maggie lashed out and knocked the king's hand to the ground. Carter broke the man's leg with one swift kick.

Foster flew at the falling necromancer like a bullet, exploding into his full size a foot from Philip. His fist connected with such ferocity Philip's neck had to be broken.

"Foster!" I said as I ran toward him and Philip. "You're supposed to be grievously wounded."

He pulled himself up to one knee, the strain obvious on his face. "I feel better."

Zola walked up to the downed man beside me. He was still breathing.

"We need to question him," I said.

"Ah just want to kill him." Her voice was flat. I'd never heard her so emotionless talking about Philip. It was almost always rage or regret, not the cold edge of acceptance.

She flipped a blade out of the end of her cane and carved a circle around the fallen man. *"Orbis Tego."* The shield snapped into existence as Mike and the Watchers made their way over to us. The zombies and necromancer were well and truly dead. And then we waited for Philip Pinkerton to wake up.

***

Edgar was standing between me and James. The younger Watcher stared at me. The look made my skin crawl. Edgar repositioned himself so James couldn't see me and said something low and intense to the man. I did my best to ignore the exchange.

"I thought you said there were two necromancers aside from Philip," I said as the radiant glow began to fade from Maggie and Carter as the soulart dissipated.

Maggie nodded. "The other is gone."

"It was Zachariah," Carter said.

"He's never far from Philip," Zola said as she squatted beside the glassy dome of power. "Where are Vik and Vassili? Dimitry and the fairies?"

"I sent them back to Rivercene," Edgar said. "There are too many strangers in this town to know who's a threat."

Zola nodded. "Wise of you."

Philip moved. He flinched as he tried to move his leg, and then looked up to find Zola.

"Fuck me."

"That ship has sailed," Zola said. "The only thing fucking you now is a barrel full of lead."

Philip actually smiled, and laughed. The laugh was wrong somehow, broken. "What do you want?"

"There are rumors," she said. "You travel with Ezekiel. Some say you control him."

"Control him?" Philip asked as his stare trailed into the distance. "No one can control him."

"Then why are you with him?" Zola asked.

"I'm not. I needed the Blessing to survive him. Did you not look over the hill yet? It should be most enlightening."

"You let him near the grave?" Edgar said.

"*Let* him?" Philip snapped. "Do you not remember his power? He is a god in all but name." Philip lowered his eyes. "He is a god in name as well, to some."

Edgar took a deep breath, and it almost sounded like a growl as he exhaled.

My heart bobbed up into my throat. "What's over the hill?"

Zola gave a quick shake of her head and started up the short rise to the crest of the hill. I followed her, and was greeted by a vision I'd seen once before. A churning mass of restless souls, trapped within the scarred earth. Nothing I've ever seen comes closer to describing Hell. The specters were younger here than those I'd seen in Stone's River, more humanlike as they clawed and threw themselves at the sides of the mass grave. They flailed silently, as others stepped on and through them, only to be dragged under in a constant, churning flow. The mass grave was below us. Dug up. Violated. Desecrated.

"Ezekiel is here." Zola said, her stare never leaving the pit below us.

My gaze traveled from Philip back to the gaping maw in the ground. "Too fucking late," I said.

"Who did he raise?" Mike asked as he strode down the hill to kneel beside the wound in the earth. "I can smell the brimstone, and there is fresh blood beneath the spirits." He leaned closer and held out a hand, pulling a thin wisp of gray toward him. It may have been a jacket, or just a bit of smoke, but Mike's hand closed into a fist, and the remnant fled. "Some of these spirits were destroyed tonight."

"I never meant for him to open that grave," Philip said, something verging on regret in his voice.

"Of course not, you only meant to raise the Destroyer and drown the earth in the dead," Zola muttered.

Philip stayed silent for a moment, watching his old lover. "When the world is dead, they'll never be able to hurt you again."

Zola slowly closed her eyes and sighed. "Ah never wanted that."

James finally lost it. "He should be put to death immediately!"

I tended to agree. We'd had enough trouble with Philip.

"I know we need allies, Edgar. Ezekiel has killed dozens of Watchers, and we don't have the men to replace them. But a soulsword?" James said, his voice rising into a hysterical shout. "He is the enemy! He is a dark necromancer without question, Edgar! What possible reason could you have to let him live?"

Oh, crap, he meant me.

James's attack came fast and hard. I was still gawking in disbelief as I raised a shield. It turned the wavy blade of a kris dagger to the side with an arc of electric blue sparks. I took a step back, my heel catching on the edge of a shattered tombstone. My head caught the edge of its neighbor as I fell backwards, sending my vision into a dangerous gray tunnel of stars and shadows.

Someone yelled. I saw a flash, an explosion, a sun? Too hard to tell. A voice screamed as I tried to roll over, a voice I knew. Zola. Another flash, yellow and orange and hot.

"Damian, no!"

Sam's voice, Sam was here. Sam. I tried to will my vision back, struggling against the grogginess. Slowly, painfully so, my vision began to clear.

Laughter and cursing. The earth shook as Mike's hammer came down on a swirling mass of shadows, and a dim red glow faded away in the center. He lifted the hammer and all that was left was a dent in the cemetery grass where Philip should have been.

"He's gone," Zola said. "You stupid little man! You dumb fuck!" she screamed and kicked James in the ribs.

James was flat on his back, unconscious. He'd probably feel those ribs in the morning.

"You okay?"

I glanced up to find Sam looming over me. I gave her my best half-conscious grin.

"Oh yeah, you got your bell rung."

Edgar sighed and raised his hand toward James, fingers splayed. A second sun bloomed in his palm. I shut my eyes and winced as shouts of protest and pain went up from Mike and Zola when night suddenly turned to noon. A voice rang from Edgar's throat. It was a huge, deep, ground-shaking basso, underscoring his methodical words.

"You shall not remember the weapons brought to bear this night by Damian Valdis Vesik. The soulsword is forgotten, the soulart lost to time."

Edgar lowered his hand and the sun vanished from it.

"Ah should kill him, Amon," Zola said, her rage barely contained. I couldn't see her face as I was still waiting for my night vision to return, but it was plain in her voice.

"That would be unwise," Edgar said. "We may need him before this night is over."

"Ah doubt that," Zola said.

"You heard it from Philip himself. Ezekiel was here."

She sighed and ran her hand over her face. "If he's still here, he'll go for the mansion."

Edgar nodded. "We practically sent him straight there."

CHAPTER SIXTEEN

W e ran.

Sam had Foster tucked into her pocket. The rest of us pushed onward, the snowfall growing heavier now as we neared the gas station. I could see the column of smoke against the clouds, a deep black where the fire still burned through the night. We stayed a block away, wary of being recognized.

"Where are the Watchers?" I said to Edgar between breaths. "The Cleaners? Shouldn't they be here?"

He shook his head. "Yes, but Ezekiel has taken his toll. I don't know what's going on." He pulled his cell out and dialed a number. We covered another block before he hung up with a curse.

That was unnerving. Mike and I exchanged glances. The demon shrugged and we kept moving.

"At least we warned Vik," Sam said. She'd gotten through to the old vampire before Edgar started trying to reach the Watchers. Whatever had been done to the city's power grid, our phones were still working.

"Surprised he carries a cell phone," Edgar said. "He's never been much for technology."

That made me blink more rapidly in the snowstorm. "How long have you known him?" I asked as my breathing grew a little harder.

"A while," he said.

Zola laughed without humor in front of us. She held the lead, her stamina and mobility almost beyond my own even though her body looked like she was in her eighties. One of the benefits of a dark time in her life. Sam sped up and exchanged a few words with her before falling back and matching my pace.

"I'm gonna puke," Foster said.

"Not in this jacket, you bastard," Sam said.

"Are you serious?" I asked. "Your sleeve is half torn off."

She glanced at the damaged arm and cursed.

I took several deep breaths in a row, too much talking while trying to run.

"It's almost two miles back to the mansion," Sam said. "Are you going to be winded?"

"Winded?" I said with a short burst of laughter. "Nah, I'll be alright," I said. The quick inhalation of icy air tried to say otherwise.

"We're over halfway there," Mike said as we ran up an alley and came back out on Main Street.

"Move faster," Zola shouted back. "We'll be safe in the mansion. We just need to get there."

We all shut up and increased the pace. We were damn near sprinting by the time we crossed the bridge to cut through the snowy grass and the damaged silos of the construction yard.

The first necromancer was there, peeking around the silo, but looking in the wrong direction. Sam put on a burst of speed and his cloaked neck broke with an audible snap. She barely even slowed her stride. Idiot should have been watching with his Sight, not his eyes.

Carter misted in beside me. "Damian, there are necromancers behind the mansion, five at least, closing on the cellar."

The little necromancer popped into existence beside Mike and said, "There are more by the river."

Carter gave her a nod and vanished off to the left.

I could see the mansion in the distance now as we crossed through the thin line of trees by the old river gates. Gravel crunched, slightly muffled by accumulating snow.

"Stop," Edgar hissed.

We drew up on the edge of the gravel drive and hunched down in the shadows.

"Ah can see them on the edge of the house," Zola said. She pointed off to the right side, the east, closer to the cellar entrance.

"Gods, if they wake that thing …" Edgar whispered.

A shadow of motion caught my attention off to the left. I pointed toward the guest house and focused hard. Ley lines were bent, contorted and almost appeared as though they were being braided together. It was no natural pattern.

"You see that?" I asked.

Zola grunted. "Someone's gathering power."

"Be right back," Foster said as he jumped out of Sam's pocket and took to the air.

I wanted to yell out to him to get his ass back, but it would have given us away if we weren't made already.

"Idiot," Sam muttered as she shifted her feet and brushed against my arm with her own.

There was a dim flash near the edge of the guest house as Foster suddenly appeared in his full glory, dropping from the sky like a rock with a sword. I couldn't hear anything, but the sudden release of ley line energy sent waves across every line I could see. Foster took a few quick steps around the building before he shrank and took flight again, landing on Sam's shoulder a few seconds later.

"It's bloody cold out here," he grumbled as he nested in her pocket again.

"And?" I said.

"And what?" he asked.

"Who was over there?" Zola said.

"Some idiot blood mage. He has lots of blood to work with now."

"I imagine so," Zola said.

Sam's hand jumped up to her mouth to stifle a giggle. Sometimes I worry about what's happened to our sense of humor.

"Enough, let's move," Zola said.

We moved forward onto the drive, crossing the snow covered grass and then coming closer to the edge of the house before Zola glanced to her left and pulled up short.

"No, not here," she said, and her voice trailed off to a whisper. "We're so close. Give me your staff, Damian." I did.

"What is it?" Edgar said as he too looked to the west. "Shit."

"Run! All of you, run!" Zola said, her voice now a commanding shout.

I didn't move at first as she started toward the man standing on the far side of the guest house. Such an average-looking form, arms crossed and legs spread in a nonchalant stance. The hint of a gold bracelet shone dimly in the night on each arm, half covered by the dark, fitted cloak he wore.

Zola turned and glared at me. "If you never listen to me again, listen to me now, boy. He is beyond you."

I ran.

"Ezekiel!" Zola screamed as we left her behind. "Face me so it may be these hands that tear your wretched soul apart!"

I skidded to a stop near the edge of the mansion. Ezekiel. I couldn't leave Zola to him. Could I? The others turned the corner and an eruption of shouts, gunfire, and magic exploded across the yard. I glanced back, one hand on my gun, the other aching for my staff.

"Adannaya." His accent wasn't thick, or noticeable. His inflection was simply dead, a lifeless thing. "You tried once before. You will fail again."

There was no incantation. He simply flicked out his arm like he was dismissing a fly and a firestorm erupted around Zola.

"*Orbis Tego!*" she cried as the flames bore down on her. A circle shield sprang to life and turned the spell away, sending wheels of fire roaring into the air and burning a nearby tree to ash in a heartbeat.

Ezekiel gestured with his right arm, a simple 'come here' motion, and the ground exploded all around us. Dirt and debris sailed through the air, raining down around us as dead things rose into the night. Skeletons and corpses of animals and men floated silently for a moment. They didn't move on their own. The bastard made it look effortless as he picked them up with a torrent of necromancy and began hammering away at Zola's shield. Bones cracked and shattered again and again.

"You will fail, Adannaya." Another strike fell. Sparking bolts of electric blue lightning cracked into the air as more and more dead hammered against the shield. The mass grew into a sickening cloud of bones and flesh, undulating and crashing in a never-ending assault.

"Your mentor could not stop me. What hope have you?" He raised his arms high. The swarm of corpses and dead auras and white bone crushed together in a single, vicious wedge. I saw Zola turn her head away. She was done. The blade came down fast, so fast. The shield held for a moment longer, hissing and sparking as Zola began to scream.

It occurred to me, at that point, I was running straight into something with the power to swat me like a fly. Zola's shield fell and she grunted, falling backwards. The focus at my belt was already in my hand. I wished my staff wasn't lying beside my master, but I gritted my teeth and forged an aural blade, bolstering it with a tiny piece of my soul. I stumbled a half step as my consciousness shifted, becoming less real and more focused as the blade channeled a torrent of power through my aura, into my body, and up into the soulsword.

One quick strike and the blazing golden blade broke the congealed mass of dead things bearing down on my master. A quick turn to the side and another flick of my wrist severed Ezekiel's ties to them all. Zola was quick enough to fire an incantation into the falling debris, knocking it away from us both.

I took two steps toward Ezekiel, sword at the ready. Four mages melted out of the shadows and appeared to either side of him. I pulled my gun out awkwardly with my left hand.

"Enough," a voice boomed. Gravelly, worn, the voice of a man who'd seen more things than any man should.

Ezekiel stopped. His gaze bore into my own, and then he looked at Zola. "None of you will survive this night. I will not play this game Pinkerton plays."

Six quick bursts of gunfire rang out and three of the mages around Ezekiel died on their feet.

"Thank you, Dell," the gravelly voice said as its owner wandered forward from the shadows beside the mansion. "Put that soulsword away, son. Using your own soul. Idiot." His irritated tone reminded me of Zola. I let the sword fade.

"You," Ezekiel growled, the first hint of emotion I'd heard in his voice. "You would follow me across this damned world only to die here?" Soulswords appeared in each of Ezekiel's hands as he started toward the newcomer.

The man stepped into the moonlight and I almost flinched. His face was a mass of scars. Some were hidden by his beard, but it couldn't hide them all. Mountains and valleys formed across his hands and forearms in the moonlight, all bearing scars worse than those across his face.

"You think you're the only one with a new bag of tricks?" he said. His hand snapped forward, palm to the sky. I couldn't be sure of what I saw, but it looked like something black and sickly leapt out of his scars and flew into the night. Ezekiel grunted and crossed his soulswords. An explosion of black and red and white ribbons careened off into the night, killing the last mage standing beside Ezekiel and extinguishing both Ezekiel's blades.

Ezekiel laughed. It was a low, stuttering growl that sent gooseflesh racing across my neck far beyond anything the icy air could conjure.

"One hundred fifty years, Old Man," he said, and it was as though 'Old Man' was the newcomer's name. "Your apprentice is still weak."

"She is no apprentice," the Old Man said. "She's still pure, unlike the filth you've become." Ezekiel started to say something more, but the Old Man cut him off. "We have friends in higher places than you can imagine." He raised his hand to the sky and a bolt of electric blue lightning leapt into the air with a crack.

The Thunderbird answered, crashing to the ground in a flash of its own lightning. Its head cocked toward Ezekiel, and then toward the Old Man. Neither moved.

"It could kill you," the Old Man growled.

"Perhaps, but I don't—"

The Thunderbird's wing flashed out and struck Ezekiel. It knocked the necromancer to the ground as though a freight train had fallen from the sky to crush him. Dust and snow settled around the impact, Ezekiel face down at its center. A moment later Ezekiel moved his head slightly to look up from the debris-strewn field.

Edgar was descending, gliding down from the roof of the mansion.

Ezekiel's gaze snapped back to the Old Man. "We are not finished." The blackened chaff of a gravemaker boiled up from the ground and enveloped Ezekiel's body, a void swallowing light, swallowing ley energy, until it billowed out and misted away, leaving nothing behind.

"No, we're not," the Old Man said.

CHAPTER SEVENTEEN

"What the devil are you all doing here?" the Old Man asked.

We gaped at him in silence.

"Whatever you're after, rest assured the bastard sent that thing after it."

"What thing?" I asked. "We're after my Mom."

He met my eyes and his gaze was unwavering, his confidence a seething and inescapable presence. Ley lines curled and bent around him as though they were pining to touch their god. His body had a thin yellow glow all around it. That glow gave me goose bumps so bad I finally understood every cliché phrase about jumping out of your skin. He shook his head, a jarringly normal movement, and blew out a breath. "That didn't just *look* like a gravemaker. It *was* a gravemaker."

"Ezekiel?" I said.

"It's too much to explain right now. You'd better get to your mother before she's dead. Vesik?"

I nodded and then paused, stuck between horror and curiosity. "How did you know my name?"

"Word gets around our circles." He gave Zola a significant glance before he coughed and spat on the ground. The hand that rose to rub his beard was just as cut and scarred as his face.

"You want to do something about *that*," Edgar said as he hooked his thumb at the Thunderbird.

"Bah, he's harmless," the Old Man said as he walked up to the towering bird and scratched its neck. The Thunderbird leaned into the Old Man like a puppy, arching its neck and firing thunderbolts into the air as he reached up with both hands for a more vigorous scratching.

Edgar just blinked. "But, the balance? Good and evil, it shouldn't, you shouldn't—"

Zola laughed quietly. "Edgar is trying to say it should kill you on sight to maintain a balance."

"Balance?" the Old Man said as he turned away from the Thunderbird. It nosed him in the back. "You think good can't exist without evil? Evil without good? Semantic idiocy. Some things simply are."

A distant gunshot brought me back to the moment.

The Old Man pointed to the shadows. "Dell, help the others. Stay out of the basement." Someone moved and raced toward the back of Rivercene. I could have sworn he was grumbling under his breath "Dell shoot the bad guys. Dell run here. Dell do my goddamned laundry."

I liked him already.

We all moved. I followed the shadow to the west, gun drawn and ready for killing. The Old Man's skin seemed to darken and become harder to see as he moved past me, sidling up beside Mike and Zola as Edgar took to the sky.

"Fire demon," he said before they got out of earshot. "This should be fun."

Dell came up short at the edge of the house and peeked around. He motioned for me to move up and I did, moving in a crouch to take cover beside a wide tree trunk.

"Just pick them off on the outside," he said. "Watch. The Old Man will move them out for us."

And so he did, quite literally. The Old Man and Mike went into such a frenzy the vampires backed off and gawked. The fire demon and the Old Man moved together, weaving between the seven necromancers as spells and gunshots shattered the night around them. The Old Man pushed one cloaked form into the path of Mike's arcing, flaming hammer. The weapon hissed as it sank into the ground, flattening earth as surely as it flattened the man in its way. Mike twirled to the right and launched the next necromancer back toward the Old Man as a flicker of darkness lit down his scarred arm. A jerk of the Old Man's hand scythed the necromancer in two. The next raised his arms and started to scream, but Mike cut that short with a swing like a baseball bat. The man crumpled around the head of the hammer and smashed into a nearby tree. Six went down in seconds.

The last necromancer ran toward us, screaming. Foster was behind him, running with his sword raised, ready to strike.

"I don't have a clear shot," Dell said.

"Foster, down!" I shouted.

He dropped like a rock, flattening against the grass.

The necromancer barely had time to think about stopping as I stepped out from behind the tree and pulled the second trigger on the pepperbox. His head vanished and Dell cursed as all six rounds found their mark.

"What the hell are you shooting?" he asked, his already high-pitched voice rising into a shrill squeak. "A goddamned cannon?"

"Pretty much," Foster said as he climbed back to his feet. "That was the last one."

I grinned and held my hand out to Dell. His hair looked dark blond in the square of light cast down by the sudden arrival of a porch light. Both our heads snapped up to spy the innkeeper. I turned my attention back to our new compatriot.

"I'm Damian."

"Dell," he said as he shook my hand in a firm grip. His eyes were the cool gray-blue of a born necromancer.

"Inside," the innkeeper said from her perch above us. "The others are around front." We walked back toward the front of

Rivercene. Voices grew louder as we made it back to the corner and reached the others standing around the front porch.

"Your help, it is most welcome," Vassili said as he shook hands with the Old Man. "Who are you?"

"A friend," he said.

"I have heard the stories, if all are to be believed." Vassili paused and paced silently beside the man. "If they are to be believed, you are a god, *da?*"

The Old Man laughed outright. It sounded the same as he looked, cracked and scarred. Vassili narrowed his eyes.

"Edgar is more god than I will ever be."

The Watcher shot the man a glare I'd seen directed at me on more than one occasion. I call it the 'I'm going to kill you now if you don't shut up' glare.

"Hail to thee." The sneer was palpable through the Old Man's beard.

"Enough, this is not the time for ancient things," Edgar said.

"Ancient things," the Old Man said with a bitter laugh. "That's all we are."

Edgar turned and glared once more before walking up the entryway steps and slamming the front door.

"I believe we may get along quite well," Vik said as he shook hands with the Old Man and followed Edgar through the door.

"Where's Dad?" I asked as Sam came up beside me.

"He's already inside," she said.

"We had him standing by to wake the Guardian," Zola said as she opened the door for the fairies and Mike.

I looked at Zola and blinked. She flashed me a toothy grin.

The Old Man reached out and grabbed Sam by the neck, turning her head to the side and staring at the dark, scarred patch of skin. Sam cursed and tried to throw a quick left punch, but he wrapped her up in a fluid twisting motion so she couldn't move.

"Let her go," I said, leveling my gun at his head.

"You didn't even reload yet," Dell said from beside me. I lowered my gun and my necromancy flared up around me.

"Sloppy, but effective," the Old Man said as he looked up at me. "Must have hurt like hell for both of you."

"Release her," Zola said, not sounding angry so much as being put-upon to supervise a problem child.

He released her, and then casually leaned away from the punch Sam threw. The strength he had to have to restrain Sam like that … I was pissed, but I was also a little impressed.

"Who the hell do you think you are?!" she said, fists clenched into balls at her side.

"I am surprised you were not put to death for that piece of work," the Old Man said as though Sam hadn't spoken.

"No one knows about it," I said.

He laughed, and it was rich. The rust broke away as he smiled, ever so slightly. "Edgar knows. Edgar is one of the reasons those laws exist."

"Enough," Zola said. "You forget the time."

The phrase seemed to have weight with the Old Man. He grew silent and nodded at Zola. "I am sorry Samantha. I forget myself at times."

Sam glanced at Zola, who gave her a small nod. She took a deep breath and turned back to the Old Man. "It's okay. Let's just go inside."

"Amen," Dominic said as he dropped out of the shadows behind Dell, who proceeded to jump and squeal. It was a manly squeal.

"Ah'm glad you did not attack," Zola said.

"Not the time," Dominic and the Old Man chorused together. They paused, and then gave each other a once-over.

"Nice to meet a sensible fang."

Dominic chuckled. "Fang. I haven't heard that in centuries Old Man. There are a few of us around."

"Stupid men," Sam grumbled as we all walked back into Rivercene.

***

"Who's coming with me to Saint Louis?" I asked. We were gathered in the front of the mansion again, sprawled out from the piano and past the fireplace leading into the dining room.

"Let's go," Dad said as he picked up the leather satchel of bomb lances.

"Not yet," Zola said.

"But he said—" Sam started as she pointed at the Old Man.

The room erupted into an incoherent babble of what we should and shouldn't do. The Watchers wanted to stay. My family was hell bent on getting to Saint Louis. Dominic and Vik were with us. Mike was being diplomatic and staying out of it.

"Silence!" Zola said, her voice tearing through the cacophony of sound. "We need to rest. Ezekiel could kill us all. You do *not* understand what you face." The arguments continued.

"Let me speak."

I blinked and turned toward the voice, only a shadow in my peripheral vision.

"Damian, let me speak."

I focused and found Carter standing beside me. His stare was intent on the Old Man. I nodded and pushed a wave of necromancy into him, weaving it with the golden sheen of my own soul until Carter and Maggie both blazed into reality, plain for everyone to see.

The Old Man's eyes narrowed and then shot to me. "You're full of tricks, aren't you?" His voice boomed in the suddenly quiet room.

Everyone gaped at the newly corporeal werewolves. Foster glided over and settled on Carter's shoulder. It wouldn't really hit me until later that he'd done it to show just how solid I'd made them.

"Zola is right," Carter said. "Rest now. You need to split into two groups."

"At least two," Maggie said.

"The demon they raised was sighted near Howell Island," Carter said. "I can only assume it's going to be waiting for you. We sent Vicky and the Harrowers to intercept it."

I didn't like that at all, but I knew the kid could take care of herself. "We have to help," I said.

Carter stared at me before his eyes moved slowly to Sam. "If Vicky can't stop them, none of you can either."

"I could," the Old Man said.

"I, as well," Mike said.

"With so little rest?" Carter said. "You're falling apart, Mike. Your aura is erratic."

The demon crossed his arms and leaned into the wall. "I won't argue with you about it. Yes, I am tired, but our friends need help."

"The wolf is right," Vassili said. "They will not kill your mother so quickly. Dead bait is not good bait."

"Usually," Zola said quietly. The Old Man flashed a faint smile through his scraggly beard.

"Fine, but we're leaving early," Sam said as she pointed to Vassili. "I don't care if you get grumpy in the sunlight. We're leaving early."

Vassili raised his white eyebrows and then bowed slightly to Sam. "As you say."

"Good, some of you need to stay here," Carter said as Edgar nodded his approval. "The rest, meet us in Chesterfield. We'll divide from there. Koda says some of Philip's men are showing up in Saint Charles."

"Who's Koda?" James asked from over Edgar's shoulder.

"Koda, from the Society of Flame," Carter said without missing a beat. Koda was, for lack of a better term, thrilled with the creation of the Ghost Pack. Something new and interesting for the old ghost to study.

Carter didn't acknowledge James any further. "Some of us will need to support Frank and Ashley. The rest go for Dimitry's wife. Get some rest."

Carter nodded to me and I cut the power. He was still there, a vague outline in my peripheral vision, but the house was screwing with my senses again.

"All of you, off to bed," the innkeeper said. "I'll have breakfast in the morning."

The Old Man stood and stretched. "No need to beat the horse anymore tonight." He turned and disappeared down the hallway. The rest of the group followed suit, quiet conversations echoing through the old halls as we parted ways for the night.

I felt a hand on my shoulder before I reached the stairs and turned to find Mike. He glanced away, taking in our surroundings, and then met my eyes again.

"What you did for the wolves, you brought them into this world," he said. "I could feel them here, truly here."

I nodded. "It seems to work with any ghosts, but it's really easy with those two. I think it has something to do with the Prosperine battle."

"Could you?" Mike asked as his voice trailed off to a whisper. "Would you do that for me?"

"For you?" I said. "You're already here. I can punch you and my fist will hurt."

"Not me," he said.

Face, palm. "Her," I said. Mike's little necromancer, the girl he'd given up everything for. He'd sworn an oath as she'd died in his arms almost two centuries ago. Aeros had told us the story. It was one of a thousand tragedies that lived in the history at Stones River.

A small smile quirked the corners of Mike's mouth.

"It's only temporary. I can't keep it up very long, maybe twenty or thirty minutes, tops."

"If you can give us twenty minutes to be together, I would give you the world."

"That's probably overkill," I said.

"I will owe you a favor. A true debt, Damian, a binding debt that I will repay, no matter the cost to myself."

"I thought you could already do that. I mean, you can touch her, right?"

"It is not the same my friend." His eyes trailed off into the shadows of the staircase. "You brought those wolves to life tonight. I am selfish enough to want that, if only for the time a candle burns."

"Mike, you've helped us more than I believed a demon could."

"I have forsaken the darkness and I am fallen because of it."

"Seems like a good choice to me."

"Yes."

"I'll do it, but not for any trade. I'll do it because you're my friend." I put my hand on the demon's shoulder. "Make no mistake. Everyone here calls you friend." I paused and tapped my chin. "Except James, oh, and Edgar. Maybe Vassili, I can't really tell what he thinks of you."

"He's a bit creepy," Mike said.

I chuckled.

"Say what you want, Damian, I will still owe you a favor if you do this."

I shrugged. "Suit yourself. I'll probably call you when I need to move some bookshelves."

We started up the stairs.

"Christ, making a ghost corporeal so she can get it on with her demon lover. I am so going to hell."

"Have you ever eaten meat on a Friday?" Mike asked as the stairs echoed beneath our footsteps.

"What?" I said. "Does cow count?"

"Ah, then you were already going to hell," Mike said. "This will be nothing to worry about."

"Super," I said flatly. "Is she here? This place screws with my ghost radar."

"She is," Mike said.

"Alright, where do you want to do this?"

"Hot tub," the demon said, nonchalantly.

"My room?" I said, somewhat surprised.

He nodded.

I grumbled under my breath about the awkward tub protocols in this lovely establishment, and then led the way to my room with Mike laughing all the way.

I stopped at the foot of the bed and dug around my backpack for the headphones Sam had given me.

"What are you doing?" Mike said.

I held up the small white earphones and plugged them into my phone. "Privacy and all," I said.

I focused, hard, and found Mike's little necromancer sitting on the chair at the vanity. She grinned and drummed her fingers through the wood. Bringing ghosts into our world was becoming old hat. I barely even had to think about gathering the power and lacing it with a soulart. The snake of yellowish energy lanced out across the floor and her translucent form burst into golden light. Her fingers began to beat a steady rhythm on the vanity as my power gave her flesh.

The small impish girl, the girl who played with hellfire and beings that were the sun to her own tiny world, smiled up at her lover as she came into our company once more. I knew how she felt in some ways, that irresistible temptation to find out if you were the one who could get away with it, if you could wield the weapons already known to have destroyed dynasties.

She still wore her old Civil War uniform, all color lost to a pale golden glow. She looked at me and blinked before wiping tears from her face. "Thank you, Damian," she whispered.

I smiled and nodded as I picked up the headphones and turned my music up. Mike crushed her in a hug, a reddish tear on his own cheek, as they disappeared into the old whirlpool tub behind the door.

CHAPTER EIGHTEEN

Something loud and rhythmic woke me up in the morning. My brain instantly jumped to the alarm clock and began listing reasons to destroy it. Once I finally cracked my eyes open, I realized it was my phone. The contact name said 'TNT.' I picked it up.

"Hey, Frank."

"Damian! Thank god. The video went viral. The Watchers didn't get it in time."

The video. The video of us shooting people and hurling magic. The video that finished with Ashley unleashing that cloud of absolute destruction. *That* video was out in the public eye. I head-butted my pillow.

"Bloody fucking hell." I closed my eyes and rubbed my face. All remnants of sleep were gone in a moment of shock. I barely registered the bedroom door clicking shut behind me.

"Most sites are touting it as phenomenal homemade special effects, but others are already pushing it as evidence," Frank said.

"Evidence," I said.

"Evidence of us," Sam said.

I glanced at my sister, standing at the edge of my bed. Her lips were pulled into a small frown and her eyebrows were drawn together.

"Is that Sam?" Frank asked.

"Yeah. Is Ashley still with you?"

"She's been sleeping on the couch. Bubbles and Peanut have a new best friend."

I chuckled at the thought of our indoor ponies smothering Ashley on the couch. "Be sure she stays there, Frank. There's trouble headed your way."

"Sam told me," he said. "I called her first."

That probably explained why she was now standing at the foot of my bed. I nodded, even though Frank couldn't see it, and said "Good, we'll be there as soon as we get our mom."

"Be careful."

"You too." I hung up the phone and stared at Sam.

"Edgar," we said in unison.

I pulled on my jeans and a clean shirt and followed Sam down the hall. We knocked on the Watchers' door, but no one answered. No James, no Edgar. We continued down the stairs, heading toward the faint sound of voices in the kitchen. The smell of eggs and bacon was a stark contrast to the dread settling in my gut.

The conversation was out on the porch. As we got closer to the door, I could tell it was a heated argument and I was pretty sure Zola was on one side of it. Mike motioned us into the kitchen from his seat beside the fireplace. Vassili and Dominic were already up, and the latter had a forkful of waffle stuffed in his mouth. By the look on their faces, I was thinking neither one had eaten a waffle in a very long time. My attention left the distant yells and blissful vampires behind as my gaze found Edgar.

He was wide-eyed when we walked into the kitchen, unfocused until his gaze locked onto me. I was fairly certain he'd already gotten the news, one way or another.

"How do we stop it?" I asked as the fairies all glided down to the table.

Edgar watched them for a moment as the innkeeper set out small plates piled high with eggs, bacon, and single-square pieces of waffle.

"Stop it?" he said as he slid a half-eaten piece of bacon across his plate like a chess piece.

I nodded. "Frank says the video is out. It's gone viral."

The fairies stopped eating and stared at me.

"It's viral," Edgar said. "It's everywhere." He fell silent and snapped the crisp bacon in two. "Ezekiel killed the only Watchers with enough influence over technology to do anything about it. All in the last week." He reduced the bacon to crumbles as I watched.

Waiting for him to say something else got under my skin, and I snapped. "How the hell do we stop it?"

"How can anyone stop that now?" he snapped back. "Do you think we're magic?"

He paused and blinked, his eyes darting to the side and back. I opened my mouth.

"Shut up, Vesik," he said.

The fairies burst into a subdued laughter.

"Technology is beyond us in some things." Edgar rubbed his palm across his forehead and grimaced. "At least, it's beyond most of us."

"What kind of damage do you foresee?" Vik asked as he pulled a chair up across the room beside Mike.

"I don't think it's too bad, honestly," Edgar said. "For our community at large, I mean. What the hell was that witch throwing around?"

"You saw it?" Foster asked.

Edgar nodded.

Mike coughed and his voice was sheepish. "I believe those were runic arts."

The Watcher's head rose slowly and he gawked at Mike. "The Blade of the Stone? That art is lost!"

Mike glanced at the empty space beside him. I could barely make out the form of the little necromancer. I coughed into my fist as I choked back a laugh.

"Lost to most," Mike said. "Reborn in a witch who walks in the light."

"'Reborn in a witch that walks in the—' Edgar shouted. "Are you fucking crazy?!" Edgar shouted.

Foster didn't bother to hide the huge grin on his face as he chewed on a piece of waffle the size of his hand. Aideen sighed and went back to her own food.

Edgar's shoulders slumped. "It doesn't matter right now. Later, it can wait." Edgar's voice resumed the absolute authority I was used to. "James and I are staying here. The Old Man is going after Ezekiel, which means you'll probably see him again in Saint Louis. Carter said to call Hugh, tell him to help Frank and Ashley."

I snorted a laugh. "Tell him, right, maybe ask nicely." Edgar astutely ignored me.

"You will take Sam, Vik, Mike, and Zola to get your mother back."

"I'm staying here," Cassie said.

Cara nodded. "The Guardian is shifting beneath us. We need to stay. Foster will go with you. Aideen will return to Frank and Ashley."

Foster rubbed the hilt of the sword over his left shoulder.

"I am sorry I won't be with you all. Do not underestimate Ezekiel. He is more powerful than you know."

"We watched him pull up every dead thing in a square mile and try to flatten Zola with it," I said. "How much more powerful could he be?"

Edgar met my gaze, daggers in his eyes. "Ezekiel has fought against three Old Gods I am aware of, and he still walks this earth."

If there'd been a clock in the room, I would have heard every tick in the silence that followed.

The outer door slammed, breaking the brief stillness as Zola walked into the kitchen. "Cut that crap, Edgar. He is still a man. He can still die."

The Watcher scraped a bite of shattered bacon together and chewed slowly.

"Dimitry is coming with us," she said. "Ah can't talk him out of it." She turned and pointed at Mike. "He thinks he can help with those damn bombs you gave him." She blew out a breath and looked at me. "Talking to your father reminds me where you got your blockheaded stubborn streak. Finish your food. We're leaving in an hour."

We all sat down and ate. The innkeeper was an amazing cook, serving up the flat breakfast soufflé once again after we finished the bacon and homemade waffles. She topped us off with a fresh batch of bread pudding straight from the baking dish. There were no formal serving dishes that morning. We ate off paper plates, everyone crammed around the two small seating areas in the kitchen. Sharing our food and fears in the morning brought my spirits up. We had new allies in Dell and the Old Man. Even Edgar was on our side. We were heading out soon to get Mom back, and a whole lot of Philip's men would be dead. I smiled and jabbed my fork into another chunk of bread pudding.

***

"Oh my god," Sam whispered. She leaned over the dashboard, nearly pressing her face to the window as we rolled over the bridge into downtown. "No."

Smoke rose from the ruins of Main Street. The old bricks of some buildings were burned out and blasted across the streets, leaving nothing but rubble. Bodies were mounted to the walls that were still standing. Snow fell delicately where shards of metal and rust and bone pinned the dead to the old shop fronts.

Some bodies were crucified. Others hung upside down, eviscerated. One teenage boy was almost nude, with his own shattered arm jammed down his throat. I almost gagged at the terror etched across his face in death. More bodies were strewn across the street like so much refuse.

"Who?" Vik said from the backseat. "Why?"

"There," I said as I pointed and swerved around an avalanche of shattered bricks. "Look at those bodies."

"Long dead, rotted," Vik said. "Necromancers did this."

"Bloody hell, we need to stop, help them," Sam said.

"You can't," Mike said, his tone a dark pulse from the back. "They're all dead."

"The whole town?" I asked.

"I doubt it, but everyone here is dead. I can't sense a living soul anywhere near us."

My old '32 Ford rattled over some bricks as we passed out of the devastated street. The road was clear at first, but then the bodies started up again. Torn and dismembered, they were discarded on the side of the road. Bloody skid marks lined the paths where they'd slid through the snow-covered ground. A trail of broken bodies led back to the gas station.

Edgar was on his phone in an instant. "Get the Cleaners to Boonville." He paused, listening to the other end of the line. "All tied up with the video? I don't give a fuck what they're doing! Boonville's half destroyed and the streets are littered with bodies. You pull them and get them out here now!" He hung up and slid the phone back into his pocket.

"Stop the car!" Mike said.

I slammed on the brakes, pushing myself deeper into the seat as we slid to a sideways stop. I glanced at Mike in the rearview mirror. He took a deep breath and then opened his eyes.

"Do you smell it?" he said.

I shook my head. "I just smell the burned-out station."

"I smell it," Sam said. "What is that? It's like when Prosperine … shit."

Mike nodded. "Brimstone. This wasn't just necromancers. A demon was here. And not long ago. The stench is still strong. It has to be the demon Ezekiel raised."

"We should not be seen here," Vik said. "Move."

***

My eyes were focused on the road, the gently winding highway, ash-colored below the gray skies. We wove through what little traffic was braving the snow. Our old, heavy cars had no problem in the weather, but my mind wouldn't leave Boonville. So many buildings on Main Street had been reduced to smoking piles of rubble. Bodies from the bridge to the exploded gas station. The carnage hadn't been that bad the night before. My knuckles whitened as I strangled the steering wheel.

"Who would have done that?" I asked.

"Had to be Ezekiel," Foster said from the dashboard.

"I know, but how could *anyone* do that?"

"They aren't like you and me," Vik said from the back.

I almost smiled at the inference Vik and I were alike.

"We kill only out of necessity," Vik said. "A need for survival or a lack of options. Regardless, we feel something every time we do it. Maybe it is regret, maybe it is glee, and maybe it is horror, but we all feel something. Ezekiel does not."

"Or cannot," Mike said.

Vik nodded. "Indeed. Worse though, a newly reborn demon will kill for sheer pleasure. One day it may thrive on twisting and damning souls, but killing is all that matters to it now."

Mike sighed and I caught a small nod in the mirror.

I slid the headset to the phone over my ear.

"Who are you calling?" Foster asked from his perch on the mirror.

"Hugh, I have to call Hugh," I said. "We're almost in Wentz-ville. I should have called him earlier. Frank and Ashley may need the backup." Sam's posture tightened when I mentioned them. "Hugh will help, sis. I know it."

The wolf picked up in two rings. "Speak."

"Hugh, it's Damian."

"Yes, brother. The phone told me that much."

"I'll get right to it. Ezekiel is headed your way. Probably to Chesterfield Mall where they're holding my mom."

"He is a powerful man, Cub." He hesitated for a moment. "What are you asking of us?"

"Not to face him, I won't ask you that," I said as I passed a slow-moving semi on a steep incline. "Frank and Ashley are holed up at the shop. They may need your help." I sighed. "Look, Ezekiel raised a demon last night. We don't know how strong it is, but it's a bloody demon. It destroyed Main Street in Boonville."

"Damian, if they are headed to Chesterfield, they will have to pass Howell Island. I cannot leave it unguarded."

Howell Island, the underground werewolf stronghold for the River Pack. My hand slid over the series of ridges on my arm where Hugh had marked me, bonding me to the pack. I still didn't know what all that entailed, but it was one hell of an after party.

"They won't know it's there," Foster said. "They may sense a concentration of power, or a distortion in the lines, but the river will mask most of it."

"I will send Alan and Regina," Hugh said.

Alan I knew. He was a mountain of a man, but a gentle soul. He's a strong fighter, and someone I am glad is on my list of friends. "Regina?"

"She is Misun's little sister," Hugh said.

"Misun?" I asked.

Hugh chuckled. "I believe you told him he looked like a tabby cat at your initiation."

"Oh, right. Misun," I mumbled. Long story.

"Regina is lithe and deadly as a fox, Damian. She will protect your friends." He paused briefly. "Our friends."

I smiled. "Thanks, Hugh. Sorry to bring this down on you."

"No, this is no fault of yours. It takes many voices to weave this tale. I must go."

"Thanks again," I said.

He grunted an affirmation and hung up.

"Two werewolves, two cu siths, Aideen, Frank, and Ashley," Foster said. "I think they'll be fine."

"I would not want to stick my nose in that hornet's nest," Vik said.

"Not even for a ferret?" Sam asked.

Vik paused, and then said, "Perhaps."

Zola's blue 1957 Chevy Bel Air pulled out and started to pass us as the hour wound down and we closed in on Chesterfield. I gave Dad a one-handed wave as they went by.

"Almost time," Mike said as we started across the bridge into the Chesterfield Valley.

The snow picked up, larger flakes turning to mush against the windshield and limiting our visibility. The tree line and riverbanks wore a stark blanket of white.

"I'd rather be stopping for pancakes," Foster said under his breath.

"There's Howell Island," Sam said as she pointed out the window to her right. "Hard to believe the entire compound is under there."

We exited at Boone's Crossing, heading west until we caught Baxter Road and wound through a small row of old homes. They lined the foot of a hill to the south, opposite a small, well-kept mobile home park.

"Edgar," I said. "How should we go in?"

"Most of the stores are already closed. Park by Dillard's on the west side and we'll start a sweep."

I exhaled a breath I didn't realize I'd been holding. That was right by the northern parking lot where we'd found Vicky. Where we'd found the van and killed the murdering bastard that hurt her.

"Vicky," Foster said.

I ground my teeth and nodded.

"Another time," Edgar said. "We need to focus. Your mother needs us."

Sam put her hand on my shoulder as we pulled into the lot behind Zola. I slammed the car into park and got out.

CHAPTER NINETEEN

"Door's locked," Dad said as he turned away from the glass.

"Stores shouldn't be closed," Edgar said. "They know we're coming. On your guard."

I glanced up into the falling snow as the Carol of the Bells boomed from the speakers above. For a moment I was thrown into the past, playing a duet with Sam on Christmas Eve at our grandparents' house. A night of family, one of those rare times everything goes right. Pine and gingerbread filled our lungs with every breath as we pounded through our performance. Mom and Grandma clapped and smiled while Dad sipped his eggnog and flashed us a fake smile. This performance, this song, in a time all but lost. The Carol of the Bells rang out and my skin crawled with anger. I snarled as the chorus boomed.

Rage makes everything easy, but cleanup's a bitch. Ley line energy leapt into my open palm, growing and pulsing and burning as the concentration grew to be too much. Foster marched beside me, full-sized and off to my left, with Sam to my right as the wind snapped at her trench coat with winter's chill. Zola's training echoed in my head, "A fist to strike the darkness."

Five feet from the door I closed my hand around the ball of power and simply punched at the air. A fiery blue comet smashed through the doors, melting glass and steel and sending shrapnel skidding twenty feet across the tiled floors.

Glass fell from the mangled door frames, a tinkling accompaniment to the sudden silence that wrapped around us as we crossed the threshold into the mall. The music from the outdoor speakers was only a whisper in the quiet stillness of what should have been a bustling shopping mall.

"That was probably unnecessary," Mike said.

I looked at the demon with my palm open flat.

A small frown crossed his face. "Right, your mom. Never mind." He ran his hand over his head and pushed forward.

My shoulder was crushed in an iron grip. I turned to find Zola at my side.

"Keep your head boy. That fire in your gut may help with some arts, but it'll bite you in the ass."

She patted my shoulder gently and moved to walk beside Edgar. They exchanged hushed words before Edgar nodded and broke off to the left with Mike. She moved back between me and Sam and whispered again.

"Edgar, Vik, and Mike are sweeping the top floor. You, Foster, and Sam take the bottom floor, mirror their movements."

"And Dad?" Sam asked with a glance at our father.

"With me," Zola said as she tucked my staff into her cloak at an angle across her back.

Sam nodded.

Dad jammed a bomb lance into his cannon and scooted off into the shadows behind Zola. They didn't wait for us as we reached the first courtyard, instead moving quickly ahead of us to the right.

"Wait up," I said to Sam in the quiet. I pointed up the escalator as Mike and Edgar reached the top. Vik was already out of sight. Mike tried the gates on the first few shops, to no avail.

"Who could've locked this place down?" Sam asked.

"I don't know, but it's too quiet," Foster said as he unsheathed his sword.

The squeak from Sam's shoe a moment later sounded like a gunshot. "It's so quiet."

I nodded as I moved underneath our companions on the second floor. "Try the gates on that side."

We tried them all between the first courtyard and the center courtyard. Nothing. Every silver- grated wall was locked down, from the clothing stores to the artists' gallery. We slid around and hugged the left wall, bunching together again as the carousel loomed into view, dominating the area around us. A shadow jumped across the top of the double-decker ride and vanished, leaving a chill down my spine.

"What was that?" I asked.

"On it," Foster said as he took wing. He landed on the carousel top a moment later with a light thump. His head snapped back and forth before slowly strafing around the top. He pointed toward Mike and Edgar above us.

I glanced up at them as Mike leaned over the railing.

Mike was frowning. "Demon," was all he said.

I took a deep breath and started to nod. The lights flickered and the color seemed to leech out of the mall, leaving a gray pallor over the entire scene as the sulfuric stench of brimstone washed over us. I felt a small vibration in the floor beneath my feet.

"Belphegor," Mike hissed from above us.

"I'm a little behind on my demonology," I hissed back, narrowly keeping my voice from shaking.

Sam grabbed my arm. "The room's getting darker. What the hell is happening?"

The tiles beside me cracked open as Mike leapt down from the second story. "It's not an illusion. He's trying to open a gate."

"What?" I said, all thoughts of whispering gone as I tried to imagine a hellgate opening in the middle of suburbia.

"Foster!" Mike said. "Find him!"

The fairy flashed up to the ceiling, sweeping across the hollows of the skylights. "Left, now!" He shouted.

Mike's weapon burst into life, exploding into a fiery war hammer. The flaming head swept in an overhand arc, dispelling the shadows around it. The large floor tiles shattered when the hammer struck. Laughter rumbled out from the shadowy murk floating toward us. It started low and rose into the stuttering giggles of a young girl.

"Oh, brother mine." The voice was a discordant harmony, a deep growl and a sinewy girl's soprano. It felt like a metal file on my teeth.

"Belphegor," Mike growled. "You are not my brother." He swung the hammer in a lateral strike and the darkening murk flew backwards with another jarring laugh.

I raised my Sight and saw … nothing. Barely a red smear in a sea of darkness. It told me where the demon was, but nothing more.

I started as Edgar pulled Sam away from me. "Call Vicky, now," he whispered, and there was an undeniable authority to his words.

I nodded and backpedaled, crouching behind a kiosk. I could see the cloud and Mike's hammer striking in the dim gray, but everything else was blurring into blackness.

At Vicky's request, I'd been practicing calling the bear. The two were inseparable, the Guardian and his … his what? His student? I frowned and closed my eyes, latching my necromancy onto the nearest ley line. I sent my consciousness racing east, hunting for my friends. I was aware of the passing landmarks, the hospital, another mall, and finally Forest Park exploded into my senses.

Happy's head rose the instant he felt my presence.

"Chesterfield Mall. Bring Vicky," was all I voiced before the gray cloud began choking my connection to the ley line.

We come, he said as my vision of his black-and-white fur faded to nothing.

I tried to release the ley line, expecting the tile and stone of the mall to come back into focus, but it didn't. The power buzzing across me felt like honey, stretching and adhering as I tried to release it. Everything started to dim, my vision narrowing as the blue lines of power began to pulse with a sickly red glow. Panic clawed at the back of my throat and tried to overcome my senses. Something was pulling on my necromancy. I could feel it distending my aura, and I had no control of it.

I screamed as the power turned into knives, like alcohol poured over a fresh wound. My body burned and seared as fire cut into me. My first instinct was a soulart, but I couldn't focus well enough to think of one that would help. My next thought was an aural blade. My right hand curled into a fist and I forced my aura through the circle my thumb and forefinger made. A dim red blade sprang to life. It was short and inconsistent, but it was still a blade. I ground my teeth together and hacked at the pulsing web of red ley lines, scraping them from my arms and legs. The power fractured and fell away, brittle as a long-dead branch.

I gasped as my consciousness fully snapped back into my own body. The lights were brighter now, but changed. A red glow pulsed at the heart of the cloud, close to the carousel. The creature within was growing, no longer an obscured smear of red.

Belphegor walked upright, on human legs, but thin snake-like whips pulsed and writhed where his arms should have been. He was nude from the waist down, and there was no doubt it was a he. His skin was blacker than the pages of a burned book. I shivered as I looked at that face, for there was no true face. A row of metallic teeth gleamed in his elongated head where a man's nose would have been. Two glowing red coals sat in the void of his eyes.

"Come, Smith," Belphegor growled. "Let me taste your hammer." His arms snapped skyward, nearly reaching the top of the double-decker carousel.

Sam moved forward and Mike put his hand out. "No, this is my fight." Much more quietly, he said, "Find your mother."

"Can you match him?" Edgar asked, teetering on the balls of his feet.

Mike's lack of an answer was all I needed to hear. Christ, he was just buying us time.

"Foster, Vik!" Edgar said. "Warn Dimitry."

The fairy saluted and flashed into his smaller size, following Vik's blur of motion.

Mike strode out to meet Belphegor in the pulsing cloud of darkness. Mike the demon, the Smith of legend and lore, a man I was proud to call my friend.

"Kick his ass!" I said as I grabbed Sam's arm and pulled her toward the food court off to our left.

"I'll watch for Ezekiel," Edgar said. A moment later he added, "As we look for your mother, of course."

"Will you step in if that fight gets out of hand?" Sam asked as we began to move faster.

Edgar nodded. "Yes, but Belphegor is powerful."

"How powerful?" I asked.

"Very."

As if on cue, Belphegor struck. He moved fast, near-vampiric speeds dragging the cloud with him as he moved. His right arm rolled out to the side and forward, a mass of reptilian tentacles spiraling out towards Mike. Mike dove to the left and a scythe of fire leapt from his arms. A small pile of Belphegor's tentacles fell off, but his left arm was already in motion. I could see the grimace on Mike's face as the mass of Belphegor's arm hit him squarely in the chest. He flew into a bubble tea stand closer to us, shattering glass and plywood as he landed. The hammer fell from his grip and went dark. Belphegor took a step back and inspected his burned tentacles.

"Mike!" Sam said.

He pulled himself up and glared at her. "Get your ass moving! I can't keep this up all night."

I ran over to him while Belphegor was still distracted. "Vicky's coming."

He grunted and nodded, his hammer springing into burning life once more as he scooped it up and charged into the cloud. Tentacles and flames flew as the demons started hacking away at each other in a nauseating blur of motion.

Next thing I knew I was over Sam's shoulder and we shot up the unmoving escalator.

"Someone else is up here," she said as she set me down.

I stumbled a couple steps and nodded. I didn't need to raise my Sight.

"Necromancers," I said. I could feel the waves and the pulsing pressure of the dead against my senses. "They have something with them."

"Yeah, a demon opening a bloody hellgate," Sam said.

I nodded, but I also noticed my vision was clearer with Mike drawing the attention of the other demon. I prayed he was slowing that thing down. The pulsing red and black presence of the demon was far less pronounced as we moved across the second floor. The pepperbox was in my hand without so much as a second thought.

I was looking at Sam when it happened. Saw Edgar's mouth open in what I can only assume was a curse as my vision was turned into a searing ball of red and orange light that sent a blast of scorched air past us. The earth shook and I fell, knowing I was screaming, but hearing nothing but a basso roar I believed was nothing less than the end of the world.

The entire southern wing of the mall vanished in one enormous explosion. Deafening doesn't cover it. Neither does terrifying. Fire and rubble and shrapnel came at us faster than I could think. I rolled over, throwing myself on top of Sam to protect her, only later realizing how stupid that was. She clutched me and buried her face in my shoulder until the crash of debris and the roar of the fireball subsided.

"What was that?" Sam screamed into my ear.

I could feel her shaking as we stood up, brushing away dust and chunks of the old mall. My hands showed cuts and blood. My back stung where something'd hit it. I winced and stared at the gun still in my hand, surprised I'd held on.

"Not magic," I said as I stared at the gaping maw of the inferno before us. A series of small collapses and gouts of flame rose from the rubble.

"Fucking hell, what are they thinking?" Edgar said as he stepped up beside us. A gash across his forehead was bleeding badly.

"You're cut," I said.

"I'll be fine. The necromancers?"

I took a shaky breath and pushed my own necromancy out before nodding and pointing toward the west wing by Macy's.

"Madness, this is madness," Edgar said as he snapped his wrist forward and a piercing ball of light spun on his palm. "We kill on sight."

I nodded and followed Sam along the edge of the glass railing, as far as we could get from the jagged cliff of steel and concrete hanging over what used to be the southern wing. The dying sun lit the sky between columns of smoke and dust. And death. I stumbled as the deaths hit me, falling to a knee as a hundred voices screamed at once.

"Damian!" Sam said as she hauled me up from the floor.

"Christ, so many," I whispered. "Wing wasn't empty."

Some part of me registered Edgar staring at the ruined stretch of shops. I heard him curse and then he was propping me up with Sam.

Almost there.

I stumbled again as Happy's voice echoed in my head, unbidden. "How in the—"

"What?" Sam asked as she started moving faster.

"Happy, he just spoke to me, but I didn't make the connection."

"Doesn't matter," Edgar said. "Focus, get through this."

Edgar was right. I put it out of my mind and clamped down on my necromancy, focusing on everything but my overwhelmed senses. Then I noticed the surge of power around us. I stopped and Edgar and Sam let go. I focused on the surges of necromancy around us again. It didn't take much to follow those black-and-white bands of power back to the cluster of zombies waiting in ambush.

"There!" I shouted as I leveled the pepperbox at the shadowy stairwell beside Macy's.

Edgar didn't fuck around. He flicked his wrist and the small ball of light in his palm rocketed into the stairwell. I saw seven or eight unnervingly fresh corpses staring at us, eyes blank, waiting for the command of the man screaming behind them. The ball of light flashed out like a supernova. It was there, then huge, and then gone. I could see the ghost of the necromancer in the charred hall, still screaming, his aura a slowly churning ribbon of black and white.

I lowered my gun and glanced at Edgar.

"Move," was all he said, his voice strained.

And we moved.

Sam reached the gate first. She ripped it out of the wall and it fell in a clatter of steel and drywall.

"I can smell her," she said as she stared intently into the darkness beyond.

"Mom?" I asked.

Sam nodded as she closed her eyes. They flew open a moment later and Sam vanished. She reappeared by the railing in the center of the store. Edgar and I ran after her.

Someone screamed and it cut me to the bone. Mom.

Sam leapt the railing as we reached it. I watched as her coat snapped in the air once before a necromancer's bones shattered when she landed on him. Sam curled up around him and jammed her fangs into his neck. A violent twist tore his head off. She held on to the gory thing by its jaw as its cloaked body fell silent.

"Behind you!" Edgar said.

Three men moved up behind her. Shots rang out. Sam jerked backwards, grabbing her waist before she fell to a knee. I didn't think. I jumped. Three stories straight down. The air felt dead around me, my resolve iron. Three feet from one of the bastards I screamed, "*Impadda!*" He had time to raise his eyes before he broke like a deer on the front of a semi.

My gun came up and killed another man, one I hadn't seen closing on Sam.

"*Inimicus Dele—*" the third didn't get to finish. A lance of light struck down from above, piercing his skull.

I dove away as the fourth man opened fire on me. Something tugged on my pants leg, but I kept moving, angling around a rack of clothes. I was moving for Sam when I heard the hiss of a rocket followed by the wet crunch of a watermelon meeting a sledge hammer. I glanced back to find a bomb lance protruding from the necromancer's face. He fell backwards slowly, and then the lance detonated. It sent a grisly, burnt rain into air around us.

I slid up beside Sam and rolled her over. She winced, bleeding like a stuck pig on blood thinners.

"Shit, why isn't that closing up?"

"Need blood."

"You okay?" Dad asked as he came up beside us. "Oh hell, Sam. You're bleeding everywhere."

"Use me, sis," I said as I rolled my sleeve back.

"No," she whispered. "You're already bleeding. Ankle."

I glanced down at my jeans. The tug I'd felt earlier. I pulled up the cuff and stared at the grazed bullet wound.

"That was close," Dad said.

"Shit." It was still bleeding, but I didn't think it wasn't bad enough not to help Sam.

"Me then," Dad said. "If she needs blood, she can have mine."

Someone grunted and it was followed by a loud thump. Dragging sounds accompanied Edgar and Zola's arrival. Zola's hands were wound around the hood of a necromancer. He looked young for Philip's crew, mid-thirties and a bit pudgy.

"Snack time," Zola said as she foisted the unconscious man on to Sam.

Sam frowned, a slight hesitation as she glanced between me and Dad before she wrenched the man's neck back and bit into his jugular. He'd never wake up again. The rivers of blood from Sam's chest slowed almost immediately. A small knot untied itself in my gut.

"We would have shot him anyway," Edgar said.

"Yep," I said. I can only assume he was trying to justify feeding someone to my sister. "Where is she, sis?"

Sam pointed to the customer service counter as something inhuman screamed and wailed back in the courtyard with Mike and Belphegor.

Dad offered his hand and picked me up. His left arm was soaked in blood. A thin red slit showed through his coat. I hadn't even noticed it.

"How bad?" I asked.

He glanced at the arm. "Done worse to myself with a fillet knife."

The memory came back to me. Mom had freaked the hell out when he came in from the garage one day, the tip of his middle finger in a paper towel. All he said was "Who wants to take a field trip to the hospital?"

"You okay here?" I asked Sam.

She nodded.

"I'll stay," Edgar said.

"Thanks," I said as Sam rolled her eyes.

"I found her!" Foster said as he zipped into the group. "Sam was right on, she's behind the customer service desk."

We broke into a run. Dad led the group as we wove between clothing racks and came out into the aisle leading to customer service. Another roar and what sounded like a small explosion followed us from the outer courtyard.

I didn't hear the incantation, but a burst of lightning lanced out from the corner of the hall. Dad slid to the side, ramming a shelf full of Godiva chocolate and triggering a cascade of metal and glass shelving. I was firing without hesitation, the barrel on the pepperbox rotating with each flash and thunderclap as I sent bullets screaming through the wall.

Foster dive-bombed the wall and exploded into his full height a foot away from it. His sword slid through the barrier like butter. There was the start of a scream, followed by a choking gurgle.

We rounded the corner. Mom was on the other side of a counter, beaten and bloodied. Her expression settled somewhere between hope and disbelief as she saw me and Dad come in. Dad saw her and his face hardened. He turned back to the hallway, to the dying man trying to push away from us with his feet while he held a hand over the blood pouring from his neck.

"You goddamned mother fucker," he snarled as he raised the butt of the whaling gun to his shoulder. The bomb lance hit with enough force to fling the necromancer to the back of the hall and put him through a door before it exploded.

"Nudd be damned," Foster said. "Those things sure are inconsistent."

Dad smiled as he lowered the cannon. I hoped I'd never see a look like that on his face again.

The fire alarm went off as we all gathered around Mom. Sprinkler heads sprayed stagnant water that felt slimy and stank like rust mixed with rotted eggs.

"Damn, that burns," Foster said as he snapped back into his small form and buried himself in Zola's hood. "Steel pipes, must be rusting."

"You okay?" I asked as I scooted up beside Zola.

"I'm good," Foster said. "Oh, you mean your mom." He laughed to himself.

Dad pulled a folded knife out of his pocket as Mom reached for him with her bound hands, clutching him as if to confirm he was real. The antlers of some unfortunate beast were attached to the knife handle. He pulled the blade out and started sawing through her bonds. Layers of nylon rope had been used. Her wrists were bruised and burned. Her raven hair would soon be matched by a swelling black eye. The blue eyes peering out from her thin face were a stark contrast. She'd been hit more than once, and the discoloration was a brutal contrast to her pale skin. My own hands started to shake and Zola hung her head.

"Ah'm sorry, Andi," Zola said. "Ah'm so sorry."

Dad finished cutting her bonds and pulled her close. She threw her arms around him and lost it utterly. My own cheeks were wet from more than the sprinklers as she sobbed into his shoulder. The back of her shirt was broken open and the white cloth was red. A whip? A blade? Something far deeper than mere rage took up residence in my gut.

"He has to die, Zola," I said.

"For this?" she said as she looked at Mom. "Ah would kill my own brother."

I heard a shout from outside the room. "Mom! Is she okay?"

"Is … is that Sam?" Mom asked, her voice shaky between sobs.

"Let's go see the grumpy vampire," I said as I pushed the dripping wet hair out of my eyes. Mom smiled, and I wished she'd never stop smiling. Dad helped me pull her to her feet and I put my arm around her shoulders, careful to avoid the wounds on her back.

"Get me out of this sprinkler crap and I'll heal her," Foster muttered. "Feels like I have a sunburn, and I don't get sunburns!"

Dad and I smiled slightly at the fairy, but Mom just looked at us, bewildered.

"She can't hear him?" Dad asked as he looked across at me.

I shook my head.

"Hear who?"

"A friend," I said.

"We'll fix that later," Foster said. "Just get me out of the damn rain."

We are here, Happy's voice thundered through my brain.

CHAPTER TWENTY

"They're here," I said. "Happy and Vicky."

"Good, Ah don't know how long Mike can keep that up," Zola said as she rabbited over the counter and landed beside Mom.

"How are you?"

"Zola?" she asked, bewilderment obvious on her face. "What are you doing here?"

"The boy would never let me live it down if you were eaten by zombies." Zola smiled and put her arm around Mom. "Come, let's get you out of here. Ah'm sure Sam's worried."

"Sam's here too?"

I smiled at them both. It's easy to forget how lucky you are to know the people in your life. Almost losing Sam once, and now Mom, were hellish reminders of that. We walked back outside the customer service area. Sam was still attached to the necromancer. I was glad to see Vik crouched beside her.

"Good to the last drop?" I asked.

Vik let out a low laugh.

Sam looked up, her eyes glancing around the group. She smiled and pushed the body to the side as she stood up. Sam wiped her mouth with one of the few dry spots on her sweater. She was a tower of gore.

"Better?" I asked.

"Much."

"Sam, what happened?" Mom asked, instantly transforming from victim to mother hen as she blotted Sam's face and looked at the holes and the rivers of red marring her clothes. She fussed over Sam as Zola stepped up beside them.

"Where's Edgar?" Zola asked.

"He went to help Mike when the holes …" she glanced at Mom and changed whatever she was about to say. "When I got better."

"Good, that's good."

"I am going to assist Edgar," Vik said as he ran his thumb over the amulet Zola had given him.

Zola nodded as he left. "Dimitry, stay with Sam and Andi. Damian, come with me. We have issues to resolve."

"No, we have balls to cut off," Foster grumbled from Zola's hood. "Not issues, balls. To cut off."

Zola drew my staff and rapped it on the wet tiles. "You have a way with words."

I bent down and kissed my mom's head.

"Be careful," she said.

"Always," I said as Foster and Sam both looked up at me with something like disbelief.

A burst of flame from the front of the store set us in motion. No words, just movement, running up the escalator, back to the same floor as the carousel. The murk was thinner, but it was vomiting red light, pouring across the floor as it began to climb the walls in spasms and arcs.

"It won't hurt you," Zola said.

"Okay," I said, really wanting to believe her as I glanced into the burning remnants of the wing to our right.

"Start of a hellgate." She answered the question I hadn't asked. The pepperbox was in my right hand, the focus in my left, as soon as we cleared the sprinklers.

Foster climbed out of her cloak. "Mike!" he said as he drew his sword and started forward, growing into his full size. Mike's hammer was a beacon in the darkness. Sweeping lines of flame followed him through the shadows as he struck and parried Belphegor. His face was cut, showing a huge gash, leaking black blood, from his left temple to his chin.

As we got closer, I could see him wobbling. His legs were unsteady and bloodied. Belphegor was moving in for a kill, the tentacles of his right arm intertwined with a shadowy scimitar. His left slid a silver tooth out of his face and it dimmed and grew into a matching blade. I stumbled a step, wondering what the hell I was looking at.

"Damian, save him!" The scream was right beside me. The little necromancer's cry punched through into our reality without me having to focus at all.

My gun snapped to the demon and I pulled the second trigger on the pepperbox. All six barrels fired, perforating Belphegor and knocking him to the ground. Mike fell to one knee, breathing hard.

"I can't beat him," he said between gasps.

"Foster, get him out of here!" I said.

"But—" he started, but I just pointed at Mike and put myself between him and the demon.

Belphegor chuckled as he righted himself. "The Smith cannot win, little boy. You have no hope."

I dropped a speed loader into the pepperbox and snapped it closed before I smiled. "Ah, but I have friends."

Zola shouted. "*Modus Glaciatto!*" The air froze and a torrent of razor-sharp hail swarmed Belphegor. The demon grunted and stumbled as wicked bits of ice tore into his body. A fluid that stank of roadkill and decay began to leak from the demon's wounds.

Vicky came through the skylight, scattering glass and steel in her wake. She still looked like a child, small and lanky, but her spirit showed color now. Her hair shone a less translucent blonde and the jacket she wore was almost identical to my own black bomber. I wondered how she'd changed clothes, incorporeal as she was. Then it started. Flames burst from her shoulders and raced down to the fists crossed before her body. The scream that followed bore the rage of a thousand broken children.

Belphegor's head snapped up and he started to slither away.

"Demon!" Vicky's voice thundered like a god, and it stopped Belphegor dead.

He spun and his arm struck out toward Vicky. She grabbed the mass of tentacles in midair as she cracked the floor with her landing, and where her fiery hands touched the demon, it was destroyed, bits of fire and ash bursting from his wounds. Belphegor screamed. The harmonized wail sent shivers across my entire body like a fork scraping a plate, only infinitely louder and far, far more disturbing.

I watched her. My gun hung uselessly at my side, and I knew the only weapon I could raise against that monster was a soulart. God, but I didn't want to touch Belphegor's aura.

The remaining tentacles of the demon's right arm lashed out and knocked Vicky's legs out from under her. She grunted as she landed hard. The demon ran, his legs unraveling into dozens more tentacles and propelling him through the north wing of the mall with astounding speed. Vicky was on her feet a second later, running down the demon. I followed.

"It's strong," Mike said as he swooped in beside me.

"You already healing?" I asked.

"The hellgate," he said as he grimaced. "It helped."

"At least it did something useful," I said as we entered the next courtyard. There was a smoking hole in the gate for Dillard's.

"It's strengthening Belphegor too," Foster said as he glided between us. "He's taking her back there, Damian."

"Back where?" Mike asked.

"Where she died," I spat. "Bloody hell, what's that going to do to her?"

"No," Mike said. "She can't handle that."

The certainty in his voice made my eyes burn. I didn't have the heart to ask him what would happen. Vicky. Goddammit, we'd already been too late to save her once.

"We won't be too late again," Foster said. I must have spoken my thoughts out loud, or the fairy was reading my mind.

We cleared the melted gate. I could feel the heat emanating from the metal, and then the battle came into view. So fast, strikes and counterstrikes, lunges, screams, and bursts of ash.

I saw them go over the edge then, a writhing explosion of darkness and flame, falling to the basement, falling beside the door that led to garage as we ran through the smoldering remains of the perfume department. Wretched smells of melted plastics and superheated beauty supplies gagged me.

"Vicky!" I screamed as she vanished from my line of sight. "Stay strong kid, we're here!" None of us hesitated as we reached the railing. Mike and I hurdled it, breaking the tiles as we landed twenty feet below, me with a sparking shield and Mike with the Smith's Hammer. Foster went into a straight nosedive, sweeping past us and drawing his sword in one smooth motion.

The fairy came down behind Vicky. Belphegor was hunched over in front of the dark-tinted glass doors, shattered crystal and dinnerware strewn all around him. A halo of fire lit Vicky's entire body and every step burned the floor, melting the stone beneath her.

Belphegor looked the child up and down, cradling the charred stump of his left arm. "Destroyer," he hissed.

"No, demon. I am one of the Ghost Pack," she said, her voice low and dangerous, entirely wrong emanating from a kid. "I am a Harrower!" She snapped her wrist forward, pointing with the middle and index fingers on her right hand. It looked like one of Zola's spells. A roaring spiral of flame erupted from her forearm and blasted Belphegor through the doors. Glass and steel and the demon screamed as one.

Vicky stalked forward, paying the burning metal as much mind as I would a mosquito. Belphegor was still moving. More of his body was gone and a trail of ash followed him as he dragged himself closer to the edge of the garage.

"Vicky, left!" I shouted as the demon picked up a car with its remaining tentacles. I was only a few steps behind her, but I couldn't do a thing. I saw her eyes widen as she turned left and the car smacked her across the garage in a barrel roll of vehicular carnage. The demon started laughing, only to retreat as Mike started to run him down. And then I saw where Vicky had landed.

She was frozen on her hands and knees, staring at the place Foster had eviscerated the vampire that had killed her. Killed her in so many ways.

"Kid, come on," I said. "Move!"

She started to turn to me, and then Ezekiel was suddenly there, materializing in a haze of black beside Vicky as he moved to strike. "Little lamb," he said as he struck her so hard and so fast I'd barely even registered he'd joined the fight.

Vicky's head rebounded off the ground from the force of the blow. She rolled to the side in a vain effort to escape Ezekiel. She groaned and put her hands over her face, blood pouring from her forehead.

"What the fuck, she's bleeding?" I said.

Ezekiel raised his foot to strike Vicky again. I raised my gun at the same time.

"No!" Foster screamed as he swooped in on Ezekiel. The necromancer unleashed a black beam of I can only imagine what. Foster dodged left and scored a hit on the bastard's arm with a fully extended sword. Foster slid to a stop beside Vicky.

Ezekiel glanced at the gash on his arm and then summoned a shield. Only it wasn't just a shield. It flashed out and smashed

Vicky and Foster against the far wall with the force of a tsunami. The pair fell limply to the ground as Ezekiel turned back to the rest of us.

"Damian," said a muffled voice. Vicky's voice. "Damian!" The terrified little girl cried out to me as she bled in the corner.

"You son of a bitch!" I pulled the second trigger, six bullets sparked against another shield as Ezekiel took stock of his resistance.

"I am untouchable," he said in that dead, papery voice.

"Tyranno Eversiotto!" The lightning burned as it left my hand, channeling so much power from the ley lines the hair on my arm began to smoke. Ezekiel's shield began to crack as bolt after bolt crashed into the translucent surface. His eyes widened slightly as the blue sparks began to dim and the shield gave way in a puff of static. He looked irritated as the last bit of the spell got through and hit him in the right leg.

"I'll kill you last," he said as he brushed out the small fire on his cloak. "For that insult."

Happy made himself known then, phasing through the wall beside Vicky and closing his jaws on Ezekiel's shoulder. The bastard just grunted as Happy flung him out of the garage into a rolling heap. Belphegor was outside with Mike, each looking beat down and exhausted. Mike's shoulders were slumped, but he still shifted to block Belphegor as Happy bounded after Ezekiel. Ezekiel rolled and flung out his left arm, smashing Happy across the parking lot with a fierce backhand.

Belphegor lashed out at Mike, knocking the Smith's Hammer out of his grip as I moved to help him. Mike gave a shaky hop backwards to dodge the next strike and I cut in front of him, a soulsword forged without a thought. Belphegor's legs came off with one sweep of that blazing sword and I screamed bloody murder as visions of the demon's circle of hell seared my brain. Women and children, skinned and hung and beaten to death atop their own fathers and husbands. The terror of war paled compared to the sight of families killing their own, not knowing it until their "enemy" died by their own hand, and then being struck senseless by the knowledge, only to be killed and resurrected by a demon so it could start all over again. I retched as the visions of torture and war etched themselves into my brain. I tried to stand—having fallen to my knees without realizing it—wanting to move in for a kill and then take down Ezekiel, but the Old Man beat me to it.

He came down on Ezekiel from the sky. It took me a second to realize the Old Man must have jumped from the top of the building. Something flashed over his right arm, a jagged bark-like darkness. It only took a split second to know where I'd seen it before: the skin of a gravemaker. Only it was the Old Man's skin.

Claws erupted from that darkness, striking Ezekiel across the back. Ezekiel grimaced and spun away, revealing four slashes through the back of his cloak. He gestured with his right hand, a simple flip of the wrist, much like Boonville, and a thousand dead things sprang into the air at his whim, shattering the pavement they rose through and forming a smoky cloud of death above us.

"No," the Old Man said, both his arms covered in rough tree bark. He clapped his clawed arms together and it felt like a bomb went off. My vision shook as the shockwave of power reached me. Ezekiel's flood of necromancy simply cut off. Everything under his control dropped to the broken asphalt. Animal corpses and skeletons and even ancient human bones clattered unceremoniously back to earth.

"This is done!" I barely recognized my Dad's voice. The rage and emotion boiling out of him turned it into a war cry. My eyes found him in time to see his finger pull the trigger. Mom and Zola and Sam stood behind him, and I wondered what the hell they were doing out there. The bomb lance shot forward like a rocket.

A smoking rocket that screamed and cried and groaned in a thousand maniacal voices. Belphegor's mouth opened but whatever the demon was about to say or do was lost as the bomb lance punched into his blackened and burned chest.

His red eyes widened as his teeth fractured and shattered and he screamed. A scream never meant for the ears of the living. I fell back to my knees, hands over my head trying to shield myself from that shrill cry. The cry I'd heard when I'd touched him with a soulsword. The shock hit me a moment later. I'd used the focus, I shouldn't have had any visions, any knowing, when I struck Belphegor. The explosion was almost quiet. A little pop and Belphegor was thrown to the four winds in streamers of fire.

Ezekiel stared at the fading fires of Belphegor's impromptu pyre before he turned back to the Old Man. "I'd like to know how you did that. I think I'll rip it from your mind." His left hand curled up and the Old Man started sliding forward, propelled by an unseen force. As I raised my Sight I could just barely make out that force. Wisps of black and red power swirled around the Old Man's aura. The Old Man crossed his arms and laughed. Laughed from his gut as he threw back his head in what seemed like an unending, inevitable procession.

"You want me closer, Ezekiel?" he said. "You only had to ask." His right arm thickened in my vision, claws growing and sparking with a dim yellow glow.

"A soulart?" I muttered to myself.

The Old Man cut the black power around him with a simple arc drawn through the air. Ezekiel stumbled backwards, staring at his hands. His face bore no expression. He was still dead inside, for all I could tell. He almost missed the Old Man's attack.

Claws slashed out, sending explosions of lightning toward Ezekiel as the Old Man closed the gap. Ezekiel threw up a shield to parry a golden beam of power. His lips slowly curled into a grin.

"You mean to kill me." That dead, papery voice crawled its way into my head.

"I *will* kill you," the Old Man snarled. The canyons and shadows of his skin flared up to cover his neck. He paused then, taking a deep breath and the bark-like texture receded to his arms.

"You don't have the power. You've never had the power to kill me. I was worshipped. You are a maggot unfit to grace a beggar's corpse." Ezekiel bowed his head a fraction of an inch and pushed forward with both hands. His cloak blew backwards as a wall of fire, bristling with red and orange and blue flames, enveloped the Old Man. The ley lines in the area bent, drawn into the maelstrom.

I watched it happen or I wouldn't have believed it. The Old Man opened his mouth and *consumed* the fire as though he was a demon himself. The Old Man took a step forward. An explosion of necromancy followed. All the dead things Ezekiel had called rose into the air, crying for blood, screaming their allegiance to the man. The man who freed them from the monster. It was a power I'd felt. It whispered and called to me. It was a power I knew.

I remembered.

It was the power that had flooded me before I killed Prosperine.

It was the Old Man.

The realization staggered me. I watched, partially aware of the soulsword in the Old Man's grasp, the union of the dead, the auras, the souls. But the rest of my mind was back at Stone's River. Back in the vision: the dying man, his family tied down and slaughtered on his back so he'd feel the blood of his own children running into the ground.

That hadn't been Belphegor's circle of hell. That had been the Old Man's memories.

Ezekiel, he had been there. He stood by and watched. He gave the order. What wouldn't a man do to take revenge on an atrocity like that? "Gods, no."

The Old Man lunged and laid open a huge section of Ezekiel's leg. Ezekiel cauterized his own wound in an instant as he spun and countered.

Something flung me to the ground as lightning cracked over my head. I rolled my head to the side to find Zola.

"What?" I said slowly, seeing her lips move, but not fully comprehending her words.

"Ah said, get the fuck down, boy!"

"It was Ezekiel," I said. "Ezekiel killed his family. He raped his … his … while they were … oh my god."

"What?" Zola said. "What are you talking …" and then her face twisted into an expression of utter horror. "Christ, that's what he never told me. He's going to lose control. This fight has to stop." She was up on her feet and running at the fight full speed. I could have sworn she shouted a name, but he paid no mind. "Old Man! You have to stop!"

He may not have looked, but Ezekiel did. The strike that followed laid his chest open, the wet white glint of bone exposed to the night air. The Old Man followed with a quick stab to the bastard's chest.

Ezekiel raised his arm and an explosion of wind sent the Old Man and Zola into the air. I was fast enough to get beneath Zola, breaking her fall, but the Old Man hit hard several yards away. He was laughing.

Ezekiel vomited blood, hands sealed over his chest as he stared at the Old Man. Something between disbelief and absolute rage crawled over his face. He never saw the panda bear storming in behind him.

Happy wrapped his jaws around Ezekiel's waist, shook his head like a rabid dog, and flung Ezekiel further into the parking lot. Ezekiel rolled to a stop with a shout of surprise. I stared as he slowly rose to one knee, holding a hand over the worst of his wounds and the blood staining his dark cloak.

"We are not done," he said, a small spark lighting in his voice.

"Not until you're dead," the Old Man said.

For the second time, I watched the chaff of a gravemaker rise up and then vanish with Ezekiel, leaving no traces behind.

"*No!*" the Old Man shouted. "No." He stared at the vacant patch in the dirt and debris where Ezekiel stood a moment before. He kicked at a smear of blood and sighed as the ley lines around him gradually resumed their natural flow.

Mike picked his hammer up and slid the innocuous-looking tool into the loop of leather on his belt.

"Where's Dell?" Mike asked. "I thought you were travelling together."

"I sent Dell to your shop, Damian," the Old Man said as he looked my way. The rough, dark carapace slowly slid back into his skin, leaving nothing behind but a mosaic of blood to trace the lines of his scars.

"Thank you," I said as I ran back into the garage. Foster was there, his wing bent at an odd angle, but he was up. Vicky was cradled against his chest, showing no signs of the power she'd been wielding.

"You okay, Vicky?"

She glanced up and forced a little smile before immediately breaking down into tears. She pushed off Foster and ran over to me, bawling. I picked her up. She was heavy and she felt as real as Nixie or Sam or any one of us. Vicky buried her face in my neck.

"It's okay. We'll get you out of here."

Edgar was waiting in the destroyed doorway, Vik just behind him. "The Watchers are on their way. We need to move."

CHAPTER TWENTY-ONE

I glanced back at the burning ruin of Chesterfield Mall in the rearview. Black smoke rose against the fading light, lit from below by the fires that birthed it.

"Edgar, can you really cover this up?" I asked.

He rubbed his hand over his forehead. "I don't know. All the employees are dead. The few Cleaners we could send found them in one of the theaters. I'll spare you the details."

"How many?" I asked.

"It wasn't just employees," Edgar said.

"How many?" Foster said from his perch on Vicky's shoulder.

Edgar sighed and lowered his head. "Not in front of the girl."

"Tell me," Vicky said. "I want to know how bad they really are."

How bad? As far as I was concerned, the whole lot of them just needed to be put down. Philip, Zachariah, Ezekiel, kill them all.

"Damn," Edgar whispered. "Damn them," he said as his voice started to rise. "Damn it all to hell! A hundred and sixty-one." He said it so fast, but his words hung in the air, choking us all into silence.

My heart sank, and that's a goddamned understatement. "A hundred and … and what?"

Sam cursed. Vicky tried to say something but her voice cracked. She tried to hold her tears down to a muffled sob, but she broke into a wailing cry a moment later.

"Sorry, girl," Edgar said as he reached up and squeezed her arm.

Vicky undid her seatbelt and crawled into the backseat beside Sam, snuggling up beside the vampire and shaking in her arms.

Foster cursed from his new perch on the dashboard. He unsheathed his sword halfway and then slammed the blade home with a metallic smack. "We kill them all."

Silence reigned the rest of the drive. One hundred and sixty-one people dead. And for what? Some kind of perverted temper tantrum by the world's scariest necromancer? My knuckles paled to white on the steering wheel as I took the exit back to the shop.

We pulled in right behind Zola in the small rear parking lot. I took a deep breath before stepping out of the car. Everyone was already out and headed to the shop. Sam carried Foster on her shoulder, walking closer to Mom. I was relieved to see Mom looked whole again. I stepped up the pace a little and hurried to the back door.

"You look like you're having a fine day," the little face on the lower deadbolt said.

I pulled my leg back and swung my foot like a punter. The deadbolt screamed and cursed and slid open with a crack.

"Calm down, Damian!" Mom snapped. "There is no need to break things."

I looked back and started to explain the deadbolt until I remembered she couldn't even see it. Instead I just nodded and fixed a small smile on my face as we walked inside.

Bubbles came pounding down the stairs as Peanut tried to shoot beneath the saloon doors. I sighed and tried to go limp as the miniature-pony-sized cu siths began to bat us back and forth with tongues and well-meaning hip rubs.

"They're adorable!" my mom said. She started gushing out some string of incoherent baby talk a moment later and I started to worry.

She crouched down between Bubbles and Peanut, scratching one's stomach and the other's scruff. They, in turn, were giving her a growling, purring approval.

Dad watched as Mom played with the bristly green and black cu siths. Peanut happily flopped his braided tail from one side of the room to the other.

"They've grown more," Edgar said, crouching down to scratch Peanut's neck.

"Bubbles!" Ashley called from the front of the shop. "Peanut!" Both the cu siths vanished through the doorway in a symphony of claws on hardwood.

We filtered in behind the pups as Frank came out from behind the counter.

"Frank," I said as I extended my hand and traded grips. "Glad to see the place is still standing."

"For now," he said as Sam pulled him away into a rib-cracking hug.

Dell was already there, standing beside Ashley. He nodded to me and resumed his conversation with the witch. Ashley laughed and curled a lock of hair behind her ear.

"Tell him," Dell said.

Ashley's eyes moved from Dell to me. "The video is out of control Damian," she said as she turned to me. "The Watchers can't shut it down. There aren't … one of the Cleaners told us their Mage Machina are dead."

I nodded. "Edgar thought that might be the way of things." I rubbed my face and glanced toward the back room. "I need to run upstairs for a minute," I said. "Check something in the Black Book."

"That thing gives me the creeps," Sam said as she dragged Frank into the back and settled onto the couch beside Mom.

"Me too," Frank said from the other side of the saloon-style doors. "I can't pick it up without getting goose bumps."

"I want to come with you," Vicky said.

I smiled and held my hand out. She grabbed it and squeezed with both hands, wrapping thin fingers around my palm. I started to lead her through the back.

"Damian, who is that girl?" Mom asked.

The grandfather clock ticked once, twice, and more in the following silence.

"You can see her?" I asked.

"Of course I can see her," she said with a huff. "She's right there."

"Umm, this is Vicky."

I locked eyes with Zola. She glanced away, returned my gaze, and then shrugged. "Ah'll think on it."

I nodded and started to turn away before I remembered one other thing.

"Oh, Ashley?" I said

She looked up. "Yeah?"

"I think Edgar may want to talk to you about something called 'The Blade of the Stone.'"

I saw her stiffen and then she slowly scratched her neck. "Figured that might come up. Mike said something?"

"Mmhmm." I flashed her a grin as I led Vicky up the stairs. I heard footsteps coming up behind us and turned to find the Old Man. He nodded and we continued up.

It felt good to step onto the carpet and take shelter between the aisles of books. An old friend was sitting in the circle near the far wall, studying an ancient grimoire we'd come to know as the Black Book. The circle was set with wards, giving ghosts just enough power to interact with the physical world if I gave them a 'key,' as Ward called it. I had a few ghosts I now considered regulars.

"Koda," I said with a nod to the ghost at the reading table. His cowl was shifted back slightly on his bald head. He adjusted his grayish cloak as we came closer. His order wore brown in life, but his cloak would be gray now until his ghost was no more.

"Damian," he said as he turned the page of the Black Book and shook his head. The movement caused a string of oversized prayer beads to sway from his neck, each bead bearing a different rune. "This is a grave tome. A threat to us all."

Vicky jerked on my arm as we got closer to the old ghost. I glanced back at her.

"What is it, kiddo?"

"Where did you get that?" she asked.

"What? The book? Frank got it from Vassili in a trade. Not sure where Vassili got it."

"I have to go." She started to pull away from my hand.

"You've no reason to fear me, child," Koda said.

Vicky paused and smiled. "It's not you. I've seen that book. It shouldn't be here."

"And where should it be?" Koda asked, his sallow cheeks lifted by a small smile.

"It should be in the Burning Lands."

"Go," the Old Man said from behind us. "The Ghost Pack should know."

Vicky nodded and ran back down the stairs. I could hear every footfall and a thump as she skipped the last three steps.

I closed my eyes and pushed my aura out. I could almost see it racing through the streets of Saint Charles, across the Missouri River and down the highways. *Happy, Vicky needs you.*

I am coming. His voice rattled my brain, his speech a low and powerful growl.

I opened my eyes and looked at the Old Man. "What's your name?"

His lips quirked and the scars around them followed. I'd hardly call it a smile. "Old Man is fine." He started toward the circle, passing the floor-to-ceiling bookshelves and pausing briefly before a small section on Roman occultism.

I settled into one of the overstuffed leather chairs and the Old Man did the same, seating himself below a small bookshelf mounted to the wall beside Koda. He stared at the floor, and it took me a moment to realize what he was looking at.

"Those are old wards," he said.

"They aren't all that old," I said. "We only put them in a few months ago."

The Old Man let out a little laugh. "What do you know about wards, boy?"

I shrugged. "A bit."

"As I thought. Your master laid these wards, and I'm fairly sure of where she learned them."

"Actually, Ward laid them," I said, thinking of the same man who had designed Zola's hidden chest.

"Interesting," the Old Man said as he glanced up at me. "Let's see what our friend has learned."

"Friend, you say?" Koda said with one raised eyebrow as he closed the book. "I do enjoy your boldness."

"When you're as old as I am, you'll have little time for anything else."

"Oh, I think you know I'm quite a bit older than you," Koda said.

"Did you find anything?" I asked as I leaned forward, my eyes locked on Koda's.

He cupped his chin and nodded. "There is nothing in here to label you a dark necromancer. The use of a soulart is nothing more than an art. I remember times when they were not so uncommon, but I did believe them to be damning. Now, I think they may have been forbidden for another reason."

"It is what you *do* with the soulart that makes you a dark necromancer," the Old Man said as heavy, deliberate footfalls started up the stairs. "But that is the case with any art. Stop worrying about Pinkerton's accusations, boy."

I leaned back in the chair and stared at the black book. "I'm trying."

"Pinkerton's not long for this world," Koda said. "Not with Adannaya out for blood."

I nodded agreement, but I wasn't sure. I'd seen her balk at killing Philip already. Maybe now. Maybe he'd gone so far off the deep end she'd do it as an act of mercy.

"Have faith, Damian. Your master will not shirk her duty. She is no Sunday Soldier."

A broad-shouldered silhouette appeared at the end of the aisle. The light brought his face into focus as he came closer, flat lines and soft eyes beneath his black hair. Hugh smiled as he nodded to each of us and sat down in the last chair.

"You are nothing like him, Damian," Hugh said as he pushed the thick braids in his hair behind his shoulders.

"You heard that?" I asked.

The werewolf nodded.

I glanced at Koda, and then back to Hugh. "Part of me knows all of you are right," I said as I tapped my foot. "But look at what I did. Throwing around soularts and controlling a gravemaker? Wielding a soulsword? It's what Zola has *always* taught me a dark necromancer would do. I just ..."

"Enough," Hugh said. "You did these things to protect your friends. To avenge your friends. Had you not acted, we would likely all be dead. Alan still talks about the battle with Prosperine." Hugh steepled his fingers and leaned forward. "He tells everyone we were wrong about necromancers, that some are good and some are evil, just like the rest of us."

A small smile formed on my face.

"And you know something? He is right. Do not judge yourself so harshly."

The Old Man let out a low laugh like he was choking on a bag of gravel. "Listen to the wolf. If there's a dark necromancer at this table, it's me."

Hugh held up his hand. "Before I forget," he said. "I am glad to see you intact after your encounter with the Piasa Bird."

"About that," I said as I looked at the Old Man and then back to Hugh. I stuck my thumb out at our scarred compatriot. "He scratched its neck like it was a pet."

"Ah, indeed." Hugh smiled and leaned back, lacing his fingers over his stomach. "Even gods have friends."

I waited. And waited a bit more. "That's it?" I asked.

"It's not why I'm here. Though the awakening of the Old Gods is a dire thought, there are more immediate concerns. Foster, would you please get Edgar, Zola, and the vampires?"

A cough sounded from above us. I glanced up to find Foster crouched on the edge of the top shelf near the high ceiling. "Sure thing," he said as he took flight with a sheepish grin.

"We have a problem," Hugh said. "And it's not only a werewolf problem, or a vampire problem. That recording, of the blood mage and Ashley and the rest of you." He bowed his head over his interlaced fingers and rubbed his thumbs over his eyebrows. "I've already spoken to everyone who was here."

"Technology," the Old Man grumbled. "More advanced ways of killing each other. That's all it has ever been."

"There is truth in your words," Koda said, "but you should not always ignore the fantastic in favor of the evil before you."

The Old Man stared at the old ghost. "I have seen evil beyond anything you can conceive. I have fought it. I have killed it. I have lost everything I am to it. Do not think to lecture me."

Koda smiled a huge smile as he rubbed a prayer bead between his fingers. "You would have enjoyed Sherman as much as Adannaya enjoyed Sheridan. Sherman was bleak, dedicated, and teetering on the edge of reason."

"I rather liked General Sherman," the Old Man said. "I was there."

Hugh raised his eyebrows slightly, and I'm sure my own surprise was far less subtle. Koda took it in stride.

"I will always wonder if there was another way," Koda said. "But those men gave their orders a long time ago, and it cannot be changed now."

"There is always another way," the Old Man said. "There's not always a better way. I rode in the First Alabama. I was there. I took part in the march."

Zola snorted from the end of the aisle, Edgar, Sam, and Vik trailed behind her with Foster and Aideen fluttering above them.

"'Ah was there'," Zola said with a laugh as she came up beside Koda's chair. "No need to be coy. There were times you *were* the march."

The Old Man took a deep breath and nodded. "I know what you mean, but let's not reminisce on those times."

"I was there too," Mike said as he followed the others up the stairs. His gaze trailed to the shadow standing just outside the circle of wards.

I focused, only a bit, and the little necromancer came into view. She waved, curling her fingers a couple times near her cheek. I waved back and nodded to Mike when he smiled. She'd died in the south, in Mike's arms. I wondered if it was during the march.

"Hugh?" the Old Man said.

The werewolf nodded and turned his chair a little so he could cast his gaze around our circle. "This is not an age for secrets. There is so much coverage of that fight, it's causing people to delve into decades' worth of archives. They're digging up other recordings. Things written off as hoaxes. A major effects house just released a statement saying they could find no evidence of CGI."

"Jesus, this has all happened in a day?" Sam asked.

"There will be a witch hunt unlike anything this world has seen," Hugh said.

"A witch hunt?" Edgar said. "The commoners will go to war with us. I always thought we'd be exposed because some idiot would blow up a city." He shook his head and frowned. "And now? We're being outed by a cell phone camera because Ezekiel killed our best Mage Machina?"

"Yes," Hugh said. Silence hung in the room.

"I have to go back," Edgar said. "I have to consult with the Watchers." He paused and turned his attention to Koda. "It's good to see you again."

Koda nodded. "And you."

"Edgar," Vik said. "You know we cannot focus solely on this footage. It has been viewed by millions. It's beyond the Watchers' power now, but Philip and Ezekiel are raising demons. If they loose a beast from one of the lower circles …" He paused and shook his head. "Gods, a war with the commoners will be the least of our worries."

"Philip will gather whatever forces he has left," Aideen said. "He'll use them as a distraction to evade Ezekiel or as an offensive force against us."

"He will use them against us," Zola said. "He will strike where it will hurt me the most. Where Ah have fond memories of my student, my family, and him. Where we started a life together, and where it must come to an end.

"Coldwater."

CHAPTER TWENTY-TWO

"Foster?" Mom asked as she stared at the fairy. She'd heard a lot about Foster, especially from Sam, but she'd never actually seen him.

"Ma'am," he said in a horrendous cowboy drawl as he tipped a hat he didn't have.

Bubbles and Peanut scooted in front of her to perform countless hip bumps for more attention. Peanut got this bizarre shuffle-hop-shuffle motion going with his rear end.

"Wow," Mom said as she stared at the fairy. "It's so nice to meet you, Foster. I always thought you were just Sam's imaginary friend. Some kind of head trauma from becoming a vampire."

Dad laughed from behind the counter. "Head trauma," he muttered as he shook his own head.

"Head trauma is an apt description some days," Vik said.

"Cara, you do that?" I asked as the fairy glided past me. "Oh, and how's the Guardian?"

"Yes, I did that. There is no sense in your mother being blind to the things happening around her. The Guardian is fine, or I wouldn't be back already, obviously."

"Sometimes ignorance is bliss," Vik said as he scooted around me and headed for the front door.

"You can't argue that," Frank said as he held his arm out to Sam. She wrapped her own around his and leaned her head on his shoulder.

"Please," Sam said. "Damian tries to argue with werewolves and vampires. Why not argue with a perfectly logical statement?"

"Yeah, well that runs in the family, Sam," Foster said as he settled on the counter.

"I am going to talk to Vassili," Vik said as he pushed the front door open.

"Do you want me to come?" Sam asked.

Vik paused and then said, "No, I do not know how he is going to react to this conversation. It is best if you stay here."

"You're a wise old vampire," Zola said as she leaned on the doorway to the back room.

"And you are ..." Vik smiled and coughed before he said, " ... old."

Zola let out a small laugh. It was good to see her smile, even now. They both waved as Vik left.

"Hugh?" I asked.

"Yes, Cub?"

"Is the pack going to be around for this?"

"I'm sorry, but we have another matter to attend."

"Another matter?" Edgar said. "What on earth could be more important than this? I mean no disrespect Hugh, but are you thinking this through?"

Hugh smiled and nodded slowly. "Yes, my friend. I have thought this through a great deal. We are meeting with two other packs. For a truce."

"A truce?" Edgar said as he scowled. "Yes, that's important, but we have to stop Philip. If we can't stop the damn video, we have to stop Philip."

"You are not wrong, but there is a greater battle looming." Hugh glanced at Zola and then returned his attention to Edgar. "I trust Zola. I trust her with my life, and if she believes Philip will attempt to destroy her home, I have no reason to doubt her.

She and our eclectic little clan have stopped him before. He will seek revenge, no matter how petty."

"That has nothing to do with a truce between packs," Edgar said with a quick flick of his right hand and a rising edge to his voice.

"No, it does not." Hugh crossed his arms and took a deep breath. "More important than Philip is the coming conflict with Ezekiel. We all know it's coming, but there are still questions we have no answers for. What will Ezekiel bring down on us? What creatures will we fight to save ourselves, to save our world? A truce with any pack is a boon. Without more allies, as we stand now, I doubt we can defeat him."

"I can kill him," the Old Man grumbled.

Hugh smiled. "Oh, I have no doubt you'd give him a good run, but this is not a time for chances and possibilities. We have to kill him. Philip must die, but when that is done, we must hunt down the God of Death, the man known as Ezekiel, the god named Anubis, and destroy him. And you, Amun-Ra, you will tell us how to kill an immortal."

Edgar's eyes narrowed. "This is no place for that name."

"Nudd. Be. Damned," Foster said as he plopped down on the counter beside Aideen, jaw slack. He glanced over at Cara. "Did you know?"

Cara just smiled.

"Ra?" Frank asked.

"The Sun God?" Mike said as his hand slid over the head of his hammer

"Lord of *truth*," Zola said with a bite to her words that shocked me.

The Old Man laughed. It started low and quiet and built into a bellowing thunder. "Lord of truth. Father of lies. Creator of wars."

Edgar sighed and his shoulders hunched forward.

"Your magic," I said. "It's all solar. You're a Mage *Solis*. Christ!"

"I am," Edgar said with a weary smile.

"You were Ra?" Sam said. "Or you are?"

"I was. A very long time ago."

"Not so long ago for some of us," the Old Man said. "If you had acted, if you had stopped that war, my family…" He curled his hands into fists until the scars on his knuckles were stark white.

"I am sorry," Edgar said as he plucked the bowler from his head and ran his fingers along the brim. "I regret much from those days."

"This was necessary," Hugh said. "Everyone in this room should know who you are." He glanced at my parents. "Well, almost everyone. Congratulations, you've met a god and will live to tell the tale."

Mom slowly scooted around the counter and slipped in beside my Dad. They whispered something and then my Dad gave her a huge hug. I did not want them to see this side of my world. This darker side where we made plans to kill, hoped to stay alive, and prayed all our friends would stay alive with us.

"How do you kill an immortal?" Aideen asked as she unsheathed her sword an inch and then slammed it home with a metallic ring. "I know how to kill many things, but not an immortal."

"Not many know how to kill us," Edgar said. "It's one of the reasons we became gods." He stared at his palms and frowned. "You may not know how to strike us down, but it is only the Fae who can kill us."

"I've heard no such stories," Cara said.

"There is only one story you need to worry about," Edgar said.

Two Blessings, bound as one

Twisted, tortured, burned upon earth

Purest flame, hammers fall

Darkest blade

Death's embrace

"You speak of the *splendorem mortem*," Mike said, his eyebrows creased and a frown pulled on the corners of his lips.

"I do."

"Madness," the smith said. "That kind of weapon could rend the fabric of the world's ley lines. Open the gates between the Burning Lands and this world."

"Or it could kill an immortal," Edgar said.

"Two Blessings," Cara said. "It is a weapon fashioned from two fairy Blessings?"

"Ezekiel is worse than Philip?" Ashley asked from the corner of the room beside the shelves of amber and gemstones.

"Yes, what of it, witch?" the Old Man said.

"What of it?" Ashley said as her lips peeled back like a wolf. "He has to die. After Philip's men …" Her hand trailed down to the nine tails on her hip. "After they hurt me, I came to understand many things about this world. If we don't protect ourselves, we cannot expect anyone to do it for us."

I almost choked on the guilt rising up in my throat as I sat down on the stool behind the counter. If Ashley hadn't known us, if we'd been there to help her … always the *ifs*. Foster saved her life, but—bloody hell—they broke her.

"I'm sorry," Foster said from the counter. "I let you down."

Aideen put her arm around him and whispered into his ear.

"Foster," Ashley said. "You didn't let me down. I *am* stronger because of it. I won't be so helpless ever again."

"But you were a green witch," he said in a small voice.

"It is still a part of me. It is still the best of me, but my coven will not fall victim to my weakness. My coven is my family, much as you have all become my family."

"Ashley is right," Cara said. "I do not know what consequences await the destruction of two Blessings, but Ezekiel has fouled the air with his very existence long enough."

"I will not make that abomination," Mike said. "You risk hell on earth to destroy one man."

"We may not have a choice," Edgar said. "Think on it. Ezekiel's death would make the world a safer place for your soul mate."

Mike frowned and glanced at the shadow beside him. He took a deep breath as his eyes slowly trailed back to Edgar. "I will think on it."

"I'm afraid we will all need to do more than 'think' before this battle is won," Hugh said. "And for that, I am sorry."

Something cold shot through the back of my pants. At first I thought I'd leaned up against some metal, but then it got worse.

"Dammit, what the hell?" I said as I leaned forward and rubbed my right ass cheek. It felt like I'd sat down on a small coaster made of ice. I stood up and glanced at the stool. Nothing.

"What is it?" Foster asked as he landed on my shoulder.

"I don't know. My ass got cold."

He cursed and leapt to the backrest on the stool. "Is Nixie's token in your pocket?" He pointed repeatedly at my pants.

"The Wasser-Münzen?" I stuck my fingers in my pocket and wanted to recoil at the intense cold. I eased the disc out, expecting to see its blue obsidian surface, but I almost dropped it when I saw what it had become. The entire surface was crystalline blue with a pulsing core in the middle. It beat as a heart would, blood red and glowing like some kind of demonic fire-fly.

"Nudd's balls! Get to the river, now!" Cara said.

I was torn between panic and laughing outright at Cara's curse. Seeing the look on her face caused common sense to win out immediately and I sprinted out the front door. During the run I realized what it must be—some kind of alarm, some kind of emergency from Nixie—and my heart rate spiked even higher.

I was slow compared to the fairies and Sam. They were waiting on the riverbank by the time I crossed the cobblestones and made it down to the water's edge. I stepped into the river and my teeth wanted to chatter instantly.

"That's fucking cold," I said as I fumbled the Wasser-Münzen out of my pocket. I held it between both hands, plunged it into the river, and grunted as Nixie's power battered my senses. There was nothing gentle or sensual about her arrival. The waters rose up immediately, outlining her face and cascading into a series of waterfalls below her neck.

"Damian, thank the gods," Nixie said. "Falias is under attack."

"Are you safe?"

"I'm … I …" She nodded and then her face began to fall. "I have sisters there. It's not … their walls, they can't be breached, but they are falling!"

"If someone has found Falias," Aideen said as her voice trailed off. "If they've found one hidden city, they're all at risk."

"It's not *them*," Nixie said, her voice edging hysteria. "I mean, there are many men, but one man brought the walls down. One man!"

"Why has no one called through the Warded Ways?" Aideen asked as she walked into the river beside me.

"I don't know," Nixie said. "The Ways, they are blocked to us all. Glenn can't break through them. He's going to destroy his own city in a fit of rage."

"The Ways are the only path to Falias," Foster said.

A black pit of helplessness welled up inside me as I watched Nixie's tears begin to fall. Her eyes focused on something behind me.

"Levi!" Nixie said.

I turned and found no one but the Old Man. The light bulb detonated in my head a moment later. His name.

"Yes, I heard," the Old Man said. "Did you see Ward? He was journeying to Falias."

Nixie nodded. "Yes, I watched him go. He's there. Oh gods, he's there."

"Then they have some chance. However small."

"I can't hold this connection open, Levi. I don't know what they're doing, but it's breaking down the lines. Our magics can't travel through it. Without my connection to Damian, I couldn't even do this."

"Ezekiel," Zola said. "He's the only one mad enough to attack the cities of Gwynn ap Nudd."

"He's one of the few with enough power to do it," Edgar said.

"The courts here," Nixie said as her image started to fall back into the river. "The courts here are talking of war. Open war! Do you know what that means?"

She cursed, her face contorted in pain. "I can't hold the connection."

"Go, Nixie," I said. "Be safe. I love you."

"I love you too," she said as the water collapsed back into itself.

The Wasser-Münzen warmed immediately and took on the deep blue obsidian tones I was used to seeing. It was a stark contrast to the icy river we stood in. I pulled it out of the water and stood up straight, the cold chill of the water forgotten amidst Nixie's message.

"What does this mean?" Sam asked as Aideen and I left the river. "Open war? With who?"

"With Ezekiel, for one," Hugh said. "Do you think she meant humanity as a whole, Cara?"

Cara frowned. "I hope not. Glenn may know something about the video. Something we don't know."

"If Ezekiel has damaged Falias, Glenn will destroy the world to cut the Fae's vengeance from the bastard's soul," Foster said. "And I don't know if we should stop him."

We all fell silent. I was trying to wrap my head around the potential disaster that was waiting for us in the back of a pitch-black alley. A disaster that was ready to smile at us as it stuck the knife in and twisted.

I remembered the number then. I pulled out the napkin from my coat and started dialing.

"Hello?"

"Euphemia?" I asked.

"Yes."

"Falias is under attack. Nixie and the others need you, but the Ways are closed."

"Gods, we'll head for the oceans. They'll be the first to open when the King strikes." The line went dead.

"Damian?" Sam said. "What now?"

"We fight."

Mike took a deep breath. The air whistled like wind through a cavern as he exhaled. "I will forge the *splendorem mortem*."

CHAPTER TWENTY-THREE

We slept for a while, if you can call nightmares, nervous speculation, and whispers sleep. Some of us stayed at the shop. Sam, Frank, Dell, and I went to my apartment while my dad took Mom and his cannon to a hotel. The next morning, well, early afternoon, we regrouped at the shop and then went our separate ways.

"Is splitting up the best idea?" Frank asked from the back seat.

"Yes," Foster said from his perch on the rearview mirror. He adjusted his sword as we bounced over a pothole. "There's too much to do, too fast. Aideen can take the Ways to travel most of the distance back to Rivercene. They may be blocked completely overseas, but some of them are still open here."

"I wish the wolves were coming with us," Sam said from the back beside Frank.

I nodded in agreement as I steered with my left hand and ran the fingers of my right over the series of scars on my left arm. They were a constant reminder of Hugh binding me to the pack. If anything, it was a reassuring presence.

"So where does that leave us?" Frank asked.

"We make for Elephant Rocks," Zola said as she balanced her giant quickie mart mug of coffee in the slightly too small hanging cup holder beside me. "Aeros will not need to hold back. Our secrecy is coming to an end."

"You can't know that," the Old Man said from the back seat. He looked cramped, but not uncomfortable wedged into the small seat beside Sam.

Dell snorted from the passenger seat. "Old Man, all you ever talk about is Adannaya's gut feelings and how *uncanny* they are. You going to write her off now?"

Zola chuckled and elbowed Dell.

The Old Man didn't say a word. I like to think he was blushing.

"Can we stop for barbeque?" Foster said.

Three of us said "Yes!" as my mouth started watering.

"We don't have time to stop for a meal," I said. "We'll get some carryout. Will you call it in, Sam?"

"Consider it done. I can sauce Frank up and have a tasty snack later."

"Good god," Dell said. "That's just … that's more than I needed to hear."

"It was funnier when Frank was still kind of round," I whispered.

Zola and Foster burst into laughter.

"What?" Frank asked. "What was that?"

I caught a glimpse of Sam grabbing Frank's face and trying to suck out his soul in the rearview mirror.

"Damian's just jealous," Sam said as she released Frank.

"I'm pretty sure Damian's just worried," Frank said. "You know, Nixie and whatever's happening with the Fae."

"You aren't wrong about that," I said.

"We're all worried about Nixie," Foster said. "And the rest of our friends. Hells, Ward comes back from exile and gets trapped in Falias while it's under attack?"

"Who is Ward?" Frank asked.

"Ward gave you the runes for your ghost circle," the Old Man said. "Isn't that right, Adannaya?"

Zola's laugh was deep in her chest. I didn't have to see her face to know her lips were pressed together in a tight grin.

"Who is he?" I asked. "I mean I know he's known for his use of wards, but who is he?"

"That's an easy question with a convoluted answer," Foster said.

"He's a badass," Dell said. "Hard. Core. Badass."

"He will not be able to defeat Ezekiel alone," the Old Man said. "He takes his vow very seriously."

"What vow?" Zola said.

"His vow not to kill," Dell said. "What kind of nonsense is that, right?"

"It's good nonsense," Sam said. "I wish we never had to kill."

Zola turned in her seat and then stared out the windshield for a moment. "Ward helped Gwynn ap Nudd rise to power. Ah hear he destroyed the Old Guard."

"So why did he take a vow like that?" Sam said.

"The Old Guard was his brother," Foster said.

"Christ," I said.

"If Ward is in Falias, Neil will be with him."

"Oh Foster," Sam said. "I'm so sorry."

The fairy raised his head and spared her a weak smile. "We don't know what's going to happen. They could still be okay."

I wanted to ask who Neil was, but it didn't seem the time with the sad look on Foster's face.

The car fell silent but for the constant hum of the highway as the miles rolled by. Sam ordered the carryout and it wasn't much longer before I pulled in to Warehouse BBQ to grab the goods.

"Drop it on the seats and I'll fashion a new seat cover out of your ass," I said as I handed the bags to Zola and Frank.

"He's serious," Frank said. "Crazy bastard."

"I can get behind that," Dell said. "I love this car. I usually like to see them unmodified, but the extra space is great. It's a hell of an antique."

"Not the only antique in here," Frank said under his breath.

We all stopped and stared at him for a moment before everyone burst into laughter.

"Bloody hell, Frank. I didn't think you had it in you," I said as I started the car.

"He's just quiet around all you freaks," Sam said.

"At least *I* don't try to eat him all the time," I said.

"Don't knock it 'til you try it."

"Oh, Ah do not like where this conversation is going," Zola said.

"Just stop talking and hand me the food," the Old Man said.

We managed to clean out most of the sandwiches before we reached the park. I took a sip of water and dropped the cup into a hanging holder on the door. Foster was laid out across the dashboard with a string of pulled pork the length of his arm hanging out of his mouth. Dell was snoring from the passenger seat, and I was utterly impressed at his ability to sleep at a time like this.

"Hey, Foster?" I said.

"Mmmph?" he mumbled around a mouthful of food.

"What did you mean when you said Ashley 'was' a green witch?" I asked.

"I meant she is not a green witch," Foster said with a small smile barely lifting his lips. "She is a Power now. No green witch can become a Power. She ascended."

"Power," Zola said. "Ah haven't heard a witch called a Power in a century. That's a dated way of thinking. Ashley will always be a green witch."

"Maybe," Foster said. "But she'll be a green witch with some serious weight to throw around. The Blade of the Stone was lost for a reason."

The Old Man grunted from the backseat. "The Blade of the Stone was lost because it was made to fight the Eldritch Gods. Your witch does not wield the power to battle the Eldritch. She may be able to stand her ground against an Old God, but the Eldritch Gods are beyond us all."

"I didn't think anyone outside the Society of Flame knew about the Eldritch Gods," Foster said. "At least not anyone that wasn't Fae."

"I was in Alexandria, Foster," the Old Man said. "The knowledge in that place, the knowledge we lost ..." He sighed. "It took centuries to regain it. Some of it we may never have again."

"Okay," I said. "Alexandria's amazing and all, and the fact you were actually there blows my mind, but I thought you just said Ashley could stand up to an Old God with that art."

"Yes, I did."

"Bloody hell. No wonder Edgar flipped out," I said.

"Who gives a damn what Edgar thinks," Frank said. "Ashley is a good person. I'll go out on a limb and say she is one of the *best* people any of us have ever known."

"That's not much of a limb," I said. "That's like a going out on a wide flat surface with a safety harness."

"Yeah, but Frank's right," Foster said. "I don't care if she turns into some kind of demon witch, she'll still be a good person."

"You know, if anything ever happens to her, the River Pack will eat whoever causes it," I said. "Hugh told me they still feel it was their fault Ashley got hurt last year."

"Hurt is a bloody understatement," Foster said.

"I think Alan's got it the worst," Sam said. "He feels like he let his Alpha down."

"Some days that man is one big idiotic bag of muscle," Zola said.

"Umm," Foster said. "You know he has like *five* graduate degrees, right? The guy's a genius."

"Why are geniuses always idiots?" Zola asked, barely hiding the chuckle in her voice.

"They're not idiots," Dell said as he stretched and knuckled the sleep from his eyes. "It's more like they don't have all the answers when they think they do."

"I think my idiot apprentice has a point to make," the Old Man said.

I turned on the signal and started to turn into the park.

"Any man who thinks he knows all there is to know in the universe is mad," the Old Man said. "No one knows everything. Half the world thinks Foster's people are myths, vampires are nothing more than Halloween costumes, and people can't live to see their second millennium."

"They're usually right about that last one," Foster said.

"Oh god, I'm going to explode," Sam said.

"Off topic much?" I asked.

"Too much food."

"Little heavier than your usual bloody morsels?"

"Barbeque is worth any price," Sam said. "Even exploding in your damn car."

"That's fine, just remember I will be making upholstery out of whatever parts of you don't explode."

She laughed, and then groaned. "I need to walk around."

"You're in luck. We is here," I said as I pulled into the u-shaped parking lot. The sun was starting to fall below the horizon, turning the forest into an unending mountain of hands trying to claw their way out of a blackened orange hell. Out of the Burning Lands.

I took a deep breath as I put the car in park. I couldn't even think of calling my '32 Ford by its old nickname anymore. Vicky was Vicky, a ghost, a little girl, and my friend. Everyone piled out, grabbing weapons and packs from the trunk.

"What's that smell?" Frank asked.

"Clean air," Zola said as they stepped away from the car. "You sure won't find it around the city."

I hung back as they headed toward the pavilions at the front of the park.

"What is it, Demon?" Sam asked.

I glanced up as I let the trunk fall closed. Most of the group was halfway across the parking lot, following Zola.

"I was thinking about Vicky," I said.

"It's not your fault."

I smiled. "I know, but look at her now Sam. She's running with the Ghost Pack? She calls herself a Harrower?"

"She doesn't just call herself a Harrower," Sam said quietly. "She's been to the Burning Lands with Carter and Maggie. She's helped rescue most of the Ghost Pack."

I ran my hand through my hair and blew out a breath. "I know, but to do that Sam ... It's all there in the Black Book. To do that she has to be ... fuck, I can't even say it."

"She has to be a demon," Sam whispered and she wrapped her arms around me. "It's not your fault."

I sagged into my sister's arms.

"Come on D, we get through this, then we see what we can do to help Vicky. We already got Mom back. Be thankful for that."

I stood up straighter and took a deep breath as I squeezed Sam's arm. "You're right, of course."

"Of course," she said with a smirk.

"Thanks," I said as I adjusted the pepperbox under my arm. "Now you just have to talk to Mom about your tendency to bite people."

Sam smiled at me, but she didn't say anything more. She knew damn well what I meant, and I knew she'd feel better for having that talk with Mom.

Sam and I started trailing the group. I waited for Foster to clear one of the little green huts before I turned to Sam again.

"Who is Neil?" I asked. "I don't think I've ever heard Foster talk about him."

"Neil is Foster's cousin. Don't you remember? He was friends with Colin and Foster when they all lived in Falias."

I glanced at Foster, fluttering over the Old Man's shoulder. He'd already lost Colin. Hell, I'd barely known Colin, and he'd still managed to save my life. I'd never met Neil, but I didn't want Foster to lose anyone else.

"Closest thing to a brother he's ever had," Sam said, "next to you at least."

I couldn't keep a smile off my face. "I'd be proud to call him my brother."

"Me too."

"We should adopt him," I said with a completely straight face.

She blinked. "Umm, I don't think you can adopt siblings."

I cracked a grin. Sam scowled and punched me in the arm.

"Ow, dammit! No fair punching like a vampire."

"I spent twenty some odd years listening to you tell me I punch like a girl. You should be glad I'm not breaking your arm and saying you scream like a girl."

"A manly girl."

"Gah," Sam said before she burst into laughter. "Let's catch up to the group."

CHAPTER TWENTY-FOUR

How long had it been? A year now since I came here with Zola to meet Aeros the first time? Longer, I thought. It seemed like an impossible length of time, but felt so short. A lot had happened.

There was nothing quiet about our entrance, crunching on loose gravel and bits of torn up pavement as we made our way to the asphalt path leading to Aeros. Commoners thought the path led to an array of massive boulders near the old quarry, which it did, but Aeros made his home among those rocks.

Zola took the lead, cracking her cane against the path with every step. We followed as the old trees closed around us, standing sentinel over the ancient land. We followed the thin yellow rope where the trail was lost to leaves and mud.

"Look at the size of those rocks," Dell said as we passed a red granite outcropping the size of a car. It was small compared to what was coming.

"It's a lot nicer in summer," I said as a chill ran down my spine. "Bloody cold out here."

"Really?" Foster mumbled from within Zola's hood. "I hadn't fucking noticed."

"It could be worse," Frank said.

"Yeah, my balls could freeze off," Foster said.

Dell laughed and started to say something, but then he stopped dead in the middle of the path. "Holy crap."

He was staring ahead where the path crested. A short, wooden staircase led to a gently sloping plain of granite. Boulders the size of cars and houses were strewn across that plain. Last time we'd been here, the leaves and moss had added color to the landscape. In the dead of winter, with the sunset burning behind it, the place looked stark and lonely.

I stopped at the pools of water on top of the granite hill. It only took a minute to find the right one. It was the only one not frozen solid.

"Oh my god, Demon!" Sam said. "Do you remember these? They looked so much bigger when we were kids." She jumped to the top of one of the smaller house-sized boulders and then up to a precariously balanced boulder with a small stalk holding it in place. She tapped her foot a couple times and grinned. "It's solid."

My mind raced back to the photos we'd taken as kids. Sam and I standing beneath that rock, pretending to hold it up. Dad laughing as we climbed up the lower ones while Mom wrung her hands together, ready to catch us before we tumbled to our doom.

"What are all the names for?" Dell said as he crouched down to inspect a few bold letters carved into the granite. "They're old, not so much as the Old Man, but still."

"You're hilarious," the Old Man said. "The names are warnings."

"Yeah," Foster said. "Warnings of the 'don't fuck with me unless you want to get flattened and immortalized in stone' type."

"Harsh," Dell said.

I crouched down next to the largest pool. It was exactly how I remembered it, a handful of smooth pebbles at the bottom of the water.

"Call him," Zola said.

There was no question in her voice. I'd seen the ritual once, and as far as she was concerned, once was enough.

I reached my hand out and a dull, yellow-green glow began to rise up between the rocks. Fragile fingers reached out and wrapped around their neighbors. They formed tiny fronds of light and a pattern began to rise.

"Ehwaz," I said and a glyph appeared beneath the water. It was shaped like a jagged capital M. "Uruz." The glyph dissolved and another rose between the pebbles, a lowercase n with a severe slant joining the top of each side.

The pool boiled, but there was no heat to warm the chill from the air. Bubbles broke the surface, pooling and oozing and rising quickly into a pillar of light. The entire mass expanded outward and the light began to fade. The bubbles grew opaque and then reddened into a solid granite surface. Two jagged chasms formed on the topmost boulder and a wiry crack opened below them.

"Do I need to bow my head and call you Lord?" I asked.

Dell gasped and his hand moved toward his gun.

Zola snorted a laugh.

The crack in the boulder curled up at the edges and the chasms lit with a dull yellow-green light. The earth laughed.

"Damian," Aeros said, his voice deep and grinding. "We are all friends here. There is no need for formalities."

"Good, no grinding the mortals to paste today?"

His smile grew wider. "Not today."

"Have you heard what's happening?" Foster asked.

Aeros nodded as he raised his arms and flexed his back. "There is much to hear. Falias is under attack. The wolves treat. The Watchers scatter."

"Yes," Foster said as he glided to Aeros's shoulder and settled himself. "Ezekiel has found a way into the hidden cities. We have to kill him."

"Kill an immortal?" Aeros said as his eyes swept around our group. He paused when his gaze came to Zola, and leaned forward. "Where is the Smith?"

"You do not play coy well, old friend," Zola said as she patted the boulder that formed the Old God's knee.

"So the demon rushes to his forge," Aeros said. "What fate befalls the countries when the Blessings are lost? Rome fell, Atlantis drowned, civilizations you mortals have never dreamed of vanished. *This* country will not survive another civil war."

"There won't be another civil war here," Zola said. "Uprisings, riots, perhaps. Ah don't believe we're headed for another civil war."

"No," the Old Man said. "We're headed for a war with Philip and Ezekiel. Only now it's a war on two fronts. I don't think Philip plans on being anywhere near Ezekiel."

"Philip Pinkerton," Aeros said. "He is powerful. I have faced him before, as you know. Powerful as he is, I do not believe Pinkerton would be foolish enough to lay siege upon the hidden cities. To invite the fury of Gwynn ap Nudd …"

"Is to invite the fury of the Wild Hunt," Foster said. "No one stands against the Hunt."

"No one with a soul," the Old Man said. "A creature with no soul to lose can wade through the Hunt like water."

"We cannot let it come to that," Zola said. "Ezekiel dies before it comes to that."

"You are not wrong, Adannaya," Aeros said. "Do you understand the consequences of forging the demon blade and slaying an immortal with it? It will take life not meant to be taken and a Seal will fall because of it. What will you unleash on this world to stand in Ezekiel's place?"

"A Seal?" I asked. "A true Seal?"

"Yes," Aeros said.

I raised my eyebrows in question. Aeros stared at me and cocked his head to the side.

"Seals keep our world safe," Aeros said. "Some were built by the Old Gods. Some were built by the Fae. And some too were built by human hands, though those hands did not realize what they were building."

"So why will killing Ezekiel affect them?" I said.

"Some Seals are woven into nature. Tied to the very fires dwelling inside the earth or the seas where your Nixie used to hunt. Those Seals will endure until the world itself is destroyed."

I nodded. "Zombie apocalypse, sure."

Frank and Foster laughed as the fairy grinned and shook his head.

"Unlikely," Foster said with a smirk before he turned to Aeros. "May I?"

Aeros nodded.

Foster turned back to me. "Some of the other Seals are tied to living beings. In times both older and more innocent, tying them to an immortal seemed like a wise decision." He sighed and leaned up against Aeros's head. "It seems instead to have been a very unwise decision. Depending on what Seals fall, we could unleash almost anything onto this plane."

"Ezekiel was worshipped as Anubis," I said. "Does that tell you anything?"

Foster shrugged.

"Yes, it tells us some things," Aeros said. "The immortal Anubis, his life is bound to two Seals, the gateway to the Burning Lands and the binding of the Old Gods. The immortal Amun-Ra is bound to the Seal on the Burning Lands as well. It will hold so long as he lives, though it will weaken. I need not tell you the binding has grown weak on the Old Gods, for I stand here before you, and I am such a being."

I knew that already. Zola had told me what he was. The Old Man didn't know, though. He took a step back and then rocked onto the balls of his feet. Dell did the same, slipping to the side of a boulder and reaching for his useless gun once more.

"Old Man, stop," Foster said. "He is a friend."

"Yeah, you're an Old God, and?" Sam said.

Aeros turned to my sister and blinked. "You know what I am?"

She nodded. "Vik told me. I thought everyone knew."

Clearly, keeping that secret from my sister had been an unnecessary exercise.

Aeros chuckled as he stood up, the sound like a rockslide. He took two steps and settled himself on the nearest boulder. "And how did Vik know?"

Sam shrugged. "He told me all of the Guardians are Old Gods, so I just assumed you were."

All of the Guardians are Old Gods.

My gaze snapped to Zola. "Happy?" I said. "If Vicky is becoming a Guardian, does that mean … what does that mean?"

"No," Aeros said. "She will not become a god. Some of the first Guardians were Old Gods. Nothing will rise to become an Old God in this age. That magic is gone. It will stay in the past with the dragons."

With the dragons. I met Zola's gaze. She gave a tiny shrug. Mike had bought an entire basket of dragon scales. Mike had called the lady out on the fact she had a living dragon. What the hell did that mean?

"Later," Zola said as if reading my mind.

I nodded.

"Adannaya," the Old Man said as his stance began to loosen. "You have kept things from me."

"Oh, and Ah suppose you never kept one little thing from me, yes?" she said, snapping off the last few syllables.

He sighed and closed his eyes. "Indeed. I cannot argue that."

"Tell me friends," Aeros said. "What brings you to my home this evening?"

"Ah believe Philip is coming for me," Zola said. "He will strike my home, and my friends. Ah cannot abide his survival."

"What of the wolves?" Aeros asked.

Zola closed her eyes and lowered her head. "Carter and Maggie died for us. Ah will not risk Hugh or Alan, or any of our other friends. And you already know they treat with the packs."

"Hugh is wise," Aeros said. "He would not have let you come alone if he thought you all doomed. What would you have me do, old friend?"

"Help us," Zola said. "We're heading for the cabin."

"Philip will bring his army upon you," Aeros said.

Zola's head rose slowly, her wrinkled face fracturing into a death's head grin. "And we will kill them all."

God, I hoped she was right.

CHAPTER TWENTY-FIVE

"A re we there yet?" Sam asked as I climbed back into the car after opening the gate.

"Just about," I said. "You grumpy ass vampire."

Frank choked back a small laugh as we started moving forward again. My car was not cut out for a gravel road, and Dell cursed as his head bounced off the roof.

"Seatbelt's advisable," I said.

"Yeah, I noticed," he said as he rubbed his head.

"Can we trust Aeros?" the Old Man asked.

"Yes," Zola said. "Ah trust him with my life. He should be there already. He'll stop us if it's an ambush."

The car bottomed out as we crossed a creek.

"You okay?" Foster asked. "You didn't even curse."

"Just distracted," I said. "I'll curse later. Probably a lot."

"Oh, good. You had me worried."

We passed a field and quickly drove into another tunnel formed from the forest's canopy.

"Now this is a place I have not seen in a century," the Old Man said.

"It's changed," Zola said.

"The city is gone, it would seem," he said as he leaned toward the window. "The old sawmill, the homes, they're fields and forest now."

"Yes," my master said in a quiet voice.

"I'm sure it is still beautiful in the day," he said. "It seems a bit spooky at night."

"Did you seriously just say spooky?" Foster asked.

"We're here," I said as we rounded a turn and an open field of grasslands spread out before us, climbing a gradual slope. The old oak waited to greet us before the house.

"It's all shadows and nature at night," the Old Man said.

"Is the cabin really from the Civil War?" Frank asked.

"It's a little older than that," Zola said.

I parked the car next to the well off to the west. Sam and I paused to look at the night sky. It was clear, and the moon was starting to rise.

"God but you don't see that from the city," she said as we started pulling weapons out of the trunk.

"No," I said as I smiled. "No, you don't."

I strapped on my black body armor. A dozen speed loaders were already mounted in the elastic straps across the front. Frank brought some of his old favorites, Uzis and the like. Real subtle stuff.

I glanced at the steel-shuttered windows as we approached. Nothing made a sound aside from us and the car's quiet clicking as it cooled.

"It's too quiet," Dell said.

"Yes," Zola said.

"Foster, stay on me," I said. "We'll take the front. Dell, Old Man, watch our backs. Make sure no one comes up the drive behind us. Zola, Frank, Sam, take either side and circle back."

"Drive?" Dell said. "It's an open field a mile wide. They're not here. No one's here."

"Shut up, Roach," the Old Man said. "Damian's right."

We split and I crept up the three short stairs to the covered porch. I stayed to the left side of the first step, avoiding the squeaky nails, and then skipping the rotten board two steps from the door.

"Anything?" I whispered.

Foster shook his head as he glided up and down before the front of the cabin.

I pushed on the front door and strained my ears for the faintest sound. The quiet clink of a pewter chess piece falling told me no one had come in through the front door. I could have guessed as much from the layer of undisturbed dust.

Foster snapped into his full-size form with a shout, and then cursed as he smacked his head into the ceiling. I almost shot the man standing in the kitchen.

"Fuck!" I said. "Edgar!"

He tipped his hat and took a sip from the teacup in his hand. "Zola has excellent taste in tea."

"Ow," Foster said as he rubbed his head. "That is a low goddamned ceiling."

The gun slid back into its holster without me really thinking about it. I glanced around the living room. The couch was undisturbed and the wood stove was still cold. "What are you doing here?"

"This is the endgame, son. I brought your backup." He pushed open the back door and my heart skipped a beat as my eyes flicked from face to face.

Aeros waved from behind the group, near the tree line. Scattered in front of him were Cara, Ashley, Cassie, James, Alan, and Hugh.

Hugh.

"What are you doing here?" I asked as I hopped down to the grass.

"Damian," Alan said as he grabbed my arm near the elbow and traded grips. He glanced down at my armor and smiled. "It's good to see you, Cub."

"You too, Alan," I said with a small laugh. "We never did get down to the Blackthorne for vampire hour."

"Another day, then," he said.

I nodded. "Are you still staying in north city? Trying to, how did you put it, 'Bring the city back'?"

"Yes, although my girlfriend is not a fan," he said with a smile. "But really, you can't expect to make a difference in a community if you don't get your hands dirty. We've been there for a year now. I've made friends, gotten to know the neighbors. There are a lot of good people there."

"As long as they aren't necromancers," I said. "Right, Edgar?"

The Watcher turned away, and I was pretty sure he was hiding a smile.

"Alan!" Sam said as she came around the corner.

"Ah, my bitey friend," he said as he picked Sam up in a hug. They started bantering about pizza and beer and I turned back to Hugh.

"The packs are finalizing some details," he said, "but Alan and I did not need to be there." He took my left arm and slid the sleeve back, showing the curved line of scars. "You and your friends are not alone so long as you are tied to the pack."

"What about Aideen?" I asked as Cara stepped up beside Hugh.

"She stayed behind to watch the shop," Cara said. "Bubbles and Peanut are with her. She'll be fine."

"What if Philip goes to the shop?" I said.

"He's not heading for the shop," Hugh said. "We tracked him to Pilot Knob. He's heading this way now."

Pilot Knob. The dead city. My hands curled into fists at the thought of what Philip did to that city. Men, women, children. Murdered and wrapped in a black art, fodder for his trap. A trap we'd triggered, raising an entire town full of zombies.

"I gave Mike the Blessing," Cassie said as she leapt from Aeros's shoulder and glided over to Hugh.

"And Rivercene?" Cara asked. "Does she still sleep?"

Cassie nodded.

"What's under that house?" I asked.

"Nothing we need worry about now," Cara said. "Focus on the task at hand, lest you lose your head."

A cry split the heavens. My arm flashed to my gun and I wrenched my gaze up to find the Piasa Bird circling above us.

"Um," I said. "Hugh?"

The wolf grinned. "We brought a friend."

"As long as he doesn't try to eat us, I'm good."

"He would never try to eat someone," Aeros said as he stood up. "Just because he dismembers a man with his beak does not mean he is eating him."

I blinked and stared at the mountain of granite.

"This is a beautiful place," Aeros said as he extended a massive, rocky arm. The Thunderbird circled closer and closer. It spread its wings and glided down to the Old God's arm. The Piasa Bird was huge, but its rocky perch didn't shift a bit as the bird clawed its way up to Aeros's neck and sat its head on top of the old rock.

Sam snorted and giggled. "You look like a crazy old lady with a bird for a hat."

"That he does," said a voice from the tree line. A voice I knew, and another friend I'd failed to protect.

They came from the woods, wisps of smoke and power, until I focused on them. The Ghost Pack, led by Carter, smiling like he wasn't dead. Maggie followed behind him with three others beside her. I recognized Johann and Betsy, two of the liberated wolves, but the third I did not know.

A faint glow weaved through the trees behind them, turning the trees to orange and red shadows.

"Don't tell me to put it out," a little girl's voice squeaked. "It's dark, you dumb bear."

I heard Happy chuff before he waddled into view, Vicky riding on his back with a ball of flame in her hands.

She looked up as they cleared the tree line. "Oh," she said as the fire in her hands popped out of existence. Vicky looked around the field until her eyes fell on me. "Damian!" She swung down from the panda and ran through the grasses.

"Hey, kid," I said as I bent down to snatch her up, swing her feet at Hugh, and then set her down again. "What are you doing here?"

"Ghost Pack business," she said with a grin. "Did you like my trick?"

"It was very pretty," I said. "Can you do that any time you want?"

She nodded and shot a little streamer of flame into the air.

"Wow, you're really good at that."

She curled her hand into a fist and the flames solidified into a glowing, searing, blade.

"My god," Edgar said.

I pointed at him and shook my head when Vicky looked the other way. "That's a neat sword, Vicky."

"I know, right?" she said. "I got the idea watching you. It cuts through everything in the Burning Lands."

"Yes, it does," Carter said as he ruffled her hair.

I stared at his fingers moving through her hair. "You can touch her, but I'm not giving you any energy. How?"

"I don't know," Carter said. "It's been like this for a while now. Since we rescued Art."

"You're not powering them?" Hugh asked as his eyes trailed from me back to the wolves. "But I can see them as plain as day." He reached out and pushed Carter's shoulder.

"Damian," the Old Man said as he squinted at Vicky. "Why does this little girl, and all of these ghosts, have slivers of your soul woven into their auras?"

"All of them?" I asked. "It should only be ... um ... ah ..." I stuttered and glanced at Edgar. He just smiled and gestured for me to go on. At least that's what I assumed he was gesturing for.

"I thought it was only Carter and Maggie."

"No, it's all of them," he said.

"Could it be related to the pack magic?" Hugh asked. "I don't know of any reference to a necromancer becoming a pack member."

"A pack member?" the Old Man said, his eyebrows rising as he leaned back. "Truly?"

I pushed my left sleeve up and showed him the ring of raised scars.

"Shit," he said. "I never would have imagined it. After all the hunts? All the death? To make a necromancer one of your own?"

"Sometimes the past must stay the past so we can change what is," Hugh said.

The Old Man studied Hugh's face for a moment before he nodded. "Sometimes, wolf, sometimes yes."

Happy nosed Vicky in the back, knocking her into Hugh. She laughed and scratched the bear's neck.

"Damian," Carter said as Vicky and Happy trundled off to see the group around Sam and Frank. "I want you to meet someone. Art."

The new ghost stepped up beside him, rail thin and smiling as he extended his hand.

I reached out without giving it a second thought and my hand met resistance. I stared at the wolf's hand. "What the hell is going on?"

"It's good to meet you too."

"Ha," I said as I shook his hand. "Yes, it's good to meet you. I'm just shocked you didn't pass right through me."

The Old Man pushed on Art's shoulder and Art swayed backwards. "Pack magic," he muttered. "One more goddamned variable we know nothing about." He blew out a deep breath.

James grabbed Edgar's arm and pulled him to the side. They whispered but I still caught snippets of what James was snarling. "… soularts … dark necromancer … enemies." Edgar snapped at him and James shut his mouth, looking like he'd been slapped. James narrowed his eyes and stalked off toward Aeros. I'm not too proud to admit I kind of hoped the Old God would trip and fall on him.

"Idiot," Edgar said. "Sometimes that man is more trouble than he's worth."

"Is he going to be a problem?" the Old Man asked.

Edgar shook his head. "He'll be fine. I'll make sure of it if I have to."

"We'll leave it in your hands."

I looked around our disorganized circle of allies before I said, "I guess we should make a plan."

CHAPTER TWENTY-SIX

"Zola!" Edgar said.

My master glanced up from her huddle with the fairies.

"As your apprentice pointed out, we need to make some plans."

She nodded. "Sam. Make a circle."

"Wait," Aeros said. "I will do this." He gestured with his hands, palms up and fingers curled, and the earth beneath our feet shook. Dirt and grass roiled as rocks rose up beneath the field. Red stone looked almost black in the dim light, flat and sloping toward the center of the rising ring. When the rumbling stopped, a circle of stone surrounded us.

I brushed off the top of one and sat down. It was a little short, but made for a decent seat. Zola bent down to look at the stone opposite Aeros.

"Ha! You remembered, you old rock pile."

"Of course," he said. "Seems only yesterday we buried this circle."

"Yesterday," Zola said. "Almost one hundred fifty years, now. Come on, you," Zola said, motioning to Frank and Sam. Ashley and The Old Man followed as everyone gathered inside the circle. "You fairies might want to close your eyes." Zola placed her staff deep within a hole on the rock's top. "*Orbis Tego.*"

The hair stood straight up on my arms and I shivered. A breeze rushed by like the world was inhaling, and then it spewed forth a thunderstorm of line energy. Bolts of electric blue singed my Sight as power arced between the rocks and stretched over us in a dome of pulsing light. It dulled slowly, resolving into the blue-tinged shield, flowing and shifting along the back edge of the stone circle.

"Don't touch it," Zola said.

"Safe?" Foster asked as he cracked one eye open.

"Safe as a bug zapper," she said.

"Hey now!" Foster said with small frown. "That was on a dare. Don't go there."

"What's with the light show?" Sam asked.

"Nothing will penetrate this dome," Aeros said as he settled onto the ground and sat as close to Indian-style as he could.

Hugh watched Aeros trying to mimic his pose and smiled. The more I thought about it, Indian-style probably wasn't the best choice of words. Vicky called it criss-cross applesauce, but there was no way in hell I could say that with a straight face.

Aeros stopped moving and exchanged a nod with Hugh. "Not sound nor spell nor man can reach us here."

"So we don't have to worry about ears," Frank said.

Aeros turned to look at him and Frank backed up a step, his hand slipping into the sling of an Uzi. "You have no need to fear me. You are correct. No one can hear us. We are outside of time."

"What do you mean?" Frank asked. "Outside of time."

"Time is perhaps not the best word," Aeros said. He rubbed his hand across his chin and my teeth clenched at the grindstone sounds. "We are within one of the Fae's Warded Ways, only there is no way in or out of this path. It is a bubble within the Abyss ... hmm ... a manipulation of the ley lines, you might say."

Frank's shoulders relaxed and he sat down on one of the stones. Apparently, when our friendly neighborhood rock talks at length, Frank feels more comfortable.

I stared at the center of the circle for a moment. Thoughts of training with Zola flashed behind my eyes. It was here I had practiced holding a circle shield. Holding it until the lizards would come to investigate. They'd scurry up the surface like it wasn't anything unnatural. When they got to the top, I'd drop the shield and let them fall into my hand. Always carefully. I didn't want to hurt them.

I took a deep breath. "How many people did Philip have with him?"

"Not too many," Hugh said. "Two dozen at most."

"Two dozen necromancers?" Zola asked. "Zachariah?"

"Yes," Alan said. "He was with them."

"I may not be of much use," Aeros said. "Philip and Zachariah have both managed to subdue me in the past."

"You'll still be of use," Zola said. "Even if we have to set you on fire as a distraction, you'll be of use."

I blinked and glanced at my master. "Did you just say you're going to set Aeros on fire?"

"No," Zola said. "Ah was merely entertaining the idea."

"I wish my Pit was here," Sam said. "Vassili and the others helped us so much last year."

"Not that much," Maggie said from her perch beside Aeros and Carter. "We're still dead."

"Sorry, Maggie," Sam said. "I just meant —"

She waved her hand to interrupt Sam. "You don't need to apologize. My issue is with your Lord, not you."

"I have a suggestion," Alan said.

"Then speak," Aeros said. "We are all friends in this place."

"I'd like to think we're all friends outside of this place too," Alan said.

Ashley settled onto the ground beside Alan and squeezed his foot. He smiled a moment before Hugh let out a quiet laugh.

"Well spoken," Hugh said. "Tell us of your suggestion."

"Divide and conquer," Alan said. "Take the packs into the woods. We're untouchable with trees as our armor. Use the fairies as scouts."

"Duh," Foster said with a grin.

Alan nodded at him. "Zola can be the bait in the trap. The trap we set here. Tell me if I'm wrong, but if she draws enough power from the ley lines, it will draw Philip like a moth to a flame."

Zola tilted her head and tapped her fingertips on her cane. "It could distract him from an ambush he would otherwise see coming."

"Wouldn't this shield we're in draw him in?" Alan asked.

"No," Cara said. "We're outside detection here. If it's not in his direct line of sight, he'd never notice it."

"If you drew a bigger circle ..." Cassie said and then she nodded to herself. "Draw a bigger circle and call a shield." Her eyes flickered to the Watchers. "Use a soulart. It will magnify the draw."

Edgar stared James down and the younger Watcher stayed silent.

"That could work, Cassie," the Old Man said before his gaze travelled back to Alan. "Cunning, wolf, very cunning. So, we draw straws, pick our stations, and die with honor."

"Everything but that last part, please," I said.

"The dying or the honor?" Sam asked.

I narrowed my eyes and let my necromancy expand, my aura crawling and seething across the ground, wrapping itself around my sister's arm. Sam glanced at her hand, and then her eyes shot up to me.

"Damian, don't you dare!"

"What?" I said. "Play the stop hittin' yourself game?" I let her arm go and flashed her a grin. Hell, I hadn't tried to do that to her in years. I don't even know if it would work anymore since she's fed off me so many times.

"Children," Zola said as she patted my leg. "Save it for the people trying to kill us." Zola turned to Ashley. "Priestess."

"How can I help?"

"You are the act they'll never see coming." Zola's face lifted into the twisted grin she reserved for special occasions. Like killing the shit out of something.

***

"You know she didn't mean that," Frank said as we made our way through the brittle underbrush.

"That she'd tear my head off if you got hurt out here?" I said with a quiet chuckle. "Trust me, Sam meant every word of it. That's why I love her."

"Me too," he said.

"Yes, but I love her in entirely normal, non-disgusting ways."

"She's changed my life, Damian. You know what I used to be."

"You mean a scheistering con man arms dealer?"

"Well, yeah." Frank shook his head. "Why did you even give me a chance?"

"Everyone deserves a second chance," I said. "Besides, it was a *fantastic* way to get under Cara's skin. And Sam's, actually. That part kind of backfired though."

"I hope you see it is as a good thing," Frank said.

"Fuck yes, and don't you ever doubt it," I said as I put my hand on his shoulder. "I haven't seen Sam this happy since she was turned. I shit you not. I am very grateful to you for that."

"Thanks, D."

I nodded and started down a slippery slope of dead leaves. I held up my hand and Frank stopped beside me. We looked down the steep edge of the creek and then turned to the north while I looked for a gentler bank.

"So, you want me to deliver any messages if you don't make it?" Frank asked.

"Don't make it?" I said.

"I wrote a letter and left it in Sam's nightstand. Just in case."

"No, seriously Frank. You're not dying. Sam would kill me. Besides, you've got enough firepower strapped to you right now to take us all out."

"Sure, as long as no one uses a shield, or has faster reflexes, or brings a demon down on our heads."

I nodded and swung beneath the bent trunk of an ancient tree. "I can't say you're wrong on any particular point there."

A thick wall stepped out from the shadow of the tree beside us, silhouetted in the silver moonlight. "Will you two keep it down?" Alan asked. "I could hear you a mile from here."

"That's 'cause you hear good," I said in the best southern drawl I could manage, which wasn't good.

The wolf's shoulders shook as he hid his laughter. "Alright, just keep it down."

"Any word from Cassie?" I asked.

He shook his head.

"Let's setup here," I said as I pointed to the old tree stand above our heads.

Alan looked up for a moment. "I think not."

"Scared of heights?" Frank asked.

Alan glanced at Frank. "No, I don't like the idea of being treed by an army of necromancers. The only direction you can maneuver is straight down."

"Nonsense," I said. "You could get a decent arc off that thing. Probably land in the creek on a bunch of sharp rocks."

"Indeed," Alan said in what I suspected was not sincere appreciation.

A few minutes later I was snug in the rickety tree stand, with Frank and Alan camped out in the curve of the old tree below me.

"I heard you volunteer at a boys' home," Frank said.

"Yes," Alan said.

"That's, it's really good of you."

"I don't do it for the approval of other people," Alan said.

"No, no, that's not what I meant," Frank said. "I spent a lot of time in a boys' home growing up. Dysfunctional family and all that. You hear people say their families are dysfunctional, but they don't have a fucking clue what dysfunctional is."

"You seem to be doing well now."

Frank nodded. "I just needed a kick in the ass. Like Sam. God, I never dreamed I'd get to date someone like Sam. She's just amazing. Brilliant, beautiful, kind."

"Not so much that last one," I said.

"I'm impressed you survived your childhood, Damian," Alan said.

"We all have our talents," I said.

"Look at me now though, D," Frank said. "I've lost like fifty pounds. I have a freaking waist now."

"Frank, most people would say you're ripped," I said. "Maybe not Alan, since he's a brick wall, but most people."

"You've overcome a great deal in your life," Alan said. "Is that what you are saying?"

Frank nodded. "It was a struggle, but it was worth every minute."

Alan reached out and squeezed his shoulder. "My friend, you speak my language. Hard work, good friends, and persistence verging on the insane. Those three things will drag you out of any pit you find yourself in."

"I can't believe I'm sitting here with a werewolf," Frank said.

"You'll believe it when the fighting starts," I said. "You may need a lint roller when we get home."

Our quiet laughter trailed off and silence settled into the shadows around us. It wasn't long before the woods fell eerily silent. Three deer sprinted by, followed by a veritable army of squirrels and wildlife.

"Sit, Ubu," I hissed down the tree.

Alan looked up and I could see his teeth gleaming in the moonlight. He raised his arm. "There. She comes."

It took me a moment, scanning the darkness across the creek. Cassie soared on fragile wings, gliding and lifting and diving around the branches, finally settling on the far end of the branch beside me. Her armor sounded like a distant wind chime as she shifted her scabbard.

"Hugh was right," Cassie said. "They split up. Looks like three groups, one coming in from the south, one north, one west."

"Why not surround us?" Alan said.

"They did," I said with a frown. "Philip knows the land. We can't retreat to the east. You'll hit some very steep hills and ponds. If you tried to run over that, they'd pick you off in an instant."

"This is still *our* trap," Cassie said. "They do not know what is coming."

"You don't think Philip will suspect?" Alan asked.

"I have known him a long time," Cassie said as she turned and looked back to the east. "He is cautious, paranoid even. He will suspect something, but he will not know what."

"They were friends," I said to Alan. "Back in the Civil War, Zola and Philip and Cassie fought demons together."

Alan looked up at the fairy. He was quiet for a moment. "I am sorry."

She glanced down at the wolf and smiled. "Thank you."

"How much time do we have?" I asked.

"The western group should be here in ten minutes. They are headed straight for the steepest part of the creek."

"They'll come this way," I said.

"What makes you so sure?" Alan said.

"They won't want to climb down into the creek. They'll aim to go around the sheerest parts. That means north or south. South is a steep hill. They'll try to cross here."

"Is Philip coming here?" Frank asked. There was a slight tremor in his voice, but I had to admire how normal he sounded.

"No," Cassie said. "He is with the northern group. Zachariah is in the south."

"Zachariah gets Sam, Foster, Dell, and the Old Man," I said.

"Yes," Cassie said. "It leaves Cara with the Watchers and the Ghost Pack in the north. Zola and Ashley at the cabin."

"Zola's plan," I said. "You think it will work?"

"If you are up to it," Cassie said.

"They're coming," Alan said. "Remember, strike, run, bait them."

"I'm ready," I said as I bent forward and stared the fairy in the eye.

Shining green gemstones met my gaze as she drew her sword.

"Tonight we finish this," she said as she shot into the sky.

CHAPTER TWENTY-SEVEN

Pawns and cannon fodder. Philip always sends them in first. It's what he's doing while you slaughter the first wave that you have to watch out for.

"It's too steep," the first cloak said as he looked over the edge of the creek.

The two men behind him started downhill. The rest of the group followed like lemmings. Alan waited below me, Frank behind us. Cassie would be in the trees somewhere, coming up behind Philip's men.

More hoods came into view. And then more. And then my buzz of adrenaline wrenched itself into a surge of anxiety. The wood split below me and I glanced down to see Alan, claws out, fastened to the tree just beneath me.

"There were not this many before," he said. "I only heard a few, now there are at least twenty men."

"Not good," I said. "I'm going to take down one in the front, one in the back." I drew the pepperbox from its holster and felt the reassuring bulge of a dozen speed loaders across my chest.

"If that rope breaks, you're screwed."

"I know it," I said. "It'll hold."

Alan nodded and slid back down into the leaves below. The first necromancer tapped his foot on the frozen creek bed twenty-five yards out.

"Come on, Cassie," I said under my breath.

There was a quiet gurgling sound in the distance. My eyes trailed to the back of our enemy's ranks.

"Fairy!" a man screamed. "Fair—" His voice cut off a second before his head plopped down between his feet.

The entire platoon of cloaks turned toward the man's scream. A couple of them were smart enough to raise a shield. I took aim at the closest who wasn't.

The pepperbox flashed with the light of a phoenix in the dark woods. The man crumpled to the ground. A few more raised shields, half turning in my direction. I took aim at the back, where Cassie had been, and fired again. This one screamed when the bullet hit him. He writhed on the ground.

I grabbed the rope and swung out of the tree stand. These idiots weren't seasoned. They fired off incantations in my general direction. I saw the tree stand burn from the corner of my eye as a spiral of flame hit it. A stuttering beam of white light cut through a tree branch above me. I was almost behind the tree when another flash severed the rope.

I cursed, still a good six feet off the ground, as the rope swung wildly and I overbalanced, crashing into the leaves. I didn't stop to consider how lucky I was I hadn't hit another tree, or a rock, I just got up and ran. My shoulder and thigh were sore from the impact, but everything seemed to be working.

I was at Frank's side in seconds. "Ready?" I said between quick breaths.

"Yes," he said as he handed me my staff.

"Good." I grabbed the shield rune and its glassy surface sprang to life around us. None of these fools would be able to get through.

We could see the burning tree stand now, the unnatural fire already dying to embers. The front half of the necromancers started to surge around it, throwing caution out the door as they tried to run me down. Alan waited until they passed him before he reached out and tore a man's arms off. The werewolf was a nightmare of shadows and blood as he began to dance through their ranks, swinging those fleshy maces so fast and hard men didn't get back up after he struck.

Alan grunted as a man clipped him with a staff and another managed to singe the fur off a patch of his shoulder.

"Alan!" I said. "Now!"

"No," he said as he reached out a clawed hand. It was a quick and brutal strike, and another necromancer's guts spilled out onto the ground. The man fell to his knees as Alan tossed his arm and entrails to fall among the other necromancers.

Alan made a break for us while they watched the gore. "Now," he growled as he ran by, sprinting on all fours.

Frank raised the Uzis.

I dropped the shield.

Five men died in an unrelenting hail of gunfire.

Or so I thought. One of the dying men brought his hand up. His lips began to move as I started to slide my hand up to the shield rune. I didn't have time. No time. My hand was in the wrong damn place.

Cassie exploded above him. Her sword was drawn and angled beneath her as she landed on his back, knees first. The sword slid through his head like butter, smashing the back of his skull with the hilt as Cassie drove the blade into the frozen ground. I'd seen Fae steel cut through pavement. The icy earth offered little resistance.

"Cabin, now!" I said in the lull.

We ran a few steps and then took a severe left, dodging behind a thick tangle of dried out briars. Anything they fired at us now would be a blind shot. Alan settled in beside us. We didn't run too fast. A twisted ankle wouldn't help anyone. I hung back a little, with my hand primed to bring up a shield if necessary.

Frank kept glancing at Alan. As a wolf-man, he was hulking and coated in midnight black fur. I had once told Carter his arms looked like furry bowling balls, and Alan was a hell of a lot bulkier than Carter. Alan peeled his lips back and exposed a mouthful of razor-sharp teeth. His run was awkward while he tried to slow down for us, half upright, half crouched, as he bounced along beside Frank.

"Christ," Frank said between shallow breaths. "I thought Cara was scary."

"She is," Alan said in that deep, wolfish growl.

We cut our way through the trees, Cassie leading us back in a slightly roundabout path. The necromancers would follow, and we'd lead them right into the backyard.

"We're close," she said as she hovered over a large shelf of rock on one of the hills. "Next hill and we're there."

I felt the lines bend all around us and stumbled as the power in the ley lines began to fluctuate.

"Zola raised the shield," Cassie said. "I'm going to check on the others."

"Do it," I said as she bent her wings and powered through the treetops.

A shadow moved at the top of the hill. Carter's face emerged from the murk as we closed in. He matched our pace.

"Philip is following Vicky," he said. "I don't think he knows what she is."

"He's not the only one," I said.

"Ghost Pack," Carter said. "She is light. She fights with us. Does anything else truly matter?"

"Not tonight," I said.

"Who are you speaking with?" Alan growled as he barreled through a low branch with a loud crack.

"Carter," I said. "You can't see him?"

"I can't either," Frank said.

"Zola either started the spell or we're too far away from Vicky," I said. "Carter, get the Ghost Pack. Get them to the front of the cabin. Be ready for Zachariah."

The River Pack's old alpha nodded and then accelerated faster than any mortal could move. Two fairies darted in beside Carter as he vanished into the distance. We crested the hill a moment later.

My pace slowed as a thirty-foot dome of lightning flickered across the field.

"Bloody hell, Zola," I said.

The shield pulsed and turned, lightning showering from the apex to the stones below like a hell-bound carousel. Zola stood in the middle, her head bowed and her lips moving constantly.

"We're here!" I said as we passed the circle and slid up to the back of the cabin. "How long can you hold it?"

As if in response, another cascade of lightning poured down the shield and a crack of thunder deafened the world around us.

"Get to the front," I said. "Carter! It's time!" I didn't know if he'd hear me from where he was, but he wouldn't miss what came next.

Alan crouched back on his hind legs and let loose a howl to wake the dead. I covered my ears as that howl laid its claws on the night around us. The Ghost Pack appeared beside us. Foster, Cara, and Cassie swept in behind them.

"We'll start the fog," Foster said. "Get to the front."

The fairies disappeared over the roof. The rest of us circled around the eastern side. Past the ruin of the shed where we'd fought Azzazoth.

"Alright," I said as I stepped up onto the short set of stairs. "When I start this, I'm out of commission. Try not to let me get vaporized."

"Frank," Alan said. "We'll stay behind to watch over Damian."

"Tell him that's a damn fine idea," Carter said. "Gods but I miss my friends."

"We all do," Maggie said as she leaned against her husband.

"You didn't bring any crispy rice squares?" I asked.

"It's somewhat difficult when you're dead." She bared her teeth in a wolfish grin.

I returned the gesture and nodded.

"We'll watch over Zola," a voice said from above us.

I jumped in shock and looked up to find the Watchers.

"Dammit, Edgar," I said. "Bad time for a heart attack, but thank you."

He tipped his hat and glided up past the fairies.

"Shit," I said. "Vicky's out there alone now."

"Happy's with her," Sam said from beside me, and I almost jumped out of my skin again.

I scowled at my sister. "Where'd you come from?"

She pointed south and my eyes trailed after her finger.

The Old Man strode out of the woods at the far end of the field. He could have been out for a morning stroll if it wasn't for the trail of smoke rising from his right hand. Someone kissed the wrong end of a flamethrower, and I was guessing they wouldn't get back up.

"Is that Dell behind him?" Frank asked. "Looks like he's limping."

"I'll check on him," Sam said. She blurred into motion, carving a path through the shin-high grass. They had a brief exchange before she flickered into motion again. "He's okay. Twisted ankle. Nothing too bad."

"Okay," I said. "Let's start this off with some smoke and mirrors."

"Cara!" Sam said. "Fire it up!"

It started immediately. The air around us thickened like the steam from a hot spring. Then it thickened more, forming an ominous gray thundercloud that began oozing along the ground, billowing out to waist height and then expanding into a ten-foot wall. It drifted out, obscuring our view, and more importantly, the view of our opposition.

The shouts started in the distance, laced with an edge of concern.

"Stand your ground!" said a distant voice.

"Zachariah," I said as I knelt in a circle of focusing runes carved into the front porch.

"He's ours," Carter said. "Art, stay beside me. Don't get carried away when Damian starts."

Art nodded. Johann and Betsy exchanged a long glance.

Zachariah. Son of a bitch. The cabin was my home away from it all. My childhood home. Zola's home. My training grounds. Memories of Sam and Zola and my parents lived in the woods around me. And these bastards dared to set foot near it. I flexed my aura with one sharp exhalation, my necromancy fastening to the wards around me. They began to glow, a sickly yellow-green against the darkness, as my aura began to surge with the steady black-and-white flow of the dead.

I reached out for a ley line. It would be my amplifier. Once it was in my grasp, I anchored it to the southern ward and let my necromancy flow, winding its way into Carter and Maggie and the rest of the ghost wolves. They began to glow, silver at first, then green, and then they became blinding yellow suns.

"My god," Betsy said. "This is ... this is amazing. I can feel again." She bent down and touched the grass.

I let the power slide back into the circle around me. "That's what it's going to feel like," I said. "Be ready."

Betsy's smile fell as the power receded back into my circle. And I felt guilty for taking it away from her.

"Carter," I said. "If Zola can't maintain her shield and mask you all at the same time ..."

"We are ghosts, my friend." The werewolf squeezed my shoulder. "We're already ghosts, but you should have more faith in your master."

I nodded as he turned away. My faith in Zola was strong, but I knew her better than any of the wolves. She was here to kill

Philip, and I shuddered to think what she might have to sacrifice to make that kill.

The mists thickened and turned the entire field into a murky black pit. The Ghost Pack set out into the conjured mists.

I raised my Sight and gasped as electric blue lines arced and sputtered through the gray. The fairies anchored the spell to Zola's shield, and the lines bent into a circle like a hurricane. I could see the Ghost Pack through it all, and at the far side of the storm, a line of necromancers. Spheres of power hovered and dipped around several of them. It took me a moment before I realized they were summoning power to act like a torch, using the varied corpses and dead things Zola had buried in the area. They kept moving forward.

Foster appeared at my side, seven feet tall with his hand on the hilt of his sword. "They're in position Damian."

"Drop it," I said.

Foster leapt onto the roof. The mists began to thin. Starlight poked holes in the absolute night we'd been buried in a moment before. Tendrils of gray trailed behind Foster, caressing his wings and sword as he landed at my side. His blade flickered in the light of the glowing torches before us. The wards beneath me began to pulse with a hideous deep red-orange I'd never seen in my own workings before. Hellfire. It lit the world from below, casting the faces of my friends in a ghoulish light.

Laughter echoed across the field among shouts of alarm. Zachariah stood twenty yards away, shoulders slumped and his hands on his knees. "Well, you do know how to make an entrance, Vesik."

I stared at the man.

"You can't win and I can't let you leave," he said. "You shouldn't have come."

"We buried a demon where you're standing," I said.

He glanced at his feet, a small frown appeared for a moment before his smirk returned. "Oh, did you now? And where are your wolves? Philip is scared of your pet dogs."

"He should be," I whispered as I pushed out a torrent of necromancy, which was swallowed by the wards beneath me. The light of hellfire was overcome by the glow of the wards and the grayish light of necromancy.

"Philip grows weak," Zachariah spat. "I am the rightful leader of this army. I will march our men over the carcass of this world and—"

"Goodbye, Zachariah," the words escaped me in an incoherent snarl as rage welled up at the thought of this monster living one more second.

His eyes widened as my power lanced out to the Ghost Pack. Each wolf swelled into a blinding sun mixed within the necromancer's ranks. Zola had been masking their presence the entire time. The only place I'd seen anything like it was Rivercene, where I had trouble perceiving the ghosts around me.

Maggie growled, and her growl rose into a howl as her body broke and grew and fur flowed from her skin. Her claws ripped the life from the nearest necromancer before he even registered what had appeared beside him.

The wolves went to war.

Alan snarled beside me.

"Go," I said, knowing the bloodlust would be boiling over as he watched his brothers and sisters tear into our enemy. He didn't need my permission, bloody hell I knew that, but he launched himself forward at that single word. His howl joined the Ghost Pack and I reveled in the cries of our enemies.

Carter and Maggie danced through the necromancers. Tears threatened to blind me as I watched my friends together, devouring the ranks of our enemies. Sense began to return to the survivors as blood and pieces rained down around them. Bodies were torn asunder and smeared across the shields flickering between the wolves and their prey.

Betsy and Art backed Zachariah against the old oak. Lightning thundered from his hands and ricocheted harmlessly off the Ghost Pack.

"What are you?" he screamed. "You should be dead!"

He didn't see Foster coming. The fairy dive-bombed the necromancer, running his sword through Zachariah's shoulder. The blade pierced the tree behind him and pinned him in place.

He screamed and pawed at the sword, eyes going wide as he took in the battlefield. The Old Man walked in from the other end of the field. Each step was deliberate. He raised his hand, and shields shattered into a mass of blue sparks. Dell raised his gun and fired one round for each broken shield. He never missed. They took down five men in a span of seconds.

The Old Man laughed and crossed his arms, looking at the carnage like an old friend come home.

"Carter," I said between clenched teeth as my forearms began to spasm from the effort. "I can't hold this."

I didn't think he was close enough to hear me, but he got the message. Carter wrapped his paw around Maggie's and they started toward Zachariah. The grass bent beneath their clawed feet. Zachariah's chest rose and fell in rapid, ragged breaths.

"You let him raise the Destroyer," Carter said as he reached out to the necromancer.

"*Impadda!*" Zachariah cringed as nothing happened but a hiss of pale blue sparks. "What have you done?"

"My sword," Foster said.

Zachariah stared and the blade in his shoulder and then spat at Foster. He tried to take a swing with his right arm, but Carter caught his hand.

"Get away, wolf," Zachariah said in a nearly incoherent snarl.

"I will not deny my friend her vengeance," Carter said. "So we will tear our own from your body." Carter offered Zachariah's hand to Maggie.

She bit it off. The necromancer let out a piercing scream, the likes of which I'd never heard. Maggie chewed the hand slowly, smiling as the blood ran down silvery, golden fur. She spit out the bones, one at a time. My stomach churned as she leaned into the man and bit off his ear.

"Now then," Carter said. "This is going to hurt." He wrenched Zachariah's body down, severing his left arm with the sword embedded in it.

The rest of the Ghost Pack circled.

"Goodbye," Carter said. He punched through the bastard's ribcage and ripped out his heart. Zachariah was still twitching and trying to scream as Carter started to eat that heart. He'd never scream again. Art ripped out Zachariah's throat and the Ghost Pack descended, leaving the necromancer's body in tiny pieces.

I watched his soul start to rise. I wondered if it would dissipate. Would he be sentenced to some dark corner of the Burning Lands for all he'd done?

"Oh," the Old Man said as he stepped up beside the wolves. "You won't be getting off so easy, old friend." He held his arms out before him, palms up. The scars along his hands began to glow, and the light raced up that disfigured patchwork of flesh. The Old Man inhaled and Zachariah's soul disappeared into his mouth.

I guess we'll never know where Zachariah was headed.

I laughed to myself and collapsed as I finally released the flood tide of power I'd been channeling.

CHAPTER TWENTY-EIGHT

"Where's Sam?" I asked as Alan pulled me to my feet. "She was with Dell."

Alan glanced at Dell. "Do you know?"

Dell shook his head.

"She went to watch over Zola and the fairies," the Old Man said. "Frank and Ashley are with them."

A knot in my stomach loosened just a little.

Intense light rocketed down into the woods to the northeast. I glanced up at the roof and found Edgar with his arm outstretched. I was fairly certain he'd killed something with that strike. James stood to his left, both well below the peak and hidden from anyone to the north.

"They're at the shield," Cara said. "Keep your voices down. We move to the east, past the crater."

I nodded and wobbled a little with my first step as we made our way past the remnants of the old shed. There were a few pieces large enough to identify as part of the roof, or the burnt edge of a door, but most of the structure was buried in the shed's crater under a layer of brown grass and dead weeds.

We crouched behind the stack of firewood beside the house and watched. The idiots we'd left by the creek were there, circled around Zola's shield. They unleashed fire and thunder, but their most powerful workings were swept up in the maelstrom of power and sent harmlessly into the air.

A little girl skipped out of the woods on the far side of the shield. Vicky ran at the nearest necromancer and punched through his back. "Philip is here," she said as she pulled her arm out of the man's chest and left him to twitch on the ground.

The next cloak spun towards her. "*Tyranno Eversiotto!*" Death and light shot towards Vicky and the ghost smiled. She raised her arm and that bloody sword of light appeared in the path of the necromancer's spell. The sword absorbed it all and Vicky's hand started to shake. Then she screamed, her fist opening and the blade disappearing as she stumbled away from the shield.

The necromancer pulled his hood down and Philip Pinkerton smiled like a madman. "Not so strong, little demon." He stalked toward Vicky as she fell to the ground, cradling her hand. I started to move, but the Old Man clamped down on my shoulder.

"Wait," he said.

Before he finished speaking, a black-and-white blur shot from the tree line.

Philip raised his hand to strike.

The panda bear ... *changed.* He stood up on his hind legs and his body thinned, his broad head darkened and flared into a helmet. His paws drew down into amorphous blobs before fingers began to show their definition. His legs were just that, and his body was armored, covered with metal scales. It was a yoroi, samurai armor, and his head was crowned with an ornate kabuto.

"Shiawase," Philip said in disbelief as he stepped backwards.

"That was my name, once," Happy said, his voice too deep for any mortal. "Now it is Happy." He took a half step backwards, a slightly curved sword of light extended in his right hand as he bent down and scooped Vicky up with his left.

Alan disappeared into the tree line nearby, chasing down another necromancer. Cassie followed him into shadow.

"You cannot defeat us all," Happy said.

"I did not come alone." Philip snapped his fingers.

The Old Man spun beside me. "Son of a—" The vampires came from nowhere, wearing shadows like armor. Bronze amulets glinted on their chests, shielding them from our necromancy.

Zola growled from the center of the shield. "We aren't all necromancers."

I heard the crack of the nine tails before I saw the cloud of nothingness explode above a dozen vampires. They vanished from the waist up. Legs and gore tumbled to the ground in a hideous, seizing pile.

Philip laughed. "You should work for me, witch. I'd pay you well."

"You should have killed me last year," Ashley said as she snapped two tiles between her fingers and threw the broken halves at a vampire standing beneath a necromancer's shield. "Frank!"

You can stop a lot with a shield. Almost nothing can break through a well-powered shield. Ashley's tiles settled on the surface and the glassy reflection turned red before the necromancer began to scream. Frank clamped down on the Uzis and unleashed a leaden hell.

The necromancer died, falling in a heap at the vampire's feet. Sam was on top of the vampire the instant Frank stopped shooting. Her arm snaked around his neck and she … well, the locals have a saying for opening a bottle of beer. It seems appropriate. She popped his top.

Foster and Cara appeared on either side of Sam. More gunfire erupted behind me and I had to turn away from the battle escalating around Philip. Dell was picking off vampires. Not killing them, but shattering the amulets around their neck. God damn, why hadn't I thought to try that?

The pepperbox hissed as I drew it and took aim. Just because Zola shielded her amulets, didn't mean Philip would do the same. Small bursts of sparks told us when we hit the mark. I'd tagged three of the bastards before I realized there were at least ten more.

They were fast. Damn fast. But I could sense their movements once the amulets were broken. Every fiber of their beings was open to me. All I had to do was reach out and pull them apart. But with so many vampires around, it would have been suicide to risk a vision freezing me up when my necromancy showed me their lives.

"Don't grab them," the Old Man said, echoing my own thoughts. His words came too late.

Dell dropped his gun as one of the vampires leapt at him. The Old Man was already moving when Dell caught the vampire in midair with his necromancy. His face twisted and turned to revulsion as he came to know the man trying to kill him. Came to know him more intimately than his own mother.

Another vampire moved on Dell, but the Old Man was already there. A soulsword sprang from either hand, golden and blinding as he brought his right hand up and severed the man's chest and right shoulder from his body in one slash.

They were surrounding us, and fast. Dell tore the vampire in front of him to pieces and then fell to a knee, shaken. I wouldn't be able to make it to him as the next leapt from the oak tree and landed beside Dell. I raised my hand.

"*Minas Ignatto!*" A thin rod of flame closed the distance in a heartbeat, boring a hole through the vamp's arm. He didn't scream, he just paused for a second, glanced at the damage, and pulled back his arm to kill Dell. A second can make all the difference.

I brought the focus down as I grabbed the blade rune on my staff. The soulsword sliced off the top of his head at the nose.

"Behind," Dell muttered.

I turned and caught the moonlight gleaming off the fangs of another vampire.

He turned to ash as a beam as bright as the sun consumed him.

Edgar tipped his hat from the roof of the cabin.

I grinned and set my back to Dell. The Old Man did the same on Dell's other side.

"Why hasn't Zola sprung the trap?" the Old Man said.

"She's channeling all her power into that shield," I said. "Maybe she's not aware."

"We need to have her drop it. Philip's there. The trap is set. Time to spring it."

More gunfire echoed from the other side of the cabin. I could hear the fairies' call to battle.

Six vampires circled us, far more wary than they'd been at first.

"Get down!"

I glanced to my right to see who was speaking. It was James, and he was making an intricate series of gestures with his hands, forming squares and runes and circles in midair.

"Shit," the Old Man said. "Down!" He dove across Dell and tackled us both flat to the grass.

A stream of bubbles flowed from James's hands. I almost laughed until a bubble hit the first vampire. It stuck to him and he began to turn to ash by inches. He screamed and tried to pull the bubble off with his hand. The hand was gone when he pulled it back. His scream died a moment later as his body collapsed into the bubble and vanished.

Those clear orbs of death floated past us, trailing the vampires as they started to run. Their eyes stayed locked on the spell, like it was hypnotizing them, making them move more slowly.

"Ha," Dell said as he fished his gun out of the grass. "Not getting away from that." He started shooting kneecaps. The vampires went down and the bubbles devoured them.

When I looked back for James, he was gone.

I helped Dell up and glanced at the Old Man.

He nodded. "Let's go." We started for the back of the cabin.

The scene awaiting us was gore and blood and horror. There were enough body parts I wasn't sure if we'd lost any of our own. Alan stooped over a shredded cloak, his chest heaving. A few necromancers stood in circles, some shielded, some armed with daggers, guns, and more mundane weapons.

"You alright?" I said as I came up beside Alan.

He growled and his eyes widened. I took a step back. His head hung down and he nodded. "Yes, sorry. Carter and the others are in the woods with Happy. Vicky said there is something else approaching."

"What?" I asked, not sure if I meant to ask what it was or what the hell was next.

"Drop the shield!" the Old Man said.

Zola continued chanting, her eyes closed, completely absorbed in the spell.

"Adannaya! Drop the fucking shield!"

Philip stared at the Old Man. He looked at his surroundings for a moment, and then dropped to his knees and began chanting. His aura flared and his voice began to boom in the rhythm of a march. A harsh wind rattled the trees behind him, swirling and snapping branches. The wind took form, a body made from rapidly moving debris, a sphere for the head, dozens of smaller spinning spheres formed the body. The eyes glowed, dirty and fiery like red-hot coals.

"No!" A voice rumbled from nowhere and everywhere. "Drop the shield."

At that command, Zola did. She swayed on her feet as the shield fell. The Old Man sprinted in, scooped her up, and retreated as the earth beneath the circle exploded.

Aeros rose like a mad god. Dirt and rock shot forward like shrapnel. At least two men fell in the hail of debris. Aeros brought his fists down on another pair like whack-a-moles.

Very gory whack-a-moles. He struck out towards Philip with a backhand.

"*Impadda!*" Philip said, his shield sprang to life, catching enough of Aeros's blow to spare him, but it still threw him several feet through the air.

Another necromancer called a shield. Aeros put his hands together and hammered down on the man, driving the shield a foot into the rocky earth before it shattered and the man's body collapsed into a mushy puddle.

"Aeros," the winds hissed, drawing the name out for several seconds amidst the howling debris.

"What the hell is that?" I asked.

"Gurges," Aeros said. "God of steam and winds. He will attack from a distance. Be wary."

"What now, Adannaya?" Philip asked from the edge of the trees. "You always rely on the rock. Predictable." He laughed and crossed his arms as he stepped into a beam of moonlight. "Ah, but the Blade of the Stone. I did not expect that."

A cry thundered above us. The Piasa Bird circled, eyes focused on Gurges.

"Stay back, old friend," Aeros said. The Thunderbird rose higher into the night, becoming a shadow amongst the stars. Aeros did not raise his gaze from Gurges, but I knew he was speaking to us about the Piasa Bird. "He is no match for this beast."

"Your men are dead," Foster said as he let a vampire's body fall at his feet.

"That is no concern of mine," Philip said. "They did their job well. I know every last piece you brought to the game."

"You and Ah have unfinished business," Zola said. "Ah do wonder ... if you want Ezekiel dead, why attack us here?"

"No one can defeat Ezekiel," Philip said. "I just want a little more enjoyment out of this life. And killing you and your apprentice is on the top of my list."

"You're lying," Zola said. "You've always been a bad liar."

Philip laughed and leaned against a tree. "Not always. Not always. For example, if all your friends leave now, I'll let them live."

Zola stared at him.

"Am I lying?" His lips curled up into a vicious smile.

"We should take his offer," James said from the roof.

I wanted to shoot him.

Aeros and Gurges began circling each other.

"Gurges," Philip said, "finish this quickly."

The Old God didn't respond in words. He spun and ran a translucent hand through the air in an arc. The tree beside Aeros splintered and an explosion of red rock leapt from his left arm. He grunted and put his hand over the wound. Molten rock dripped from the gouge and smoke rose from the grass where it fell.

"Bloody hell," I said. "Aeros!"

"Concentrate," Aeros said. "I am not your concern."

"Fuck this," Dell said. He leapt over the firewood and ran behind Aeros, setting up across the backyard from Philip. Three shots rang out.

Philip laughed as they hit the tree around his head. He hadn't raised a shield, the lines hadn't shifted around him at all, and no glassy shell appeared. "You can't harm me so long as Gurges shields me."

"Then Gurges dies," Cassie said as she swooped in from behind with her sword extended. It was a perfect strike, the blade sliding through the back of Gurges's head and out through its left eye. It screamed and its body turned away from Aeros. Only it didn't turn like a mortal creature, its back simply *became* its front, its left eye became its right.

The Old God spread its translucent fingers and a blade of wind cut through Cassie's chest. Dead center. Blood sprayed from her armor and her eyes widened as the tree behind her fell from the same attack.

"Now, Frank!" Ashley said from the shadows of the forest.

A handful of tiles sailed through the air. A flash of sunlight burned a hole through Gurges's chest. The Old God stumbled as Ashley unleashed a cry to send the devil running for shelter. The nine tails cracked and Ashley ran directly into the black cloud. She vanished for a split second and then reappeared on the other side of Gurges, her body covered with blood. Something glistened in her hands. It was the damaged eye of the Old God. She smiled and jammed it into a pouch on her belt.

"Thunderbird!" Aeros said, the world shaking with every syllable. "Take your sacrifice!"

The Piasa Bird dove from the stars, claws out as it neared the stumbling form of Gurges. The Old God looked up at the last moment, in time to see the Piasa Bird pluck his last eye from his head. The Old God collapsed, dissipating in a quiet breeze, and opening the view across the field.

"Cassie!" Zola screamed. "Cassie, no!"

Cassie's body started to fold in on itself. The ley lines sparked into a blinding spider web of power around her.

Cara jumped in front of Foster and held him back as he tried to run toward Cassie. "She's gone. Look away. Look away!"

But I couldn't look away. None of us could look away as the ley lines siphoned the skin from her body, tearing and shredding her wings until there was nothing left but an outline of fairy dust where they'd been a moment before. Then the screams began. And I screamed with her as the muscles spun and unraveled around her naked flesh, exposing her organs, her skeleton. Her entire being began to drift away and still she screamed. Until the end. Her bloody armor was on the ground, the outline of her body floating above it, remnants of our friend in the fading fairy dust.

And Foster's screams. The battle had stopped, both sides struck dumb by the nightmarish vision of Cassie's death.

Everyone but Philip.

"Take him, James," Philip said.

The Watcher was fast. Impossibly fast. He was down from the roof before I could blink, wrenching Dell around and forcing his arm behind his back. There was a wet pop and a grunt of pain as Dell's shoulder dislocated.

"Anyone moves and I pull the trigger." James forced the barrel of a small revolver up against Dell's head.

Zola was closest, and I wished her gaze could sear the flesh from James's bones. "You won't leave here alive." Her eyes trailed back to Philip. "She was our friend, you monster." Her voice grew low, dangerous beyond words. "How did Ah ever love such a thing?"

Philip raised the hand of the dead king.

"In all the ways this world betrayed me, you were the worst," Zola said as tears began to roll down her cheeks. "Never again."

It happened so fast, her face serene as she ripped James's soul away from his body. The Watcher collapsed, the gun tumbling to the grass. A brilliant yellow glow rose up between Zola's hands as she cried out, the soul throwing itself against her power. Her will would not be denied.

She snapped her left hand forward and a beam of white light severed Philip's arm below the elbow. He screamed as his escape plan—the hand of glory—fell from his grasp, vanishing into a black pit with his arm as they hit the ground. He fell to his knees, scratching at the earth where the hand of glory had vanished.

"No more," Zola said, her right arm shaking as the soul began to peel the flesh from her hand. "No more." She stared at Philip, her gaze unwavering. "Now girl."

Vicky emerged from the shadow of the cabin behind Zola. She raised her hands to the night sky and her body ignited. A sickly orange wave of fire burst from her feet, licking its way up to her head and trailing towards the stars.

Philip stared at Zola, wide eyed. "It was for you," he whispered as she brought his world to an end.

"*Magnus Ignatto!*" Zola's scream filled the field, filled the night around us as the soul leapt from her hands, sucked into the ley lines as they siphoned hellfire from Vicky and birthed a wall of death. Zola cried out as the lines burned through her. Flames spiraled into a sphere forty feet wide before they shot forward. The earth screamed as its flesh was scoured away by flame, leaving a wake of ash and superheated rock as the fires bore down on Philip.

By the time the searing image of fire left my vision, Philip Pinkerton was dead.

CHAPTER TWENTY-NINE

Vicky was on her knees with her head hanging limply. She was taking deep breaths and I could hear her lungs working to draw in oxygen. Lungs that shouldn't be there.

I frowned and looked away from her, staring instead at my master. "That was hellfire."

She glanced at me and nodded.

"You used her." I bit off the words, unable to prevent the anger I felt from seeping into them.

"For this," Zola said. "For this, yes."

My fists began to shake as my fingers curled up, forming fists. Would I have done the same in her shoes? I don't know, but for anyone to hurt Vicky… The things she'd been through … I grimaced and turned away from my master.

I knelt beside the girl. "You okay?"

She nodded weakly and unfolded her legs with great care, sprawling out on the scorched earth. I squeezed her shoulder and she reached up to grab my hand.

"I wanted to help," she said, her voice just above a whisper between her shuddering breaths. "Don't be mad at Zola. Don't be mad."

I squeezed her hand and bowed my head. "I won't be, kiddo. You did good."

She smiled and laid down, curling up against Happy after he trundled up beside her, just an innocent panda bear.

"You," I said.

He stared at me and blinked.

"You owe me an explanation."

He blew out a breath and nuzzled Vicky.

I narrowed my eyes. "Later then, furball," I said with a small smile. I turned back to Zola.

"Ah want …" Zola started to say before she paused to take a deep breath. "Ah want to stay here a while."

"We need you," Hugh said as he pushed a branch out of his way at the tree line. Carter and Maggie and the rest of the Ghost Pack were with him. "Take some time, but we need you soon. Gwynn ap Nudd has called the Concilium Belli."

"What?" Cara asked. "Why has he called a war council? How did you hear of this before me?"

"The king fought beside us in the woods," Happy said as he shifted a paw beneath Vicky's head. "Gwynn ap Nudd told us much."

Hugh nodded. "He was not physically with us, but we could see him, pointing out the enemy's hiding places."

"A sending," Cara said.

"Like Nixie's water sending?" I asked.

Cara nodded. "Only Glenn can do it without the elements. It is one of the blessings of the Crown." She looked up, towards Edgar. "And what will the Watchers do?"

"I will consult with them," he said. "At least, what's left of them. Ezekiel dealt us a great deal of damage."

"You are their strongest," Cara said. "There is no need to hide it here, among friends. If you count us nothing else Edgar, we are your friends now."

Edgar tipped a hat he was no longer wearing, likely lost in the chaos of battle. "I could do worse."

"We all could," Zola said as she gestured at the scorched earth. "This was no small thing."

"Friends," he said with a shake of his head. "Strange days."

"Edgar," I said, my voice quiet. "About James?"

"Ah, yes," he said as he pursed his lips and snapped his fingers a few times before pulling out his notebook. "James was a fool who got himself killed by the dark necromancer Philip Pinkerton. That's what I saw." He looked up from his notebook and glared at each of us in turn. "That's what you *all* saw."

Edgar paused and looked at Zola. "Do you want the Cleaners here? I can probably pull one or two, but Ezekiel has taken a toll on the Watchers."

Zola shook her head and leaned up against Aeros. "See, he's not so bad."

"Perhaps," the Old God said.

"Are you okay?" I asked.

Aeros glanced at his arm, where Gurges's damage was crusted and black. "Yes, it is healing quite well."

The Piasa Bird hopped up on his shoulders and nested on his head again, making a strange vibrating tone.

"Yes, my friend," Aeros said, "I am fine."

The Piasa Bird quieted and began preening its feathers.

Sam snorted a laugh and we all turned to her.

"What?" she said. "You gotta admit it's kind of funny."

"The world is a funny place," Aeros said as he scratched the bird just below the beak.

"That's for damn sure," Alan said from a tree stump beside Foster.

The fairy was still staring at Cassie's armor. I didn't know what to say to him.

"Something is coming," Aeros said he looked toward the forest. The mood shifted in our little circle of friends. Eyes widened and hands moved for weapons.

"So, little ones," a voice whispered as though shouted from a great distance. "You finally threw down the tyrant."

"Is that ...?" Edgar said. "Shit, *shit shit shit.*"

"What?" Sam asked. "What is it?"

"Ezekiel," Zola said.

"Quiet," the Old Man said as he stepped into the middle of our circle. He closed his eyes and took two deep breaths. A delicate web of yellow light spilled from his eyes and raced across the field in every direction. "He's not here."

"What will you do now?" the voice asked. It was close. A shadow shifted beside the Old Man and began to rise like a sheet pulled up by a single hand.

The Old Man growled, his arms bleeding as darkness poured out of his scars, the black pitch of a gravemaker spilling over his forearms. Alan jumped to his feet, but Foster put his arm out, shaking his head.

"You think to stand against me?" Ezekiel's laughter rolled through the hills around us, shaking the earth. "You think to stand against Anubis?" The shadow took on the lines of his face, cloaked in darkness. "I am a god. I am immortal."

"We will pay the price to stop you," Cara said as she drew her sword in one hand and a dagger in the other.

"You have already paid the price," Ezekiel said. "Falias is fallen."

"You lie," Cara said as she stepped toward Ezekiel's shadowy form. "Falias is one of the four hidden cities of the Fae! You don't have the power to strike them down!"

He laughed again and raised his arm, the chaff of a gravemaker rushing up to cover it in wicked-looking spikes, a mirror of the Old Man. A taunt.

Cara's face twisted into rage. "You lie!"

Silence flooded the field and Ezekiel's shadow turned to face her.

"I have destroyed it utterly. Your king did not raise a finger to save it."

Cara's rage stuttered.

Ezekiel's smile turned smug.

"No, oh no," she said as her hand covered her mouth. "That's why he was here. Glenn, gods, what has happened?"

"We finish this now!" the Old Man said.

Ezekiel turned to face him. "You want to finish this Leviticus? Face me on the field once more."

"Face me now!" the Old Man's voice rose, verging on a scream.

Ezekiel laughed his papery thin chuckle. "Face my horde, Leviticus. Find me in Gettysburg, we will fight upon the field of dead. As it should be. And then—"

Ezekiel's shadow was swallowed by a flash of absolute blackness. When the moonlight returned, Gwynn ap Nudd stood in the center of our group.

"I am sorry I could not be here," he said. "Ezekiel did not lie. We have lost Falias."

The fairies crumbled. Sam ran over to Foster to hug him as he started to tremble.

"Ward saved many people," Glenn said. "I did not give him the respect he has proven he deserves."

"What about Nixie?" I asked. "Is she safe?"

Glenn nodded. "The other cities are intact. They are in fact untouched. The water witches' home in the realm of the commoners is intact as well, though I suspect you are indifferent to that."

Well, he wasn't wrong there. It would have been damn convenient if Ezekiel had taken out the Queen.

"We face a war on two fronts, and even if we win, two fronts come again," the king said. "The film of the blood mage and Ashley, the ascended witch, has caught the attention of several governments around the world. Some of them are not as skeptical as we'd hoped. All our people are in danger. Take care of yourselves until the Concilium Belli. Bring the witch. Break the Seals. The choice has been taken from us."

His image swirled and collapsed and vanished with a clap of thunder.

"Fuck." I ran my fingers through my hair. "Fuck that sounds bad."

"Damian," Edgar said. He stayed silent until I turned to look at him.

"Is this about Ashley?" I said, ready for a verbal joust.

Edgar shook his head. "No, it's not about Ashley. You have to learn to battle the Old Gods."

I blinked. "What?"

"Ezekiel was always the best of us," Edgar said as his gaze unfocused. "He was the best of us, until he became the worst."

"What does that have to do with the Old Gods?" Footsteps whispered through the grass behind me. The Old Man coughed beside me and flashed a wry smile.

"Boy, you have to learn to battle the Old Gods, because we're going to release them when we kill Ezekiel."

"What?" I said. "That's insane!"

"When Glenn said to break the Seals, he meant Ezekiel," Edgar said quietly. "It won't be all of the Old Gods. They are only part of the concern. Have you come across the dark-touched in your books? Have you heard of them in any of your research?"

"Yes," I said. "They're old vampires, right?"

"You're not wrong, but there's more to it than that," Edgar said. "They are both weaker and stronger than the vampires you know. They can be destroyed by stakes and beheading and sunlight, but at night they are a plague upon the world."

"Is it even worth killing Ezekiel?" I asked. "It sounds like the consequences of that are going to be less than good."

"It's simple," the Old Man said. "Do you want a damaged world or a destroyed one? I will take damage over destruction any day of my life."

Edgar nodded. "I don't know all of the legends. The Society of Flame is formed by the keepers of lore. We should consult with them as well."

"Hugh knows some of them. Koda's the only one I know well."

Cara began to speak, her face tilted toward the starry night. "When the Seal is broken, and the Old Gods roam the earth, the dark-touched will return with them."

"Go home to your families tonight," Edgar said. "Enjoy your time with them. One day soon the world we wake up to will no longer be the world we now know."

CHAPTER THIRTY

It was waiting for me the next morning when I walked into the shop. Bubbles and Peanut stood on either side of the counter, growling. In the center of the glass countertop, perched upright with a small book in its gray fingers, was the hand of the dead king. Philip's hand of glory.

I stared at it like it was a bomb, ready to take out the entire building. But why send it here? Who sent it here? The index finger was stuck between the pages, toward the back of the book. I focused my Sight and didn't see any malevolent workings or obvious wards. A few symbols were carved into the flesh near the wrist, but they were dormant. The book was old, a couple hundred years at least. There wasn't a trace of magic on it, and the pages looked brittle because of it. I frowned, lifted the book carefully from the hand, and started to read.

I, Philip Pinkerton, have long been considered the last of my kind. The last son, the sixth son, of the one-time god known as Anubis. Now I fear there is another. My lover's apprentice.

I read that sentence again and again until the book fell from my grasp and slammed closed on the glass countertop.

Philip's words rang out through my mind, "Just like me, Vesik. Just like me."

ABOUT THE AUTHOR

Eric is a former bookseller, guitarist, and comic seller currently living in Saint Louis, Missouri. A lifelong enthusiast of books, music, toys, and games, he discovered a love for the written word after being dragged to the library by his parents at a young age. When he is not writing, you can usually find him reading, gaming, or buried beneath a small avalanche of Transformers. For more about Eric, see www.daysgonebad.com.

VESIK, THE SERIES

Days Gone Bad
Wolves and the River of Stone
Winter's Demon

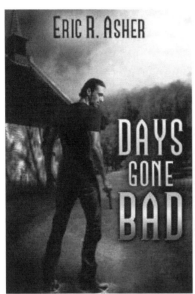
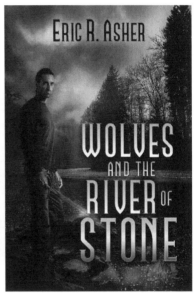

Available in paperback and ebook from
www.daysgonebad.com and all major book sellers.

Made in the USA
San Bernardino, CA
24 June 2014